I0598126

Fallbank

MAKE ME STAY

CASS SCOTKA

Make Me Stay
ISBN # 978-1-80250-727-0
©Copyright Cass Scotka 2024
Cover Art by Erin Dameron-Hill ©Copyright April 2024
Interior text design by Claire Siemaszkiewicz
Totally Bound Publishing

MAKE ME STAY

Dedication

For all the readers out there kissing frogs.
May you find your person.

Acknowledgements

This book would not exist without the love and support of more people than I can name, but I'll try. My agent Jana Hanson is such an amazing supporter, champion and outstanding human being! Thank you for choosing to believe in me and my writing. I couldn't imagine a better partner as an author.

Anna Olson, Rebecca Scott and everyone at Totally Bound and Totally Entwined Group, thank you so much for taking a chance on my book and me as an author. Thank you, Erin Dameron-Hill, for creating another phenomenal cover that matches my book to perfection. You've all made this journey spectacular and so fun! The support and resources given to me for making my book a success have been invaluable and I am forever grateful.

To my writer crew! Suleena Bibra, Rosanna Leo and Claudia Ambrose, you keep me sane and inspired. I hope we get to meet in real life one day!! The Romance and WF On Sub group chat—Joanne Machin, Suzanne Baltzar, Erin Rose, Laya Brusi, Jess K Hardy, Kimberley Ash, Despina Karras, Annia Dowell-Wiltshire, Noreen Mughees and Jannelle Drummond. You ladies keep me laughing, writing and pushing through this publishing life. I couldn't do this without all of you.

Gwynne Jackson and Ingrid Pierce, there are not words to say how much you mean to me. Thank you for reading and critiquing my work, for staying positive and encouraging, helping me work through mental blocks and plot questions. Thank you for trusting me to read your words and fawn over them before anyone else gets to. You two are amazing, wonderful, beautiful, brilliant writers who give everything you have to the writing community. I am so grateful to have you both in my corner.

The romance readers group chat—you make me laugh and smile and give the best book recs. The Elite Elevens, for not only hyping me up with my books, but also with my running. Our social club with a running problem is the best! I wouldn't trade our miles together for all the cheesecake. (LOL, we all know I'm lying... Sort of.) To the California Livin' crew, thanks for accepting me into the fold as a transplant and being the most awesome found family ever. My Colorado loves, Casey Kroepsch and Allison Simpson, you two are kindreds and sisters from another mister. Thanks for always having my back and being awesome friends. My parents, sister, cousins and Aunt Linda, thank you for the lifelong support and love to shape me into the person I am today.

Angela Santello. A. My bestie. My ride or die. My no-questions-asked, where's-the-shovel, when-you-die-the-first-thing-I'll-do-is-dip-your-computer-into-acid best friend on the planet. No words are enough to describe my love, gratitude and happiness that you are in my life. Thanks for reading my words, telling me what needs fixing and overall being a badass. You are the BEST bestie.

All of YOU reading!! The response to my books humbles me, fills me with all the love and motivates me to keep writing new stories to share with the world. An author is nothing without readers, and I am eternally thankful for each and every one of you. Thank you, thank you, thank you for reading and supporting me!!

Lastly, to my children and my husband. Without you three, my life would cease to have meaning. I love you more than all the words that have ever been spoken, written or thought combined together. Your love, support, snuggles and laughter are everything.

Chapter One

The conference room was filled to standing, with low conversations making the room buzz. Sarah dropped into the lone empty seat at the conference table with a smile that rivaled the rare, sunny early spring day in Seattle. "Hey, thanks for saving me a chair." she said to her co-worker next to her.

"Morning. No problem. I'm curious about this surprise meeting. What do you think it is?" Tyneisha replied.

Sarah couldn't hold her grin from getting even wider. The last-minute email requesting this gathering had the group texts pinging for hours last night. "I'm thinking the new senior and junior partners announcement we've been waiting for." Vibrant little bubbles of excitement rose in her stomach. She'd been at this marketing agency since her college internship. It was time for her to be promoted. And her boss had hinted that her name was top of the list. This was why she'd worked so hard. Why she went out on rare occasions and never dated seriously. Online apps for meeting up and satisfying her physical needs suited her just fine, thanks very much. She would have plenty of time for a real relationship after making partner. Thirty-one was plenty young. Her lack of dating had nothing to do with *him*.

Ty squeezed her arm. "I hope so for you! You're a lock for it."

"Thanks."

The screen in front of the room lit up and the face of their Vice President, Jimena Herrera, filled the screen. Conversations came to a halt as everyone turned their attention to her. "Good morning, everyone. Thank you all for joining on this zoom call at such late notice. We have some news to share that affects all of you."

The bubbles in Sarah's stomach fizzed and popped. She glanced around and estimated forty people present. There were another thirty calling in. Her heart started to thud inside her chest. Why would partner announcements impact this many of them?

A second square popped up and the face of their Human Resources director looked out. Why the hell would HR be on this call? A bead of sweat gathered at the back of her neck. Sarah knew this was not the announcement she'd been expecting.

Jimena spoke again. "I'm here to announce that as of yesterday, Empire State Marketing has acquired Jewel Creatives Agency. This purchase is effective immediately."

Gasps and exclamations filled the air around her, but Sarah kept her mouth shut. Her mind was stuck on the words. Her marketing company had been bought out? What did that mean for her job? For all of their jobs? *Oh, fu –*

"Please quiet down and hold your questions for now." The whispers ceased as their VP continued. "I know this is a shock to all of you and that's understandable. With this merger, there will be a reorganization of personnel due to some redundancy." Jimena paused and cleared her throat. "I am sorry and saddened to say that for those of you on this call, your positions have been eliminated."

The room fell so still they could have heard a caterpillar cough.

"I know this is a shock to all of you and you will be missed more than I can express…"

Jimena rambled on, but Sarah tuned her out. Fired. She'd been fired without warning. She tried to suck in a deep breath, but panic wouldn't let her. After years of loyalty and stellar work for this company, over a hundred campaigns and forty-five exclusive accounts signed because of her…to be fired because of a merger? What the holy hell was she going to do?

Tyneisha gripped her hand and Sarah locked eyes with her friend. Others surrounding them had expressions varying from shocked to tears to outright pissed.

"You'll all receive generous severance packages based on your time with…" HR droned on, but again Sarah lost focus. How could this happen? Not even a whisper of this takeover had reached the rumor mill. This couldn't be true. Secrets like this were never kept silent. Someone always found out and the game of telephone would begin. Yet this time, no one had whispered a word?

Her phone vibrated and a text from her landlord popped up with a picture. She blinked hard. Then again. Tiny black dots danced in front of Sarah's vision as she gasped for shallow breaths. Her entire apartment. Flooded. "Motherfucker."

Without a look back, Sarah stood and walked out of the room, then the building. She'd contact HR later to get her severance package set up. It better be freaking fantastic given it looked like she needed to find a new place to live and new furniture if that photo was anything to go off of. Racing along the streets in her red sports car, she swung into her parking spot and jogged up to the front entry.

Her landlord met her at the elevator. "Sarah, I'm so sorry. We had a water pipe burst and the whole left side of the fifth floor flooded. Yours and Mrs. Hashimoto's places were the hardest hit."

"Damn. Is everyone okay?" Sarah blew out a breath. Her hands shook and she squeezed them into fists.

"Yeah, no one was hurt or slipped and fell. All pets are accounted for." He gestured up the stairs. "The water is off now if you want to go assess things. You have renter's insurance, right?"

She nodded as a headache crept across her forehead. What the hell was she going to do? How was it not even ten in the morning and her life was in shambles?

"Good, good. I'll make sure to get you a copy of the reports and have my insurance reach out to yours. These things can take months to sort out. You have somewhere to stay for now? Your rent won't be held to you. Shit, this is a mess."

"I'm sorry, Phil." She patted him on the shoulder. This whole thing sucked for everyone involved. It hurt even worse for her since she'd just been laid-off. Finding a new place *and* a new job would be a tall order. "I guess I better go see what I can salvage."

She trudged up the five flights up since the elevators were shut off, too, then squished her way down the hall to her door. On opening it, she was hit with a wave of humid air. Sarah continued her slog into the main living and kitchen space, noting her ruined sofa and armchair, dining table and the two chairs, and most likely all of her electronics. She wound through to her bedroom where her ruined duvet dripped onto the soggy floor. The closet door caught her eye and a pulse of fear shuddered through her. Flinging open the doors, she shoved past her wet clothes to the back where several plastic bins were stacked. "Please, please, please don't be ruined."

She yanked out the second tub from the top and tossed the lid aside. Her favorite romance books. She'd spent years holding on to hard copies of a small, but select catalog of novels she loved to reread. So far, nothing seemed damaged, but there was a tiny amount of moisture. Her blood pressure dipped enough to ease the dizziness buzzing inside her head. She could salvage them. She turned her attention back to the wardrobe where another box awaited her inspection. "Be okay," she whispered as she lifted the worn container. Biting her lip, she lifted the top and peered in. Relief soaked through her limbs and the backs of her eyes stung. With shaking fingers, she took out the notes tied with a red ribbon and sighed, finding them dry. The necklace with their initials, the teddy bear with the red heart he'd won for her at a festival, the hoodie she'd "borrowed" and never given back. All free from water destruction. And there at the bottom, the picture. The one he didn't know about. The one that had broken them without him ever knowing. "I'm so sorry, Corey."

Her phone vibrated and jerked Sarah away from the avalanche of memories threatening to bury her. Her emotions were far too volatile at the moment. A glance at the screen showed her sister calling. "Hey, Bridge."

"Jack and I set a date! I expect my maid of honor to be here June third." Her giggle came through the speaker. "Well, you need to be here before that, but you know what I mean. We're planning a wedding!"

"That's great. I can't wait for it." Sarah winced at how false her enthusiasm came across. Ugh, she was a terrible sibling for not being more excited, but how could she when her life had imploded?

"What's wrong?"

"It's fine. Or it will be. Don't worry about it, B." She would not unload on her family. Would. Not.

"You're my sister and I can tell something is way off. I'm going to worry about it. Tell me." Bridget's no-nonsense voice brought the first smile to Sarah's face since the meeting this morning. *Bossy little sister.* Sarah loved Bridget's newfound strength and take-charge attitude. Still…

Clenching her eyes shut, Sarah ripped off the metaphoric Band-Aid. "Okay, okay. Today hasn't been great and it's only…nine-forty-five in the morning." She sighed at the weariness dragging her down. "I lost my job."

Bridget gasped.

"And my apartment flooded."

"Oh my God, Sarah, I'm so sorry. What happened? What can I do?"

She looked around for a dry place to sit and ended up on top of her toilet. In an ironic twist, her bathroom had been spared from the broken pipe. "Where to start? My agency was bought out and something like seventy of us had our positions eliminated because we were redundant." Anger boiled inside her again saying the words out loud. How could they all be redundant? This was ridiculous.

"That's terrible! They didn't give any kind of notice? You've been there over ten years and this is how they treat you?"

"We'll be given 'generous severance packages' according to HR." Sarah rolled her eyes. "I didn't stick around to get all of the details because I got an alert that my apartment was underwater. A pipe burst."

"Oh, no. How bad?" Bridget's soft voice almost loosened the tears Sarah kept choking back.

"Bad. Almost everything was soaked. Tons of wall and floor damage that will need fixing. Most of my stuff will need to be replaced. Who knows how long insurance will take to cough up the money for it all?" This whole situation was a nightmare. She didn't know how to take the first step in fixing things.

"Come home, Sarah."

She shook her head with a self-deprecating laugh. "And do what? My life is here, Bridgie."

"At least stay in Fallbank for the time being. It'll take a while to find a new job and apartment. You said yourself the insurance payout wouldn't be completed right away. Don't waste your savings on rushing into a new lease based on what happens to be available right away. You don't know what part of town your new job will be in and you don't want a terrible commute. Stay with me. Help with the wedding planning and at Three Sisters. I'll even pay you."

A laugh stuttered from Sarah's lips. "Gee thanks, sis." She sighed. Her sister was right. She should take a minute before jumping at whatever apartment could be found on short notice and secure a new job before signing a lease. "All right, you win. Give me a couple of days to pack up what I can and I'll head home."

* * * *

Cornelius looked over the job schedule for Timber Logging Company as the office door swung open. He glanced up with a wave at his business partner and best friend. "Hey, Jack."

The satisfied grin on Jack's face bordered on obnoxious. "Good morning, indeed."

Cornelius snorted. "I don't recall saying anything about the morning. Good or otherwise."

His friend laughed and shook his head. "It's still the best one I've had since Bridget said yes to marrying me. We set a date."

"A date. For the wedding?" His former roommate turned co-owner of TLC had proposed to Cornelius' long-time neighbor this past December. He was glad for the two of them, yet they were a niggling reminder of his single status.

"You know it. My honeybee wants to get married in June. She wants an outdoor wedding surrounded by blooming flowers at the Wild Rose Inn's garden. We walked by yesterday when we got ice cream in town. She decided then and there. We booked June third, then we celebrated back at home." Jack's smugness overflowed. "And again this morning."

Cornelius rose and pulled his friend into a bear hug. "I'm thrilled for you two. That's great news." He shoved down the jealous surge inside as they stepped back. Jack and Bridget were perfect for each other. He couldn't begrudge his friend or the girl who was almost his little sister their happiness. But was it too much to ask for something of his own? Maybe he'd used all of his up too young in life. Or perhaps he needed to put himself out there for real.

"I, uh, have a question for you." Jack stroked his beard. "Would you be my best man?"

"Me?" Stunned, Cornelius cocked his head to one side. "You don't have anyone better? One of those fancy, rich friends of yours back in Seattle?"

Jack shook his head with a laugh. "Nope. Maybe a few of them will get an invite, but nothing more. Fallbank is home now and the people here are the first real genuine folks I've met. You're the truest friend I've had."

"How can I argue with that? Of course I'll be your best man. It'd be an honor." Cornelius grinned, excited at the prospect of Bridget and Jack's wedding. Then it hit him. Oh, hell. This was going to do a number on him. He knew without asking who the maid of honor would be. Bridget's older sister and his ex-girlfriend. What had he just gotten himself into?

"How much do you see us doing for the wedding? June third isn't too far off. Just around three months," Cornelius ventured to gauge what amount of time he'd spend with his ex. The freaking love of his life who'd left for college then broken it off two years later. By phone. Damn if that hadn't ripped him apart. It was over twelve years ago and he'd yet to move on. But he couldn't go back. *Once broken up, stay broken up.*

On the plus side, she lived in Seattle and he couldn't picture her coming back every weekend for wedding planning. That would be excessive...right?

Jack furrowed his brow. "I...have no idea. I know Bridget wants small and intimate, which I'm on board with. But I guess the rest is up to her. I don't know how elaborate she'll want things. You're right that three months isn't a ton of time." He shrugged. "We also have the house we're building to keep tabs on. The timing of the wedding and finishing the house should align well."

"Right. That'll keep you crazy busy. You sure I'm going to have my partner around to help run things here?"

His friend's laugh made Cornelius smile. "Man, you know I'm too invested in TLC to ignore it. You just might get your wish and have to be more involved in wedding stuff." Jack plopped down at his desk.

"I don't know that I said that exactly..." Cornelius grumbled as he sat back down. How was he going to get through this wedding knowing Sarah would be everywhere he turned? Despite the years, his heart gave a pang at the thought of her. She'd been it for him from the moment he'd laid eyes on her. Ten years old and smitten with the girl next door. When she'd kissed him at twelve, that had sealed the deal. He'd have followed her to the ends of the earth. Until they turned twenty and she hadn't wanted him anymore. And that was that.

He pushed his glasses up and scrubbed a hand over his jaw. He tried to focus on work, but thoughts of Sarah kept floating through his brain. It wasn't that he hadn't dated since her, because he had. He just hadn't met another woman who had made him feel that way again. Maybe he needed to get off his ass and make a true effort. At the very least, Cornelius needed a date for the wedding. *Screw it.* He pulled out his phone and opened the lone dating app he'd installed two years ago.

Chapter Two

"Sare-bear! You made it," her sister exclaimed as Sarah walked through the door to Three Sisters Apothecary.

Sarah grinned and held back a sigh, feeling like a failure. Coming back to Fallback felt like she'd taken a thousand steps backward. After being within reach of becoming a junior partner at the agency to jobless with a ruined apartment and moving back to her childhood home, it seemed like life had hit the back button and screwed everything up. Of course, if she were her sister, she'd look at this as a reset instead of a rewind. Alas, Sarah was Sarah and much more of a pragmatist than an optimist. That was what her romance books were for. Happily ever afters weren't real life.

However, Bridget's enthusiasm at Sarah's homecoming did ease a bit of the sting of loss. "Hey, Bridget." She wrapped her sibling in a tight hug. Leaning back, she said, "You're glowing, little sis. Engagement agrees with you."

Her sister ducked her head with another bright grin.

"It does agree with her," Gran announced as she walked into the store from the back hallway. "And having you back home agrees with me."

Sarah found herself enveloped in a Gran hug and she struggled to keep tears at bay. She held her grandmother tight, thankful for the unending support from the woman who had raised her. While Seattle had been good to her, not having her family nearby had sucked. Gran, her sister and her cousins — they were the most important people to her growing up.

And Cornelius.

Her chest tightened at the thought. No, she wouldn't think about her ex-boyfriend. Or how close he was going to be while she was back in Fallbank — in the most literal sense. No need to dwell on the boy next door. The one whose heart she'd shattered along with her own.

Sarah straightened her shoulders. They'd both moved on and it was all water under the bridge. They had grown in different ways and their lives would never overlap at this point. She had to keep telling herself that. With a glance around, she saw the shop decked out for spring. Pots of pink, blue and yellow flowers dotted counters and tiny carved wood animals sprinkled the shelves. Sarah crossed to the far wall and picked up a bird. "These are cute. Where'd you find them?"

Bridget walked back around the checkout counter to her spot behind the laptop. "Oh, Cornelius made those. Aren't they adorable?"

"What?" When had he learned to make something like this? She didn't recall him having a crafting hobby.

Her sister looked up as her cheeks turned pink. "Um, I mean, Jack and Cornelius. Jack's grandpa taught him some woodworking and he picked it up again after moving here. Cornelius wanted to learn. He's really gotten into it. They use leftover scraps from Timber Logging Company and we sell the items here." She shrugged. "They donate all of the proceeds to the local animal shelter."

"Very cool," Sarah said. She was at a loss for how else to respond. A sense of pride filled her that Corey had made the little wooden bird she held. It was simple, but created with meticulous care. The curves and lines of the figure showed the craftsmanship put into it. A pang of sadness hit that she'd had no idea about this new hobby of his. But it wasn't her right. Not anymore.

Placing it back on the shelf, Sarah turned and plastered a forced smile across her face. "So, what's the latest news?"

"Nothing much, just wedding planning," Bridget replied. "We have about three months. I'm freaking out a bit. There's so much to do."

Sensing her little sister's anxiety, she kicked into oldest sibling mode to protect Bridget. "I'm here now and as your maid of honor, it's my duty to help however I can."

Gran smiled and cocked one brow at Bridget. "I told you Sarah would take care of things. She'll put together a plan in no time."

Sarah laughed for the first time in three days and it felt good. She wasn't sure what else to do with her life at the moment, but Gran was correct. Sarah would have a design for her baby sister's wedding. If anyone deserved to have a perfect day with the spotlight on her, Bridget did. Her sister took too much on for others and put herself last. It was time for Bridge to be center of attention for once. Although knowing her sibling, she'd be too intent on Jack and oblivious to all of the focus on herself. Sarah clapped her hands together. "Tell me what you have in place so far."

Her sister scrunched her nose. "We have a date and a venue? No more than fifty guests."

"Okay. We'll go from there. How about I go to the house and get settled? Then when you get home, we can talk through a few things like flowers, catering, music, cake, invitations. That sort of thing. Sound good?"

Judging from how wide Bridget opened her eyes, it did not sound good to her. "Sure…"

"Don't worry, sis. I've got you covered. Once you pick out a few things like colors and general aesthetic, I can take it from there. I know what you like."

Bridget sighed. "Perfect. Thanks, Sarah!"

"What are big sisters for?" Sarah waved then made her way up Main Street toward her car. She passed by the local bookshop and couldn't resist going in. While she didn't have space or spare money for more books, the comfort of a story and world she could fall into and forget about everything around her was too tempting.

Sarah slipped inside and inhaled the familiar scent of dust and paper and coffee. Shelves lined the walls and filled the spaces between until they parted at the back to leave space for a small coffee bar and a couple sets of two cushy chairs. Soft music in the background and an instant peace settled in Sarah's bones. Strolling the aisle, she rounded a corner to find three massive freestanding shelves and one entire wall dedicated to the romance genre.

A delighted gasp escaped her. Clasping her hands together and giving a little wiggle, Sarah embarked on investigating the offerings. She was ecstatic to find a whole subsection on sports romance with a heavy showing of hockey-based love stories. She was a sucker for those. Plucking three from the shelf and continuing on her way, Sarah added one romantasy novel with a winged elf on the cover and a contemporary romance with an adorable illustrated cover.

As she checked out, a sense of relief settled over her. Books made her feel better. That was why she gravitated toward romance—because she was guaranteed a happy resolution. Real life was hard enough and she knew she came off as cold and stony. This was her soft underbelly and she guarded it with a fierce exterior.

* * * *

Cornelius was bone tired after a long day filling in on a logging site. Even if he'd just been strapping the cables around logs for hoisting them into the backs of trucks, and not running the hill to drag them up, the work was exhausting. His evening plans consisted of a beer, whatever sports game he could find on television and nothing else. As he pulled onto his cul-de-sac, he saw something that derailed his night. An unusual car was in the driveway of the Wildes' house. Familiar, but not one that should be there.

What the hell was Sarah doing in town on a Monday? A trickle of worry slithered through his belly. Was Gran all right? She'd had a heart attack a few months ago, but had been as healthy as could be since then. Cornelius parked his truck and hopped out, peering at the sporty red car.

The sound of a door opening was all the warning he was given before Sarah appeared from the house. As she always did, the sight of her was like a punch to the gut. Her beauty never faded or grew mundane to him. From her golden blonde hair falling around her shoulders, to her dark green eyes the color of the fir trees at twilight, her full lips that still made his blood flow south and her svelte curves his hands had once upon a time memorized — they all called to him on a primal level. Time had done nothing to change that.

No getting back together. That's what Hop had taught him and God knew Hop had all kinds of experience with on-again-off-again relationships.

"Sarah?" he called and she turned those incredible eyes on him. He almost faltered in his steps.

She swallowed then lifted the corners of her mouth into a small smile. "Hey, Cornelius."

"What, um, what are you doing here?" He shuffled closer to her car. Awareness prickled along his skin at her nearness.

Sarah yanked open the back passenger door. "My apartment flooded at the end of last week," she mumbled as she snagged an overflowing box. On instinct he reached to grab it from her, but she resisted. "I've got it."

"I'm just trying to help." He refused to let go of his end of the box.

Another tug from her end. "I don't need it, but thanks."

A sigh escaped his lungs and he reigned in his frustration. Same old stoic Sarah. "I know you don't need assistance, but you don't have to do everything on your own. There's nothing to prove."

"Ugh, fine." She released the box and he staggered back a step from the sudden force. "Do what you want." She plucked a suitcase out, then spun and headed into the house.

"O-kay." He trailed after her. "So I guess the damage must have been bad?"

"Yeah, you could say that." She dumped her things in her old room and swung around to take the box from him. "I'm surprised I have anything left."

Cornelius winced. "That sucks. How long until it all gets fixed?"

She shrugged. "Longer than a week or two. So here I am," she barked

Her snarky tone took him off guard. Sarah didn't mince words, but she wasn't mean. Something must've happened to upset her this much. Of course, if her apartment had flooded bad enough she had to move back to Fallbank, that could put anyone in a terrible mood. "I'm sorry to hear about your apartment, Sarah. At least your job is cool with you working remote and you can come home to save on paying for temporary living."

Sarah dropped onto the bed and buried her face in her hands. An unintelligible noise came from behind her palms.

"I missed that."

She lifted her head with a heavy exhale. "I was laid off the same day as the building flooded. Overall, an exceptionally shitty day."

"What?" He jerked back. "They fired you? But you're great at your job. That's a stupid decision to make."

"No argument from me." She ran a hand through her hair. "There was a merger and about seventy of us were considered redundant. Then I got the text about my place. So here I am. Back in Fallbank, for who the hell knows how long."

Cornelius sank down on the mattress and wrapped an arm around her. When she leaned into him, he forced himself to refrain from pulling her closer and kissing those lips that always beguiled him. His heart raced behind his rib cage. Her floral scent of peonies jolted electricity down his nerves. Being this close to her was never good for his emotions. Instead, he focused on not being a perv who took advantage of a vulnerable woman and concentrated on comforting her as a friend. "I'm so sorry, Sarah. That is a total shit deal."

"It is, isn't it?" She snorted a laugh then sucked in a breath. "No use moping around about it. That won't change anything." Sarah stood and crossed to the door. "Better get back at it."

Cornelius followed and together they emptied her car within thirty minutes. Then he stood awkwardly by the front door. "I guess I should go."

"Yeah. Thanks for all the help. And sorry for being so grumpy earlier."

"I get it. That's a lot to have happen in the same day, let alone the same morning." It surprised him that she appeared so unflustered by the terrible turn of events.

"Yeah." She closed her eyes and sighed. She lifted one corner of her mouth into a half-smile as she opened her eyes. "I guess we'll be seeing each other around now that I'm back next door."

He nodded. "That and the wedding."

Her green eyes widened and she swallowed. "Wedding?"

A vision of Sarah in a white dress filled his imagination. For a second, he struggled to breathe. Sarah had been the only girl—woman now, he'd ever dreamed of. With a cough, he said, "Bridget and Jack. In a couple of months? I assume you'll be there?"

Sarah looked away before stuttering out a giggle. "Right. I'll be there. Maid of honor and all. Can't believe my little sister is getting married."

Cornelius smiled. "Kind of crazy. She and Jack are great together. Perfect match. Anyway, I'm going to be

28

the best man so I guess we'll be helping with all that...
You know. Planning and stuff." He waved a hand in a
vague gesture.

Her chuckle this time was real. "Yep. Planning and
stuff. We'll get through it together."

Cornelius' phone dinged with a new alert, startling
them both. A quick glance at the screen showed he'd
gotten a hit on the dating app he'd signed up for that
morning. He blinked at it, unsure what the tightness in
his chest meant. Shoving his phone into his back
pocket, he looked at Sarah. "Well, I should get home.
Early morning tomorrow at a job site."

Three little lines appeared between her brows.
"Sure. Bridget will be home soon."

"And Jack. He lives here now instead of my place."

She crinkled her nose and damn, if that didn't hit
him hard in the stomach. She was so cute and her
expression reminded him of when they used to catch
frogs. She'd loved it, but also was always just a bit
grossed out. "Right. Him, too. Not awkward at all."

They both laughed as headlights came down the
road. "Speak of the devil." He waved as Jack swung his
truck into the drive next to Sarah's.

Bridget hopped out from the passenger side and ran
over, hugging her sister with a squeal. "I'm so excited
to have you here. I know things have been a total
nightmare and coming back to Fallbank wasn't in your
plans, but I love that you and Cornelius can both come
to all the wedding planning events and give input."

Cornelius' phone chimed again and he said his
goodbyes to everyone. Once he was inside his house,
he sank onto his couch and rubbed his eyes under his
glasses. His phone sat on the coffee table like a bomb
about to go off.

Should he look at the alerts from the dating app? Was there someone else out there better for him than Sarah? Not that it mattered, because she didn't want him. Not anymore. With a grumble, he grabbed up the offending device and opened the application. Two notices waited. Heaving out a breath, he tapped the first one.

Chapter Three

Sarah woke the next morning to the sound of rain and the smell of bacon. After dressing, she headed for the kitchen where she found Bridget at the stove with Jack wrapped around her from behind and kissing her neck. A pang seared her heart. It had been years since anyone had held her like that. Dating hadn't taken top priority in her life and now she realized how empty it was.

The goal of making junior partner had reigned in her world. She'd made friends, though, hadn't she? They'd gone to bars and dinners together, talked work strategy. She bit her lip. Not one of them had texted to check in since the layoff meeting.

A giggle from Bridget broke Sarah's train of thought and she shook her mind clear. They'd all gotten fired a few days ago. It made sense no one had reached out yet. Everyone was still reeling from the news. Sarah stepped into the kitchen. "Morning."

"Hey, good morning." Bridget turned and tried to wiggle out of Jack's arms, but he followed with a grin. "How'd you sleep?"

"Oh, fine." And she had. One of the best night's sleeps in a long time. Fallbank was so quiet at night and her mattress here was softer than the one she'd bought fresh out of college back when her budget was super tight. "Why aren't you at the store? And why aren't you on a job site?"

"I'm on desk duty today and don't have to be there for another hour," Jack answered. "I get to have breakfast with my honeybee and future sister-in-law."

Bridget blushed, but her grin stretched ear to ear. "Gran is opening up the shop this morning and has Arianna there to help."

Sarah couldn't help her smirk. "So I was right in hiring her. Things worked out, huh?" It was so satisfying to be correct.

Bridget threw her a baleful look. "Arianna is great and a hard worker. You still shouldn't have hired someone without asking me. Three Sisters is my store."

Well, look at that. Her baby sister had just put Sarah in her place. *Good for Bridget.* They all sat and filled their plates with eggs, bacon and toast.

Sarah was proud of her sister's newfound backbone. She'd come into her own confidence and Sarah loved seeing her thrive. "Noted. So, store owner, do I get to come work there for a while, too?"

Bridget pursed her lips. "I could use someone for marketing and keeping the website up to date with products we have in stock." She glanced down at her plate. "I'm not sure how much I can pay you. I need to look at the books and see what's feasible."

Sarah reached out and covered her sister's hand. "That's okay. You're not charging me rent and I have money saved. I'm not saying I'll work for free, but I'm sure whatever we can sort out will be all good. I'm just grateful to have family to lean on right now."

Bridget grinned and Jack threw Sarah a smile, too. "I'm so happy to have you home, Sare-Bear. I missed you. Now let's go get dressed and see what's happening in the shop. I have a new employee to put to work."

* * * *

"Hey, Gran? Do we have any more of the muscle salve in the back? There's an online order for three and that would wipe out what's on the shelf." Sarah glanced at the wall from her perch behind the computer on the counter. As she looked over the list of orders on the screen, it appeared website shopping had taken off since her last visit to Fallbank in the autumn. She shuddered at the remembrance of Gran's heart attack. That phone call had caused a panic she hadn't felt since — well, since she'd had to break up with Corey. *Cornelius*. But that wasn't a memory trail she wanted to revisit. Ever.

"I've got the last five here." Gran came out with a small box and a smile.

Sarah snagged what she needed and put the rest on the shelf. Then she added the salve to the restocking list Bridget kept. By the looks of it, they'd need to make a few things tonight if there wasn't more at the house. A slight brush of wind accompanied the tinkling of the bell at the door. Turning, Sarah grinned. "Becca!"

Her cousin returned her expression and strode across the floor to give her a tight hug. "It's good to see you, Sare. Too long since you've been back."

Despite Sarah's angst at losing her job and the flooded apartment, she had to admit being in Fallbank was nice. She still needed to find a new job as quick as she could and get back to Seattle and her life there, but maybe updating her resume and searching job postings could wait until the weekend. Ease into the job scene. There was a four-month severance package her company had given her to keep her savings from getting completely drained.

"Being home is a good break. I wish I hadn't gotten fired and had a water pipe apartment disaster as the reasons for it, but silver linings and whatnot." She waved a hand and shrugged off her melancholy moment.

"Oh, I love this," Gran said, beaming. "All three of my granddaughters here again. Now if we could get your brother to come visit, Becca."

Becca shook her head. "Don't look at me, Gran. I'm lucky he texts me on the regular. Phone calls are almost impossible to get Hop to answer."

Gran sighed. "One day he'll come back home. Until then, I'll enjoy having my girls here."

Bridget came out from the back room with an arm full of candles. "Hey, Becca. What brings you by?"

Becca pressed her hand to her heart. "I can't just come in? I need to have motivation to come by my family's store?"

With an arched brow, Bridget waited.

"Okay, okay. I have goat milk and some fresh plant clippings in my truck for you."

"Oh, perfect. I need to make some products this week. Thanks," Bridget replied as she placed candles on different tables around the store. "And since you're here, maybe we can talk wedding dress shopping?"

Both Sarah and Becca grimaced, then laughed at each other's expressions. "I don't know why you're not enthused," Sarah said to her cousin.

"Ha, ha. Me and dresses don't go hand in hand. I can't even remember the last time I wore a skirt or dress." Becca gave an over-exaggerated shudder.

Bridget leaned against the counter. "I guess you're lucky that I'm just picking a color for my two bridesmaids to wear and not the actual outfit. I'm sure you'll find something that fits your style in a pale sky blue."

"Hell yeah!" Becca fist-bumped Bridget. "I knew you were my favorite cousin."

"Hey, now." Sarah mocked offense and crossed her arms. "What about me? What about all those times I told your parents you were sleeping over at our house so you could sneak off to do God knows what with Julie Kennedy back in high school?"

"That was then and this is now. Besides, Julie moved to Colorado, is married to her college girlfriend and has three kids." She lifted her shoulders in an exaggerated shudder. "We were never going to work out long term."

"Speaking of…" Bridget plastered on a smile as the door chimed. "Hey, guys. What brings you by?"

Sarah glanced over and saw Cornelius along with a couple of other loggers she assumed he worked with. The sight of him in dusty jeans, a well-loved flannel shirt, messy hair hanging over his forehead and those black rim glasses did things to her. Things like her heart missing a beat and her chest growing tight, not to mention a distinct tingling lower in her abdomen and heat making her skin fell tight. How did he still have such sway over her after all this time? Shouldn't she have moved on already?

"The guys need some hand lotion. The good stuff that keeps skin from cracking." Cornelius rubbed the back of his neck. "And I, uh, I need body wash."

Interesting. What had him embarrassed to ask for that? Sarah focused back on the laptop screen in front of her, doing her best to ignore the men in the store. When the two others approached, she rang up their items and found Cornelius waiting behind them.

"I'll check you out," she said and immediately wanted to kick herself. "I mean, you know." She gestured to the bottle he held. Ugh, she was acting so awkward.

"Yeah, thanks." Cornelius handed over the item and adjusted his glasses.

She made the transaction quick, but as she looked up to hand over the bag, she found Cornelius watching her. For a moment, their gazes locked and all she could do was fall into those deep blue eyes of his. She'd always loved how beautiful the blue of his irises were. Like the ocean just as dawn was breaking. Frame them with those glasses and she could combust from desire. He licked his lips and she drenched her panties. The vision of him peering up at her from between her thighs while he did wicked things with his tongue hit her hard.

A hand clamped down on his shoulder, making them both jerk free of their staring. "Ready to go?" one of the loggers asked.

"Sure thing." Cornelius turned away, but not before Sarah caught the blush creeping across his cheeks to the tips of his ears.

Sarah worried her lower lip with her teeth. What was that moment about? Did Cornelius still harbor feelings for her? A wave of sadness crested through her. As much as she might wish it, they couldn't be together again. He would never forgive her if he found out what she'd done.

* * * *

Cornelius looked over the files Jack had sent to him. Jack was on their latest job site today while Cornelius worked at the office. He read over their list of upcoming sites and the requests coming in from timber companies. His exhale ruffled the papers on his desk. They needed to recruit more people if they wanted to keep up with timber requests. Otherwise, they would need to say no to some distributors and timber purchasers would look elsewhere. If they found another reliable business that could handle the workload, those businesses wouldn't come back to Timber Logging Company.

How to get new blood in town, though? That was the big question. He'd need to figure out where to start advertising for new loggers then entice potential employees to come to Fallbank. He rubbed a hand over his forehead, then poked at his glasses. Maybe Jack would have some brilliant idea in his fancy business arsenal. It wasn't a bad problem to have — too much demand, not enough workers to keep up. But it was still an issue needing solving.

Cornelius rolled his head on his shoulders to loosen up his tight muscles. Shutting down his laptop, he packed up for the evening. Making his way home, he thought about stopping over at Jack and Bridget's, but then he saw Sarah's flashy car parked in the drive and went straight to his house. He wasn't sure he could deal with seeing Sarah so soon again. She brought back too many memories and emotions. He wasn't up for that tonight.

Instead, Cornelius found himself warming up a lasagna he'd prepped and frozen a few months back. Then he took his plate and his beer onto his back porch to enjoy the early spring evening. As he settled into his chair, a familiar head popped up over the edge of his fence.

"Hey, partner," Jack said as he glanced at the plate of lasagna and the beer sitting on the table. "How's my best man doing?"

Cornelius went on instant alert. Jack was being way too congenial now — he must be up to something. Cornelius narrowed his eyes at his friend. "What do you want, Jack?"

Jack's answering laugh was at once reassuring and alarming. "Nothing major. It's that the ladies decided the invitations for the wedding needed to go out as soon as possible. You know, since the wedding is about three months away."

"Uh-huh." Cornelius took a bite of his food, savoring the taste of cheese and marinara sauce.

"So, we thought tonight would be good for us to get those put together."

"Tonight?" Now all of the bells in Cornelius' mind were blaring. "By 'us' you mean..."

"Me and Bridget. Becca..." Jack's voice trailed off as he mumbled something that sounded like "you and Sarah."

Cornelius adjusted his glasses as he leveled a glare at his business partner across the fence. He refused to think of Jack as his best friend in this moment. "I missed what you said at the end."

Jack threw Cornelius a no nonsense look that was eerily similar to one of Gran's famous ones. "You and Sarah. There. You happy? As the best man and maid of honor, you two are obligated to join in the envelope-stuffing and address-writing fun." He sighed. "Look, I know you don't love hanging out with Sarah because of whatever happened between you two, but *I* would be grateful if you helped. I promise to supply beer for the endeavor. And Bridget made chocolate chip cookies."

That last sentence had Cornelius up and moving. "Well, you should've led with that. I don't pass up Wildes' cookies." He knew giving Jack a hard time over wedding stuff because Sarah was involved was a jerk move and he needed to squash the instinct to react that way. Whatever he felt toward Sarah didn't need to be dragged into what should be a happy and fun time for his best friend and the girl who was almost his little sister. Cornelius would focus on that and not ruin the vibe by being an ass.

Plus he really did love Bridget's chocolate chip cookies. Those damn things were magic, no matter how hard she denied it.

A few minutes later, Cornelius was sitting in Bridget's living room with a pile of envelopes and custom-printed invitations in front of him. He and Jack were on stuffing duty while Sarah and Bridge wrote addresses and Becca sealed and stamped. A half-filled plate of cookies sat on the coffee table in the middle of their little circle.

"How did you get these done so fast?" Becca asked as she studied an invitation. "And is this QR code how people RSVP?"

Bridget smiled. "Yep. I decided to save money on stamps and extra paper by having the QR code link to a site for me to track who is and isn't coming. Plus you'd be amazed at what you can design and print on your own these days."

Her cat, Candle, jumped down from the perch on her cat tower and sauntered over to where Bridget sat. She then rolled onto her back and batted at the pile there. Bridget gave Candle scritches while shifting her stack out of reach.

Cornelius paused and looked closer at the invitation. They were pretty and the cardstock was quality. "Impressive, little B! Look at you being tech savvy. Who knew you'd get one website under your belt and become a computer genius."

Bridget smirked. "This was all Sarah. She has mad marketing skills."

"Plus the print shop up the road did the heavy lifting of production," Sarah chimed in.

"*You* made these?" Cornelius blurted out. He cringed at how offensive that sounded. "Not that I don't think you couldn't make these, but you've been here a couple of days. When did you find the time?"

Sarah shrugged. "I'm not all that busy. There's only so many job postings out there for me to apply to. Plus Three Sisters seems to be a pretty well-run machine." She grinned at Bridget. "So I offered to come up with some ideas and they liked this one so much that here we are now."

"I think you're being too humble. These look awesome." He wasn't lying. The invitations had a simple but elegant font, the border showed intricate, detailed geometric lines intersecting and the overall effect was very Art Deco and sophisticated. The perfect representation of Bridget and Jack. Neither of them was flashy, but they were more traditional than hippie. And not hipster-like at all. Cornelius looked up and caught Sarah's gaze. "This is impressive, Sarie." He hadn't meant to let his old pet name for her slip out, but he'd been so awed, it had happened without thinking. He hadn't made that mistake since the night he'd called and begged her to take him back a week after she'd broken up with him. His chest ached at the memory.

He wanted to close his eyes, but was captivated by the sight across from him. Ugh, he didn't need these feelings. He wasn't getting back with her.

Sarah's skin flushed pink from the roots of her hair down past the collar of her shirt. She mumbled a thank you and fixated back on her pile of envelopes to address.

Buzzing with desire while at the same time feeling awkward, Cornelius pushed his glasses up his nose and went back to stuffing invitations. He wasn't sure if her embarrassment stemmed from the use of the nickname or his praise or both. Either way, he'd done a fine job of making everyone at the table uncomfortable.

After a moment of weird silence, Becca said, "Cornelius, have you ever thought about getting eye surgery or contacts?"

"No," both he and Sarah exclaimed at the same time. They locked eyes again and Sarah stuttered out a laugh that sounded forced to his ears.

He cleared his throat. "I, uh, I mean, it has crossed my mind, but sticking my fingers in my eyes for contacts doesn't appeal and lasering my eyes seems aggressive for what a pair of glasses can fix." And Sarah had always liked them. Especially in bed. Or anywhere she could kiss him enough to make them fog up. She had a thing for glasses, said they were sexy. He'd never wanted her to not find him sexy, so here he was. A thirty-one-year-old single man who wore glasses and couldn't seem to shake off the hold of his childhood girlfriend over a decade after she'd dumped him. God, he was pathetic.

Chapter Four

After Cornelius had departed and Jack had gone to take a shower, Sarah was left with her sister and her cousin as they finished up organizing the wedding invites. She turned over the moment he'd called her Sarie in her mind again. For maybe the thousandth time. Her heart still tripped each time she recalled it. He hadn't called her that in…twelve years? Not since he'd called her heartbroken and crying and wanting to get back together. It had killed her to stand firm and say no. When she'd hung up the phone, she'd crumpled into a ball and cried for the rest of that night. The depression that swept her up had lasted a year.

Yet here he was, calling her by that pet name and keeping his glasses. The glasses that still got her hot and bothered, as evidenced by tonight — one intense look as he'd called her Sarie and her panties were ruined. *Sarah* was ruined and she knew it. There was no lying to herself that she wouldn't fantasize about that moment in bed later tonight.

"Hey, Sarah! Hello in there." Becca waved a hand in front of Sarah's face. "Are you still with us or are you too caught up mooning over Cornelius?"

"What?" Sarah coughed in a poor attempt to cover up her daydreaming. "What are you talking about? I was thinking about job possibilities."

Becca snorted. "Sure you were."

"Anyway," Bridget said as she elbowed their cousin. "Would you be able to drop these at the post office tomorrow morning? I've got to open the store and I want these to get delivered as soon as they can."

"No problem. I'll stop by on my way over to Three Sisters. I have some ideas about updates to the website and maybe a social media campaign that I wanted to go over with you and Gran."

Bridget wrinkled her nose. "I like the website updates, but a social media campaign? Is that necessary? I don't want us to get too bogged down by online business that we can't keep up with."

"That means expansion and growth, Bridgie. All things any business owner wants." Sarah threw her sister a know-it-all look.

Her sister tossed the same expression right back at her. "Not this business owner. Three Sisters Apothecary is meant to be a small, local business with the intention of serving those in the nearby area. Not a conglomerate that doesn't give a crap about people and only cares about money."

Jack walked up and wrapped his arms around Bridget's waist as she went on her rant. "It's an argument you won't win, Sarah. I've had this conversation with my honeybee multiple times. She's not budging." He pressed a kiss to the top of Bridget's head. "And that's okay. As long as Three Sisters is going strong with the customers it has, then we're all good."

Bridget beamed. "Case closed." She turned and kissed her fiancé. "This is why I love you."

"Ugh, please stop," Becca teased.

Sarah joined in. "Or at least get a room so we don't have to bear witness." The two of them were so in love and so damn cute. Sarah hated the jealousy that flexed its claws inside her stomach each time they got this way—which was daily. Sometimes multiple times a day.

Candle took this moment to come racing in from the hallway with a long *yowl*. Sarah laughed. "See, even your cat agrees with us."

"Whatever," Bridget said and scooped up her pet. Candle then proceeded to climb from her arms up onto Jack's shoulders and lay there. "See, she loves her daddy, too." She took Jack's hand and led him down the hall. "As we were told, let's go get a room, baby." Jack called a 'good night' to both Sarah and Becca as he grinned at his fiancée.

Sarah chuckled and rolled her eyes. "Well, at least I won't see them going at it and fingers crossed, I won't hear it either."

"I guess I should head home. The animals never let me sleep in." Her cousin stood and stretched her arms over her head.

Sarah gave her cousin a hug when Becca dropped her limbs down. "It was good to hang out tonight. We should do that more."

Becca arched one dark brow at her. "We could make this a regular thing if you stayed in Fallbank." She raised her palms up. "I'm just saying."

"I need a job!" Why couldn't her family grasp that concept? The rest of them all had a steady income, but didn't think she needed the same.

"Open your own marketing firm here. There's tons of local places that would use your skills! And you and Cornelius could get over whatever it is and get back together. You know, live happily ever after? Instead of mooning over each other like lovesick puppies?"

"You're ridiculous. Neither of us does that."

"Liar. You both pine after each other like an angsty teen romance. Just get back together already."

Sarah shook her head. Her cousin didn't understand why they'd broken up in the first place and how there was no coming back from what Sarah had done. "You don't get it. We're not... Cornelius and I aren't going to be a couple again. Ever. I know it might seem like a simple answer but—" Her words stuck in her throat as her eyes stung.

Becca flapped her hands in the air. "Don't cry. You know I'm not good when it comes to someone crying. You're the strong one, remember?"

She hugged Sarah tight and Sarah leaned into the support from her cousin. "Sorry, Becca." She cleared her throat. "I'm fine. For real." Sarah stepped back and flashed a smile. "I get that no one understands why we aren't together, but trust me when I say first, it's not his fault. And second, we're not going to end up with an HEA."

"HEA?" Becca scrunched her nose.

"It's a romance novel acronym. Happily ever after." Sarah laughed. "You said it earlier, so I thought you knew."

Becca snickered along with her as they walked to the front door. "Whatever. I'm not into girly shit." Becca shook her short blonde bangs out of her eyes. "Listen. If you ever want to talk about whatever happened with you and Cornelius, I'm always here. It feels like you should unload to someone, but I'm not here to pressure. And if you aren't going to get your forever, then you can at least get a happy ending with him, if you know what I mean." She wiggled her brows at Sarah. "The tension between you two is off the charts. Maybe it would help get things out of your system so you can both move forward. Hit it and forget it."

"I don't think that's quite how the expression goes." Sarah chuckled again. "I appreciate the advice, even if I don't take it."

* * * *

Cornelius glared as Jack sauntered in whistling the next day. Why was his friend always in such a damn good mood? It wasn't normal.

"Good morning," Jack said as he plopped into his chair.

"Morning," Cornelius grunted. "Took you long enough to show up today."

"I'm fifteen minutes late. What's up with you, man?"

Cornelius shoved a hand through his hair and sighed. "Nothing. Just didn't sleep well." Not with dreams plagued by Sarah... Sarah teasing him. Sarah kissing him. Sarah stripping her clothes off for him. Sarah looking up at him from her knees while—

He gave his head a violent shake. With every toss and turn, he'd dreamed of Sarah and woken up with a raging hard-on every hour of the night. He'd slept like shit and was grumpy from the least satisfying shower despite his self-administration to get some relief.

"We need to talk about how we're going to handle all of the upcoming jobs. I've gotten three new requests, all at least half million in lumber. We don't have the crew to get them completed in time. I don't want to say no and have these companies go elsewhere for their supply." Best to deflect away from poking around why he didn't sleep well and focus Jack on the business. That should keep the two of them occupied strategizing for a while.

"So we'll hire new people. Easy solution. We can cover the extra salary and costs. Are you thinking temporary or permanent positions?"

Cornelius gaped at his partner. "It's not that simple. I think we need to make permanent expansions to the crews, but where do we find workers? It's not as if loggers are lining up outside the door looking for work."

"So we advertise." Jack shrugged. "There's people out there looking for good paying work. We offer competitive salaries and benefits. We might not be other companies' favorites after some of their employees come to us, but hey, free market. Ante up if you want to keep teams happy."

"How do you suppose we advertise? Do you know how to write job descriptions that entice and catch someone's eye? Where do you suggest we put these ads?"

Jack sighed. "Marketing. We find someone who can help put something together to show we loggers should come work for us." He lifted his brows. "I might have a couple of connections with firms in Seattle."

"I don't want some fancy-pants company." Cornelius waved an arm around him. "Look at this place. I know we updated the office, but we're still in small-town Oregon and we aren't bougie. Not to mention I'm not paying the price tag that comes with some big-ass firm like that. Even with your connections, they still expect to be paid."

"All right. Calm down, dude." Jack sat back in his chair and crossed his arms. "There is another solution, you know. Someone in town."

"Here? In Fallbank? We don't have…" Understanding dawned on him. Followed by instant denial. No way he wanted to include Sarah in TLC work. "Wait, no. No, we are not hiring my ex-girlfriend. Uh-uh."

"She's my future sister-in-law and why not? Sarah's great at what she does. She's local and wouldn't charge her soon-to-be brother-in-law a fortune to work with him. Plus it might convince her to stay in Fallbank." A grin spread across Jack's face. "Bridget would be thrilled if her sister lived here again. And if I were the reason why? Yeah, that's the plan. Hire Sarah and make her stay."

"Look, you get laid enough as it is. I can't stand your goofy, stupid-in-love-ness already. I don't need to add to it. Plus, as I said, I don't want to work with my ex." It would be the most divine torture and he would snap.

Jack dropped his smile, leaned forward on his elbows and arranged his expression into one of seriousness that had terrified boardrooms throughout Seattle once upon a time. "I know you and Sarah have history. Yet both of you keep insisting you don't have feelings for each other. You and she have to do wedding stuff together, so what's a couple of extra meetings? Tell you what, you find us a better alternative in Fallbank and we'll go with it. Otherwise, we at least ask Sarah. She might not even say yes."

"Okay. Fine," Cornelius grumbled. Jack had him backed into a corner and Cornelius knew it. Everything Jack had said was true, but there had to be another alternative in town. There had to be someone who could help. If nothing else, Cornelius could always go down to the local high school and see if there were any graduating seniors looking for jobs instead of running straight off to college. He knew not every kid here went to a university. Lots of them went into blue-collar work or took classes at the community college while working to save up. Maybe having someone else advertise wasn't necessary.

"You have a deal, Jack. I'll see what I can drum up here in town and I'm betting to say we won't end up needing Sarah's help." Cornelius fought to keep the smirk off his face. He'd stick it to Jack with how simple this was going to be. He couldn't wait to see the look on his friend's face when he hired the crew needed in record time—and without the aid of any marketing or advertising.

"You're going to try to recruit on your own, aren't you?"

Cornelius blinked at Jack. "How did you—"

"And you think going to find new workers is something you can do on your own. At like the community colleges or high schools, right?"

"What? Can you read minds or something? Does Bridget know about this? Because she's *not* a fan of anything magic in case you didn't pick up on that."

Jack threw his head back and laughed. "Yeah, I'm well aware of my honeybee's opinions on magic. And no, I'm not reading your mind. I'm just good at business. You do know part of my family's holdings are in construction, right?"

"Yeah. I seem to recall that from your confession to me a while back," Cornelius said in a flat tone. He was starting to get annoyed here and that wasn't going to help his mood.

"So I've been there and done that. I know that those kids need a chance to get started and I'm not opposed to that. Go ahead and hire them. Get them started in training for how to log. But for the love of all the kittens and bunnies, let someone help us advertise to hire on experienced workers, too. These jobs, the new ones rolling in and the ones we hope to have follow, can't be screwed up. We need at least three new seasoned loggers to be able to manage the incoming contracts. And if we can get an additional five young kids hired and trained over that time? That's when we'll be in a good place. Trust me when I say we'll need outside help getting not just numbers on the jobs, but quality employees to do the jobs right. Plus more job contracts to keep these new employees paid."

Cornelius flopped back in his seat, knowing he was beaten. "You win. We'll hire Sarah to help." He sat up and pointed at Jack. "But I'm still recruiting at the schools. We need fresh loggers, too."

Jack grinned. "Sounds like a plan to me."

* * * *

Later, when Cornelius was driving home, his phone rang with his dad's number popping up. Answering on his truck's Bluetooth, he said, "Hey, Pops, what's up?"

"Cornelius? Are you at home?" His dad's voice sounded shaky and thin. "Your mother and I have something we need to talk to you about."

Anxiety curled in ribbons around Cornelius' chest. He'd never heard his father sound like this before, like the weight of the world was on crushing his shoulders.

"Hi, honey," his mom piped up.

Alarms blared inside Cornelius' head now. She sounded as if she'd been crying and hadn't slept in weeks. He pulled the car over to the side of the road and switched to the phone speaker instead. "What's going on?"

"Well, sweetheart," his mother began but his father interrupted.

"Your mother is sick, Cornelius."

A cold, gaping void opened in Cornelius' stomach and ice ran through his veins. "Sick? Sick how?"

His mother spoke again. "We caught things early –"

"Your mother has breast cancer," his father announced.

Cornelius' world ripped out from under him. His mother had cancer? His hands shook and sweat broke out on his forehead.

"Boyd! If you don't stop interrupting me, so help me I will take you out and abandon you on the side of the road."

"I'm sorry, Clarissa. I don't mean to talk over you, it's just that –"

"That you're having trouble with your feelings and processing the news we were just given." His mother's voice gentled. "I understand that. But let's not send our son into a nervous breakdown, either."

He reached his breaking point. "Mom! Pops! Would one of you please tell me what's going on? You have cancer, Mom?" His heart pounded like a waterfall beating down on a rock. Was his mother dying? He was thirty-one and not ready to lose her. There was so much left in life for her.

"Honey, I'm going to be okay."

Cornelius blinked hard as tears formed in his eyes. He pushed his voice past the clog in his throat. "You will, Mama?"

"Oh, Cornelius, don't cry. I can't stand it that my baby is crying and I'm not there to hug it better." Now she sounded like she was crying, too.

He wiped his eyes using his sleeve and blew out a deep breath. His mom needed strength right now, not worrying about him falling apart. "I'm all right. Tell me what's going on?"

"Well, they found a spot on my last mammogram and after more imaging and a biopsy the doctors determined I have breast cancer. The good news is they caught it early. I'll have surgery in a few days and then start chemotherapy."

Surgery? Chemo? This sounded worse to Cornelius than his mother seemed to think. "This is serious. I think I should come down to Eureka for a while and help out."

"That's very sweet, Cornelius, but we're okay. I know this sounds frightening and my oncologist did say I'd be monitored from here on out, but she's very optimistic the cancer is treatable at this point with a high probability of remission."

"I still want to be there, at least for the surgery." He couldn't let her go through all of this without him there for support. It wouldn't happen.

His dad said, "Your mother and I would appreciate that. I could use the comfort while all that's going on. The surgery is set for Wednesday."

"I'll book flights right away."

Chapter Five

Sarah checked her email again and glared. Still nothing in her inbox about any of the jobs she'd applied to. Wasn't she qualified? Didn't over ten years in the industry give her enough experience? She'd been successful, landed tons of accounts, led hundreds of campaigns. Her references were outstanding. So, what was the deal? It wasn't the holiday season where everyone was on vacation. It was March, for crying out loud. This was a great time of year to apply for jobs. Yet, here she was a week after sending her resume and applications in with nothing in return. A frustrated sigh left her and she snapped her laptop shut. Crossing her arms, she glanced around the empty store to find something to keep her occupied.

Gran came in through the back and approached where Sarah sat at the counter. Giving Sarah a side hug, Gran asked, "What's the face for?"

"I'm just discouraged about jobs. I applied to several a week ago and haven't heard back about any of them.

I don't get it." She wanted to throw or hit something — anything to let off some frustration.

Gran tsked. "Give it time. Goodness, one week is a mere blink when it comes to business. You know that. The right answer will come when it should. Until then, it's not as if you aren't in a good place. You're much more fortunate than most who lose their jobs."

"I get it and I don't mean to sound ungrateful. You're right. I'm luckier than most, but I guess I thought I'd find something right away." Sarah grumbled under her breath. "And that I'd still have my own place in Seattle." She hated when her grandmother's logic prevailed. One week wasn't enough time for things to move in the corporate world.

"What was that, dear?" Gran cocked an eyebrow and gave Sarah a Look.

Sarah fought against the heat rising in her face. Of course her grandma's hearing was still excellent in spite of her age. "Nothing, Gran."

The older woman humphed. "I thought so." Gran puttered around the shop, tweaking displays here and there. "How are things living with Bridget and Jack?"

"Good. No complaints." None aside from having their true love shoved in her face any time they were all in the same room. It was petty to whine about that. She adored her sister and was thrilled she'd found Jack, but damn if it didn't rub salt in Sarah's wounded heart. She'd spent years moving on from Cornelius and now she felt like she'd fallen down the cliff she'd worked so hard to climb. All it had taken were a few interactions with him to throw her into emotional turmoil. Between the love birds at home and her ex living next door, Sarah realized maybe she hadn't healed as much as she'd thought...not that getting back with Cornelius was an option. *Nope.*

"How are wedding plans?" Gran asked.

Wincing inside, Sarah smiled on the outside. "Great! The invitations are all mailed and Bridget has the Wild Rose Inn reserved for the ceremony and reception. I think we're going dress shopping this weekend. Maybe some kind of meeting at Wild Rose for planning? I think Becca said she'd take care of flowers from her own garden." There was so much to do and not a lot of time. March was halfway gone and the wedding would be here faster than they could blink.

With a nod, Gran said, "Becca and I have the flowers set. We've already gotten ideas from Bridget and have early plans in place."

The door chimed and both women looked over to see who entered. Gran beamed. "Hello, my almost grandson. What a lovely surprise!"

Jack walked over and hugged her grandmother. "Morning, Gran. You're looking spry as ever."

"Flattery will get you everywhere with me." Gran chuckled. "What brings you by? Bridget isn't here at the moment."

"I know. I'm here on official TLC business." He looked over at Sarah. "Do you have a few minutes?"

"Sure, what's up?" She wondered what Jack could need from her for Timber Logging. And why talk to her here instead of at home?

He nodded his head over to the corner and they walked a few feet away. Gran busied herself with straightening shelves on the opposite side of the store. Jack cleared his throat. "Timber Logging is in need of some marketing services. We need to hire new loggers, ones with experience."

"You need an HR person. Not marketing." Sarah tried to tamp down her annoyance. This wasn't the first time someone had confused the purpose of a marketing advisor.

"I need someone who can make what I write for job descriptions sound catchy and know where to advertise. Marketing. Not Human Resources. Plus, it would be great to have some pieces for actual promotion of TLC to get more timber requests, maybe even some long-term contracts. That's right up your alley." Jack grinned.

Sarah didn't. "I don't want your pity job. I have enough saved to be okay while I find something else." Ugh, she wanted to wipe off the smug look on her soon-to-be brother-in-law's face.

"Not what this is. At all." He sighed and gave her a serious look. "I've been going through every book and spreadsheet for TLC. We're not in trouble by any means, but I know how fast winds can change in the business world. We need to expand and have backups. I'd like to hire some seasoned workers, not just the local kids who are brand-new to logging. We need both to keep moving forward, plus new job contracts to keep them employed. I'm willing to pay you market value."

She snorted. As if he knew how high her hourly rate was. "You can't afford me."

The charming smile returned. "You mean you won't give your brother-in-law a family discount?"

"You aren't married to my sister yet." She crossed her arms. Given she didn't have any current job interviews and she'd applied to all the open positions out there right now, Sarah couldn't afford to turn Jack down. She just wasn't sure what this meant for interacting with Cornelius. "Listen, I know Fallbank doesn't garner what I'd be paid by a big firm in Seattle. I'm willing to be reasonable about my rate. What would this entail? Do you want me at your office or something? I can't abandon the shifts I'm working here." Please, please let him pick up on her need to avoid his business partner.

"I wouldn't ask you to stop helping at Three Sisters. That would be sacrilege." He pressed a hand over his heart with a mock gasp. "And you don't need to come into the office. We see each other often enough. I'll email you what I have for the job descriptions and what I'm thinking for a potential advertising campaign."

"And I'll fix all of it. From the comfort of home or the store when it's quiet." Gratitude at not having to go into TLC offices weakened her resolve. As long as she could evade Corey, this side hustle could work out.

Jack nodded. "Done."

"You have a deal." She held out her hand and he shook it. "But this is temporary. Once I start getting job interviews and offers, I'll wrap up whatever I'm working on for you and that's it."

"You got it. Wouldn't want to derail your job search."

Sarah wasn't so sure about Jack's sincerity with his last comment. His cat-eating-the-cream smirk was far too suspect for her liking.

* * * *

Cornelius exited the regional airport in Eureka and made his way to his rideshare pickup while checking his phone again to see if his dad had texted. He assumed no news was good news and fired off a message that he was on his way to the hospital.

Cornelius hadn't taken his father up on the offer of a ride so that his parents wouldn't be separated. Even though the surgery wasn't scheduled for another few hours, their arrival time was far in advance. Anxiety swamped him as he sweated through the entire twelve-minute drive. Once he could see his mom in person, he knew he'd feel better...at least he hoped. He had to hold it together for a little bit longer and he'd be reunited with her. He bounced his foot hard enough the seat shook.

After navigating the medical complex and getting to her waiting room, Cornelius took a moment to breathe and calm his nerves. No reason to go in and make his mother upset or worry about him. He needed to keep focus on her and nothing else. Plastering a smile across his face, he knocked and opened the door. "Hey, Mom!"

Clarissa Hawthorne looked small and fragile in the hospital bed, hooked up to machines surrounding her. Her cheekbones stood out in her face from weight loss and her skin was paler than normal. She still beamed at him, though. "Hi, sweetheart."

Cornelius blinked at the stinging in his eyes. Dammit, he hadn't wanted to get emotional in front of her. There was no reason to add to her stress. "You look good," he lied. "How're you feeling?"

"Come here, honey," she said and opened her arms.

Like he was still five years old, Cornelius threw himself into his mother's hug—albeit with more gentleness, and let himself cry. Her eyes were wet too when he pulled back. His mom patted his cheek. "Feel better? I'm going to be okay, I promise."

"You can't promise that, Mama." Cornelius choked out the words, still tied up with his emotions that his strong, vibrant mother was having surgery, that she had cancer. A cold pit of fear in his stomach opened and refused to close shut. His mom had to be okay. No other option was acceptable.

"You're right. No one can. That doesn't mean I won't fight my hardest to recover. The doctors have high hopes that all of this will resolve." She squeezed his hands. "I know I've lost a few pounds and I'm having surgery, but I do feel fine."

Her reassurances eased some of the apprehension in his body. "That's good. You know you and pops can always call me if you need anything." Cornelius turned to greet his dad. "Hey, old man. You look like crap." This time no lies were detected. Boyd looked haggard and defeated, tired in a way that Cornelius had never before seen in his father.

His father chuckled. "I know. I'm taking this harder than your mother."

"We both are." Cornelius shoved his glasses back up his nose. "Hate to see the woman in our lives sick and we can't do a damn thing about it." He despised this helplessness.

"All right. That's enough fussing over me." His mom waved a hand at Cornelius. "I'm more concerned that I'm the lone lady in your life. Aren't you dating anyone?"

Sarah popped into mind and Cornelius just as fast shoved that thought away. She was back in town and seeing her was torture, but that was how things were. No changing that situation, either. They had broken up for a reason. Sure, he still might not know what that reason was, but it was something on Sarah's end. He needed to move past these lingering feelings for her and find someone new. The dating app notifications he'd ignored made his phone seem like a lead weight in his pocket. "I'm not seeing anyone right now, but I am open to it."

"Maybe you should get on those app things to meet girls," his dad suggested.

"Women, pops. I date women, not girls." Cornelius gave an exaggerated shudder.

His dad rolled his eyes. "You know what I mean."

"Yeah, yeah. I'm trying to lighten the mood. It's heavy in here." Cornelius sighed. "I'm on dating apps. There's not a lot of options in Fallbank. Even expanding the mileage range still doesn't give much."

His mom opened her mouth, but a nurse walked in. "Hello, Mrs. Hawthorne. We're ready to get you wheeled back to the operating room for your procedure." The nurse smiled at all three of them. "We'll take good care of her. I promise. Dr. Ateyemi is the best. She's a fantastic surgeon."

Cornelius and his dad made their goodbyes to Clarissa and both men managed to keep crying at bay. Once they were out in the waiting room, his dad went to grab coffee while Cornelius staked out a couple of chairs.

While he waited, Cornelius checked his phone. A text from Jack had come in a while back.

Jack: Talked to Sarah and she's on board. Good to go for help with the job and general TLC ads.

Running a hand through his hair, Cornelius exhaled. He couldn't begin to unpack how that made him feel, given the status of his temperament and the situation at hand. He needed to not blow off Jack, yet didn't want to commit to working with Sarah.

Cornelius: Cool. Let me know if you need any help.

Jack: How's it going? Your mom doing all right? You hanging in there?

Cornelius: Yeah, things are okay. My mom's surgery started a few minutes ago. I'll check in with you after she's done here.

He drifted his gaze up to the first text, the one about Sarah. A pang of sadness hit him in the chest. Twelve years later and he still missed her like their breakup was yesterday. It didn't make sense. He should have moved on. God knew he'd tried. When she wasn't around for long stretches, he would believe he'd gotten past all of this, that he'd stopped loving her. Yet as soon as she came back to town or someone mentioned her in conversation and Cornelius was back at square one. Maybe she would always be the one that got away, the one his heart would want more than any other.

He'd fallen for her the day they'd met — the day she had moved in with her grandparents. He'd seen her before on family visits, but never said hello. That day she'd sat on the sidewalk in a black dress, sadness draped over her like an invisible blanket. He couldn't not speak to her to try to cheer her up. His poor ten-year-old heart never stood a chance. Of course when she'd kissed him at age twelve, let him get to third base at age fifteen and slide all the way home at sixteen, he believed they'd be together forever.

Too bad life threw a curve ball he couldn't hit. Seattle had changed Sarah and with that her plans had, too...plans that no longer included him. Yet here he was, still mooning over her and wishing for one more chance at bat. He shook his head. Ugh, his stupid metaphors were annoying even him. "Get your shit together, Hawthorne."

He could hear Hop's voice in his brain.

"Let me give you advice you'll never need. Don't get back together with an ex. It doesn't work out. Ever. Trust me."

Cornelius did. He'd seen how Hop's high school girlfriend had dragged him along for years. Then there was the woman he'd met at his first mobilization post and their volatile break-up-make-up relationship. Hop spoke from hard-earned experience.

"Hey, son." His dad sank into the chair next to him and handed over a cup of coffee. "What's got you looking depressed? Aside from the obvious?"

Adjusting his glasses, Cornelius shrugged. "Thinking about life. Women. Getting married. Having kids. The fact that I'm thirty-one and single."

His father nodded. "Understandable. Your mother and I don't mean to put pressure on you. Like most parents, we'd like to see you settled with someone. A family of your own before we depart this world. Assurance that you'll have loved ones by your side."

"Jeez, Pops. Way to make this super morbid. You and Mom are *not* dying on me."

"Not tomorrow, but one day in the future we will. We worry about you and don't want you to be alone. Your mother in particular. She wants to hold her own grandchildren."

Grandchildren? Cornelius struggled with finding a date, let alone someone to have kids with. The idea was like ice cold water thrown down his back. "Dad, I..."

"I know. You're having a hard time finding someone. You don't want to settle and that's a good thing. Nothing wrong with taking your time for the right person." His dad glanced at the doors to the OR. "Just maybe don't take too long."

Cornelius patted his father on the back. "I'll do my best, Pops." As he stared at the doors, willing the doctor to come through them even though there were still several hours to go, he realized he needed to change his habits, make a real effort at meeting women and finding a real relationship. He might not be able to let go of Sarah entirely, but that didn't mean he couldn't fall in love with someone else.

Chapter Six

Sarah grinned at her little sister's excitement to go wedding dress shopping. The weather was sunny today and while still chilly, it put Sarah in a good mood. Puffy clouds danced across the sky and the damp earth was on the cusp of bursting into fresh growth and blooms. Stark tree limbs along the sidewalk were laden with buds prepping to herald in spring over the next few weeks.

The two sisters walked into Meant To Be Bridal and Tuxes alongside Becca and Gran. Even Becca seemed cheerful about the outing despite not being a lover of all things girly.

"Okay, let's start with the bridesmaids," Bridget announced after they'd been greeted and shown to their own space by the store owner.

"Bridesmaids? No way, we start with you. The bride," Sarah argued. Why on earth would they not start with Bridget? Her sister was too spotlight aversive.

Bridget shook her head. "No, starting with you is better. This will help me get the vibe of the wedding, how dressy to be or not be."

"Wrong." Becca crossed her arms. "You set the tone—your dress, your wedding, your vibe."

Sarah watched her sister chew on her lower lip. "Is it that you don't know what you want?"

"Yeah. Does that make me a bad bride?" Bridget grimaced.

Gran chuckled. "Not at all, Bridgie. All you need is to look around and try on different options. See what catches your eye and find similar styles until the right dress comes along."

"How will I know?"

Sarah leveled a stare at her sister. "You'll know." She might have to nurture her sister through figuring out what she wanted, but Sarah could keep watch for subtle signs of excitement and wanting as they tried on options. She'd convince her sister she knew what she wanted. It was all about encouraging her sister's subconscious desires to the forefront.

Bridget shrugged and glanced around. "I'm not even sure where to begin."

"Divide and conquer." Sarah nodded at Gran and Becca. "Let's all take a lap and pull some options for Bridget to try on and get a feel for what's out there." She looked at Bridget with what she hoped was an encouraging smile. "We know your style. Trust us." Time to take the worry away from her baby sibling and let her bask in the thrill of getting married.

Lana, the owner of the shop, circled back to their group. "Ladies, can I help get you going? Perhaps pull some dresses that would look stunning on our bride to be?" Lana beamed at Bridget.

Becca shook her head. "Do you have anything to drink you could get us? Bridge is a bit shy and is feeling a little nervous. We can take a look around if you don't mind getting her comfortable?"

"Champagne for everyone, then?"

Gran cackled. "You are an excellent business woman. Yes, please!" She patted Bridget on the shoulder. "Have a seat here, dear. We'll be back and then the fun will start."

Bridget sat while Sarah and the others split into different directions. Sarah perused the racks of dresses in a front corner of the store. Tulle, lace, sequins, crystals and beading glinted at her from all angles. Mannequin forms displayed dresses with voluminous skirts and trains. They were all gorgeous in their own way, but most were too fussy for her little sister. Bridget's style was understated. Simple and elegant. Perhaps a touch of lace, but nothing with sparkles. No giant skirt or cathedral-length silk flowing out behind.

Sarah grabbed a few options when an all-lace number caught her eye — sheer silk lining overlaid with diaphanous lace panels. A sweetheart neckline fell into a fit and flare skirt that pooled into a chapel-length train at the floor. The lace threads had a subtle shimmer to them, making the light catch the floral pattern and bring it to life. It took Sarah's breath away. Not for her sister, but for herself. This was the exact style she could picture wearing at her own wedding...sexy and sophisticated, elegant with a flashy touch.

Without thinking, she grabbed the hanger and walked over to a grouping of mirrors. She laid the other dresses across the back of a chaise and held up the gown. Tucking the hanger down, she pressed the cool fabric across her chest and admired her reflection. With the sweep of her blonde hair over one shoulder, brushing the top of the bodice, and the lace puddled at her feet, it looked stunning. She didn't need to put it on. She knew. It was *the dress*. Sarah's heart sped into a canter as she blinked at the image. Her palms grew damp and a lump formed in her throat. Loneliness reached its cold hand into her chest and crushed the air out of her lungs. On a strangled gasp, she stuttered in a breath and swallowed. What was she doing? Fantasizing about wedding dresses when she had no one in her life? She hadn't been serious with anyone in…years. Over a decade. Not since—

"Sarah?"

She whirled around, heart thumping triple time. His voice…how was he here at this exact moment?

Cornelius stared at her, slack jawed. He ran his gaze over her and his Adam's apple bobbed a couple of times. He looked like he'd swallowed his tongue. "You look…ethereal." He pushed his glasses up, then rubbed at his chest.

Heat flushed over Sarah from the roots of her hair to the tip of her toes. Desire flexed inside her body. Then she remembered what she held in her hands. Humiliation lashed her thoughts back to the present. Yanking the dress down, she looked at the floor and wished for a way to disappear. Could a giant hole open under her feet and swallow her whole? With a flit of her eyes back to where Cornelius still stood, she shuffled back to the pile of options for Bridget.

Her sister. Getting married. The one Sarah was here for today. Not herself. *Stupid woman.*

"Hey, Cornelius," Sarah mumbled. "What're you doing here?"

For a hot second, he blinked at her. "I'm, uh, here…Why am I here?" He furrowed his brow.

"In a bridal store?" Sarah cast around for anything to take the heat off of her fawning over a wedding dress like a real-life heart-eyes emoji.

He scratched at his head and the tips of his ears turned pink. Then he seemed to shake himself. "Right. Tuxes. I'm meeting Jack to try on tuxes."

"Jack is here?" Sarah shouted. Alarm shot through her. She scooped up the gowns and raced around the corner to where Bridget sat sipping champagne. "Jack just showed up. He can't see you!"

Her sister laughed. "Calm down. I know he's trying on tuxedos today. I wanted to watch and help."

"But then he could catch you in your wedding dress. That is unacceptable." Sarah dumped the pile of white fabric onto the couch. "He has to leave." How was Bridget so chill about this?

Jack sauntered over with Cornelius in his wake. Sarah glared at the two of them in the mirror.

Her soon-to-be brother-in-law bent and kissed Bridget's cheek. "Hey, honeybee."

Bridget giggled and again, Sarah was enveloped in the chill of her single status.

"Hi, Jack." Bridget stood and snuggled up against his side. "I can't wait to see you all dressed up."

The look between the two of them morphed into something so intimate and heated, Sarah wanted to fan herself. "Okay, okay. Save *that* kind of vibe for the bedroom. We're in public here, kids." Sarah propped her hands on her hips. "How are we supposed to wedding-dress shop with the groom here?" Why was she the one who cared about this?

Jack shrugged as Bridget still grinned. "The guys' side is way over there." Bridget pointed. "And maybe you and Becca could look at bridesmaid dresses while they're here?"

"Second option. Wanna help me change?" Jack teased with a waggle of his eyebrows.

Becca made a gagging sound and Sarah waved her arms. "Knock it off." She marched over to the two guys. Placing a hand on each one's arm, she pushed. "Go. You are not to cross the threshold from the groom's side to the bride's side of the store under any circumstances." That should quell any chance of an accidental bride sighting.

"What if there's a fire?" Cornelius quipped.

"Ha, ha." Sarah shook her head with a half-smile. "I'm serious. No peeking. This is not a joke."

Jack held his palms up in surrender. "All right, all right. We'll go. But if Bridget wants to have a say in what we pick, she'll have to come over."

"Deal. Now shoo."

* * * *

Cornelius shoved his arms through the third jacket he'd tried on this afternoon. He still couldn't shake the vision of Sarah and that dress. With her golden hair and dark green eyes and all that white lace, she'd almost brought him to his knees. God knew what would have happened if she'd been wearing it instead of holding it up. It was the kind of gown he'd pictured back when they'd been together… When he thought they'd spend the rest of their lives in love with each other, married, with babies. Maybe a pet. And all the sex.

He blew out a harsh breath. He needed to get a grip and find someone else to fill this void in his heart and his soul, to keep the aching desolation from ripping him apart. Why had Sarah's return made this feeling so strong? Sure, he'd felt alone from time to time, but seeing Sarah on the regular had caused him to realize how lonely he was. Compound that with his mother's illness and he felt like his life was a ticking time bomb. At thirty-one, what did he have to show from a relationship perspective? His professional life was amazing, but was it worthwhile without someone to share it?

Bang. Bang.

"You good in there?" Jack asked through the door.

"Coming," he said and opened the door. Stepping out, Cornelius noticed Bridget standing by the mirrors.

"You guys look fantastic." She stared at Jack and licked her lips. "Super handsome. Hot."

Ugh. He didn't want to watch the two of them eye-fuck one another. "Thanks, little B."

She jerked her face in his direction, her cheeks pink with embarrassment. "I think this is the one. The peak lapel emphasizes the lumberjack shoulders. You both should take advantage of that."

Cornelius did have to admit, the trim cut and wider, pointed tips of the fabric did make his stature look good. He didn't have quite the hefty build that Jack did, but he wasn't a slouch either. Years of logging had toned his body and he'd never heard any complaints when his shirt was off in front of the fairer sex, rare occasions that those were. "Yeah, I like it, too."

Jack nodded. "So I'll have a white bow tie and Cornelius and Hiro will have light blue to match the bridesmaids?"

"Mmm," Bridget hummed. She was drooling over Jack again.

"Bridge, what's taking so long?" Sarah walked up behind her sister and stumbled to a halt. Her gaze snagged on him and didn't move.

Bridget shifted to the side, and holy hell, Cornelius was slapped again with Sarah's beauty. She was in a sky-blue dress that plunged down between her breasts in a V, cinched above her waist to emphasize her bust and flared into a flowing skirt. A mirror in the corner offered a behind image of thick, smooth rope that traced her shoulders to twine together down her spine, then wrapped three times around the high waist before knotting in the front to let the ends dangle along the waves of the soft fabric skirt.

The style was very Roman goddess come to life. It hugged her curves and made his mouth water. Her tits looked spectacular. She'd gotten more lush over the passing years and he would give his last dollar to be able to explore every inch of her body. His blood flowed south and he shifted on his feet. Shit, he didn't need to sport his erection to everyone in the store. Clearing his throat, he buttoned the satiny jacket, but that served to highlight his growing bulge. He began reciting baseball stats from his favorite team in his head, anything to take his mind off the desire pulsing through him.

"Don't the guys look amazing?" Bridget grabbed Sarah's arm and tugged. "Come stand by Cornelius so I can see you two next to each other. I want to be able to picture this for the wedding."

With awkward movements, Sarah shuffled to pose next to him. Cornelius forced a smile on his face, but was afraid the heat rolling off him would be noticeable. He was sweating at the back of his neck. The reflection of him in a tux with Sarah gorgeously attired next to him did strange things to his stomach—and his heart. He could see the two of them receding down the aisle, one of her hands tucked in his elbow with a bouquet in her other. Except it was her in that damn wedding dress she'd been holding earlier he was now envisioning. His heart pounded so hard he could see his pulse racing at his throat in the mirror. Shit, this was bad. He was so screwed.

"Perfect," Bridget chirped and broke Cornelius free of his reverie. "You look perfect together." She clapped her hands and beamed at Jack. He grinned right back.

At least the two of them were oblivious to the tension flowing between Cornelius and Sarah. Or Cornelius at any rate. Maybe Sarah wasn't as affected... He chanced another look at Sarah and yep, she had hunger in her eyes. He knew that look. He'd seen it enough growing up that there was no mistaking it. His groin tightened again.

"Oh, my!" Gran's voice rang out. "Don't you all look beautiful."

It was the welcome dose of figurative cold water Cornelius needed. No way could he sport wood in front of Gran. Exhaling, he side-stepped away from his ex-girlfriend. Her skin was flushed and she kept her gaze on the dark-grained planks of the floor.

"Cool. I'm going back to the other side to change. Bridge, we still have dresses for you to put on." Sarah gave a brisk nod and speed-walked out of the room.

"I'm going to change, too." Cornelius jerked his thumb toward the dressing room.

"Just a minute," Seth, the store associate said. "I need to get your measurements to ensure we reserve the correct suit for you." He held up a tape measure and clipboard.

"Right." Cornelius walked over to the low platform. He refrained from urging Seth to hurry up so he could get out of view, change clothes and get rid of this echoing desire.

"So you and the lady in the blue dress make a lovely couple." Seth scribbled notes as he held the tape along Cornelius' arms and shoulders, waist and legs.

"Oh, we're not—that is, she and I used to, but not anymore. We're friends. Her sister is the bride and the groom is my work partner." He locked down his muscles so as not to give away his inner mortification over his bumbling response.

"And best friend," Jack interjected as Bridget and Gran departed. "Jeez, make me look like we're just business associates."

"That, too," Cornelius agreed. And now he'd offended his buddy.

"Although, I have to side with Seth here. You and Sarah looked pretty good together. Maybe you should give it another try."

"We're friends. That's all." Cornelius smothered the hope in his chest. He'd learned there was no going back with Sarah. She'd moved on, no matter if she still found him attractive or not. That much had been made clear over the past twelve years. He walked to the changing room and called over his shoulder, "But I'll find a date for the wedding, don't worry." He had to. He couldn't take this oppressive solitude any longer.

Chapter Seven

Sarah sipped her latte while she worked on the job descriptions and marketing pieces for Timber Logging Company at a window table in the Evergreen Espresso. The view highlighted Main Street's vintage buildings, a gray sky and a steady fall of rain—exactly what to expect from early spring in the Pacific Northwest. The cozy feel of the cafe was bright and inviting though. Tiny vases with fresh flowers sat on each table giving a hint of the warmer weather to come.

If she were honest, the job postings weren't too difficult. Jack and Cornelius had the means to pay higher wages and offer better benefits than most of their competitors. Jack knew how to find avenues within TLC to cut costs so the money could be funneled into hiring and keeping quality employees. It was a sound proposition. A reliable workforce meant getting hired to clear land, which equated to more money coming into the business to keep it progressing forward.

Finding ways to advertise for TLC was a bit trickier. She'd dug into how to pitch for some of the state and national forestry services and those were great contracts if the company could get them. There was also ensuring the local farms knew about TLC for their lumber harvesting, too. Sarah had a few ideas sketched out and was fleshing out a forestry service slide deck when another woman approached her.

"It *is* you, Sarah Wildes. I thought I'd heard you were back home and here you are!"

Sarah lifted the corners of her lips into a small smile. Dorothy Ferrars, antique shop owner and Fallbank's most notorious busybody, vibrated next to her table. "Hello, Ms. Ferrars. How are you?"

Dorothy waved a hand. "None of this Ms. Ferrars business. Call me Dori. You're not a young girl running wild anymore. What brings you back here all the way from Seattle?"

Sarah winced on the inside. She knew as soon as Dori heard the news, it would be gossiped about all over. One reason she loved Seattle was the anonymity. Small towns with small populations meant everything was big news. "Oh, just back here to help with Bridget's wedding. She and Jack set a date for June. I'm covering some shifts at Three Sisters and some other little projects."

The other woman peered at Sarah's laptop. "Looks like more than that. I'd forgotten you have that marketing degree from U-Dub." Dori puffed up like a proud mother hen. "So impressive to have one of our own make it big in the city."

"Thank you, but I—"

"Now that I think about it, I could use some marketing for my shop. Antiquing has become quite the hip thing to do these days. So many young people have learned the joys of finding treasure." The shop owner preened. "I bet you could help me."

Help her? Unease spread along her shoulders. What did she mean by that? "Well..."

"You aren't bothering my customers, are you, Dori?" Sam, the coffee shop owner, asked as he paused by the table. He flashed a quick grin at Sarah. She tossed a grateful quirk of her brows to him.

"Of course not. Just talking business with one of our own."

Irritation spiked. It irked Sarah that townspeople were more inclusive of her than her sister. It didn't make sense. Bridget was nothing but sweet, yet her shyness made people think she was standoffish. True, Bridget had always been more involved in the store and making products, but still... The way townsfolk called Bridge a witch incensed Sarah.

"Business, huh?" Sam asked. "You offering services? I'd get in on that. A couple of employees think we should start offering activities like a book club and maybe an open mic night. Don't know how we'd drum up participants, though."

Sarah nodded and made a sympathetic sound. "That would take some thought and planning."

"Well, what are your rates?" Dori jumped in. "I want on your schedule before the whole town gets in on it."

"I'm not sure—"

"Give the girl time to noodle on ideas and time estimates. Then she can let us know in a week or so. We'll circle back to you, Sarah." Sam patted her on the shoulder and escorted Dori away.

Sarah blinked at her screen. What the hell had just happened? With a small shake of her head, she murmured, "I guess I'm working freelance for now." At least the extra income would be a bonus. Focusing back on her current project, she sighed when another shadow fell over her. She looked up and froze.

"Hey, Sarah," Cornelius said.

He looked rugged and dirty, as if he'd just come off a logging job, like a lumberjack from the romance novels she devoured. His flannel shirt did outstanding things to his shoulders and chest. The sight of him did outstanding things to her lady bits.

"Hey, yourself." She licked her lips. "What're you doing here?"

"Long day. I needed a pick-me-up."

"Everything okay?" A tickle of worry brushed down her neck and goosebumps spread across her arms.

He rested a hand on the back of the empty chair at her table and she nudged it out with her foot. As he sank into it, he moved his head from side to side. "Yes and no. I hired on two new recruits from the community college and they're green, to say the least. Lots of training and watching like a hawk to keep them from making mistakes that could kill someone."

"Sounds exhausting. If you already hired new people, why did Jack ask me to work on these job postings?" Were the two guys not talking to one another? She didn't want to invest her time in a project that wouldn't be used or cause problems between Cornelius and Jack.

Cornelius laughed, but it felt flat and lifeless. "For the very reasons I just named. We need some seasoned loggers, not just newbies. Somebody needs to keep their dumb asses from falling off a cliff or getting brained by a tree."

A giggle-snort escaped her. "Yeah, that would be good. Makes liability insurance premiums stay reasonable."

"True." He sat back and sipped his coffee. "How's the job search going?"

Sarah lifted a shoulder. "Not great, but Gran says it's too early to get responses. On the plus side, I am getting freelance offers from local stores. Sam and Dorothy want help."

"That's great! Maybe you could start your own marketing firm."

Why did that keep getting suggested to her? "Maybe, but it's so hard to get that up and running. There's so many big players in Seattle already. I'd have to do a ton of planning and prep to get a loan large enough to get a firm off the ground."

He opened his mouth, but was interrupted by his phone ringing. Cornelius jumped and grabbed for it in his pocket. "Sorry, I'm just..." He trailed off as he looked at the screen. "Ugh. A stupid scam call." He set down his phone and looked back up.

Sarah was hit with those deep blue eyes framed by black glasses and it knocked the air from her for a second. Inhaling the scent of fresh ground coffee beans and fir needles, she drew her brows together. Something more was up with Cornelius than work stuff. He wasn't one to let a new employee or two get him this depressed. "Waiting to hear from someone?"

He darted his eyes at her, then away. For a moment she wondered if he would answer at all. "My parents." His voice was gruff. "My mom's having treatment today and they're supposed to call afterward."

"Treatment? Is Clarissa sick?" She sat up, fear curling in her stomach. Cornelius' parents had been so generous and accepting of her, even after the break-up. She hated to think of anything happening to either of them.

He chewed on his lower lip. "Mom has breast cancer." The words fell out on a shaky breath,

"Oh my God, I'm so sorry!" Sarah wrapped her hands around his. The open vulnerability in his eyes gutted her. All of her instincts flared to comfort him.

"She says she'll be all right. Surgery was about a week or so ago and chemo started this week after giving her a little time to heal. Mom insists her doctors feel they caught it early and will be able to beat it."

"But it's still scary as hell." She couldn't imagine his inner turmoil. Her heart thumped in an uneven rhythm.

"Yeah. Super fucking frightening."

She squeezed his hands, savoring the warm roughness of his skin. "What can I do?"

"Nothing." Cornelius shook his head. "Not a damn thing anyone but the doctors and Mom can do."

"For you? What do you need?" Idleness was not an option. She needed action of some kind, anything that could ease his distress.

Cornelius shifted moods in a nanosecond. His hands were yanked from hers and he was pushing to standing. "I'm fine. Don't worry about me." His expression turned cold and sharp for a moment, so fast Sarah thought she might have imagined it. He dipped his chin in a quick nod. "I'm all good. Nothing to complain about. Mom's my concern." He shoved a hand through his hair. "Anyway, sorry for interrupting you, Sarah. See you around."

Before she could utter a goodbye, he strode out. She was left bewildered and staring after him at a complete loss for what had caused his speedy change in attitude.

* * * *

Good grief, what was wrong with him? Cornelius punched the wheel of his truck and growled. He had to move on from Sarah. Why would he go up to her, then sit and pour out his troubles? His conscience tried to guilt him over how he'd snapped at Sarah when he'd departed, but he ignored it. She might not understand his treatment of her, but she also didn't warrant an explanation.

Cornelius drove home and stomped into his back shed where he'd set up a woodworking station. He and Jack had spent a lot of hours out here as Cornelius had learned the ins and outs of the craft. Now, Cornelius made little figures through whittling and filing and sanding, cat trees that he donated to the local shelter to give to new pet parents and the occasional larger furniture piece as inspiration struck him. He eyed his current project, a curio cabinet made from reclaimed barn wood and leftovers from logging timber. The base was complete, but he was piecing together the top half. He'd decided on a mosaic of sorts, mixing and matching different woods in a herringbone pattern to showcase the back wall that would be the backdrop for whatever knickknacks were placed inside.

He'd known this would be his wedding present to Bridget and Jack when starting the project and now felt pressure to ensure it was perfect. It would fit the rustic, cabin-in-the-woods vibe they had going with the new house, but he'd never given one of his creations to a friend. Family, really.

He often wondered if he was meant to be alone in this life. Sure, his parents were great and they loved him, yet they'd retired out of state. He had the guys from TLC, but most of them held him at a distance since Cornelius was their boss. Even as a child, his circle of friends had been small.

Bridget was almost his little sister and Jack was the missing brother from his life. At one point, Becca's older brother had been that pillar, but after joining the Army, Hop didn't make it back to Fallbank much at all. There'd been Sarah, the woman he thought would be his forever. But she'd left him, too.

On a whim, Cornelius pulled out his phone and shot off a text to Hop saying hello. They still kept in touch — so he'd know if Hop was still alive and out there, but it could be days before Cornelius heard anything back. Picking up a piece of wood, Cornelius let himself fall into the rhythm of measuring and sanding and sawing and constructing. Woodworking had fast become a love of his. The concentration gave a meditative quality to his brain and let him work out his feelings through the craft. It didn't require socializing or exerting himself outside of his comfort zone. He liked the solitude and simplicity. He could process his emotions or at least not feel quite so alone as when he sat in his living room, watching hockey or football or whatever game he could find while eating dinner for one on his couch.

A block of wood that was taking shape with slow, but steady work was waiting on his tool bench. He'd began this piece a week ago when a certain female had blown back into his life. Shying away from examining where the urge to create this piece came from, he'd accepted the creative desire and made progress as the fancy hit him. It gave him a renewed sense of purpose.

Cornelius didn't know when he'd become so dissatisfied with his life or complacent in letting it slip by, but at least with this hobby, he could have a tangible product at the end. He might not have the love of a significant other, or even a roommate anymore, but he could be productive with work. His mark on the world might not be left behind with children and grandchildren, but his business and support of the local economy in Fallbank would be worth something. Right?

His phone chimed. "Thank God," he muttered then looked at the text. To his surprise, Hop had responded already.

Hop: Still alive and well. Heading back from this last deployment in about a month. At least that's what they tell me.

Cornelius: I hope that's true, bro. How many does this make? Where are you these days?

Hop: This makes round six. Heading back from sandy places with no beaches is all I can say. Looking forward to getting stateside again.

Cornelius: Think you'll make it to Fallbank for Bridget's wedding? I know she'd love to have you here.

When Hop didn't respond right away, Cornelius sighed and went back to sanding a piece of Douglas fir that was next up in his pattern for the cabinet. He didn't know why Hop hadn't come home after those first few years in the Army, but his friend hadn't returned to Fallbank in over a decade. Cornelius should have known not to push when Hop was at least texting back, but he missed his friend. And Cornelius knew Bridget missed her cousin. She was more sensitive to family leaving her than the rest of their clan. Having him at her wedding would mean the world to her.

His cell screen lit up with another text. Holy shit, he hadn't scared Hop off.

Hop: Maybe. I'll have to see if I get back in time. June, right?

Cornelius: Yep, June third. I bet Gran and Becca would be happy, too. Your parents are making the trip out.

Hop: Yeah. Becca let me know. She's been riding my tail to get me to commit. I'll do what I can.

Cornelius paused and debated his next words, but he needed to know.

Cornelius: Hey, you still live by the 'don't get back with your ex' rule?

Hop: Shit yeah. Don't go back is my motto. There's a reason we broke up, so stay that way.

He read his friend's words with a slow nod. That was what he figured. Cornelius needed to take the advice from a man who'd learned the hard way on this. Better to move on with someone new than go back and relive the heartache.

Cornelius: Gotcha. Hope things are going all right for you. We miss you, dude.

Hop: Same here. Gotta run. Duty calls.

Cornelius: Stay safe.

This time when Hop didn't reply, Cornelius understood why. Instead, he focused back on his task at hand. He let his mind turn off for the evening and got lost in the creative flow. By the time he headed inside for the night, he'd gotten a third of the back wall completed. Between the woodworking and his brief connection to Hop again, Cornelius felt lighter than when he'd left the coffee shop. His emotions might still be a bit raw from everything going on in his life, but at least he held a strand or two of kinship with someone in the world other than his ex.

Chapter Eight

Rain poured from the dark clouds covering the sky outside...again. Spring in Oregon was an ever-changing mood — rain to sun to chilly to warm. The weather had a mind of its own and there was no rhyme or reason. The result was an unfortunate growing dissatisfaction with the environment surrounding her. Sarah scowled and pulled on her rain boots before grabbing her coat. She was leaning more and more toward expanding her job search outside of the Pacific Northwest and the dreary weather it seemed to have more often than not. She could use some sunshine in her life. Instead, she slung her bag over her left shoulder and raced out of the house to her car. After swinging by Evergreen Espresso and dropping off her proposal with Sam while picking up her caffeine fix, she made her way over to Three Sisters Apothecary.

The bell chimed as she unlocked the door and entered. "Hi, Gran. Are you down here yet?"

"Just making my way," Gran answered as she appeared from the back stairwell that led to her apartment above the store. "Good morning, darling granddaughter." She grinned. "Are you enjoying our gorgeous weather this morning?"

Sticking her tongue out, Sarah grimaced and shook her head. "Ugh. I hate all this rain. How have I never realized how wet it always is here? I swear Seattle isn't as bad." She was lying, but refused to back down from her statement.

Gran laughed. "Oh, yes it is. You just don't have time to fixate on it with all of your busy, big-city life. It's spring. It should be raining this much. We need it. Think how beautiful the wildflowers will be once it warms up in another month or two." The older woman leaned against the large wood counter and cocked her head. "What's not to love about this weather, anyway?"

Sarah puttered around the shop, making certain things were set up for the morning. Bridget would be in around noon to take over, but wanted the time to start a batch of new lotions they were low on. Sarah threw Gran a sassy eye roll and received a Look back. "The wet? The chill? The wind? The lack of sunshine?"

"You kids these days. What about the smell of damp earth? The majesty of the gray clouds moving and shifting in the sky? The brisk breeze that blows away winter and promises warmer days are coming soon, so enjoy the snuggly blanket and cozy hot tea season while it lasts?"

"I suppose. If you're into that kind of thing. I prefer the ability to go outside." Sarah came around to stand next to Gran. "What's wrong with that?"

"Nothing at all, dear. But there's more than one way to keep warm on a day like today." She winked and wiggled her brows. "You should be taking advantage of these kinds of moments."

Grimacing at her grandmother's innuendo, Sarah covered her face with her hands. "Gran, please!" She sighed and looked up again. "Besides, I don't have anyone to do that kind of thing with anyway."

"Another problem with a very simple solution!"

"Oh, is there? Care to enlighten me?"

"I seem to recall a very available young man who lives quite close to you. Next door, even." Gran threw her another Look. "You two need to stop pretending you aren't still pining for one another and get back together already."

A flare of sadness leaped and dimmed inside Sarah's chest. Try as she might, she did have unresolved feelings for Cornelius, but there was no way to go back. She'd burned that bridge to ashes and let the wind carry them away. She sighed. "I know you think Cornelius and I should date again, but it's not that simple." Her eyes stung and her vision wavered as tears threatened. "He'd never forgive me if he knew why."

To her credit, Gran didn't ask the why. She'd been down this road with Sarah before and knew that the answer wouldn't be given. "He wouldn't forgive you or *you* can't forgive you? You can't decide his reactions for him. You can give yourself the grace of forgiveness, though. The rest will follow. You owe it to Cornelius to at least tell him why. Maybe he can't move past it for the two of you to be together, but at least you'll both have closure." Gran placed a hand over Sarah's. "Neither of you can move on until the past is cleared between you two."

Tears slipped from Sarah's closed lids. "I know, but I can't. I can't tell him." She opened her eyes and shook her head. "I can't stand to see him hate me. And he will, Gran."

"He won't. That sweet boy couldn't hate anyone if he tried. Whatever this thing is that made you run away from him, from all of us here, *you* need freedom from it. That can't happen with you holding it tight inside your heart."

"Maybe..." Sarah swiped at her cheeks. "I'll think about it."

Her grandmother gave one nod then smiled as a customer walked in, giving Sarah a moment to collect herself. Gran was right that Sarah needed to let go of this secret that was eating away at her sanity, that she needed to forgive herself. Yet that felt selfish after what she'd done. And telling Cornelius would be selfish too. How could she burden him with this knowledge so she could feel better? Did he deserve to know? Yes. Would he want to know? That she couldn't answer for certain, but leaned toward no. And with the bomb he dropped the other day about his mother having cancer, Cornelius didn't need any more grief and stress and pain.

Sarah might owe him the right to know what had driven and kept her away for so long, but now wasn't the time. This burden needed to stay hers for a while longer, along with the feelings she still harbored buried beneath her emotional armor she never took off. It might be hot and exhausting to wear, but it was her penance for the past.

* * * *

Cornelius sat in his truck and stared at his phone screen. Three more alerts for potential matches. Sighing, he looked over the profiles. The first one showed a pretty blonde woman who liked hiking, hockey and lived in Portland. *Tempting, but…* He swiped left. *Too far away for a real relationship.* Maybe he should tighten his radius on this app. He'd learned the hard way that long-distance relationships weren't for him. The second match showed a brunette who was nice looking, but didn't appeal to him the way he wanted. It was superficial of him, but hey, what about these apps wasn't? At least in the beginning. He wasn't going to get a ton of information about someone from an application on a mobile device. Expecting instant chemistry via the internet was too much to ask for, but he still declined.

The third option was someone with an obvious lumberjack fetish. She listed loving the woods, brawny and bearded men and flannel. *Hard pass.* He wasn't here to make someone's fantasy come to life. And he didn't want to roleplay until the novelty wore off and this woman dumped him. Besides, he wouldn't fit into her imagined perfect man. While some of the loggers had large muscles and beards, not all of them did.

Cornelius was built with lean muscle. He just didn't have the body type to get super stacked like some people. Maybe it was possible, but he didn't put in the effort. Cornelius rubbed at his smooth shaved chin. A beard though… He could do that. He hadn't grown one in the past because Sarah preferred him without, but he had to get a grip and move on. Jack had commented a few times how much Bridget enjoyed his and recalled seeing Bridget nuzzling Jack's face. Facial hair was something to think about. He did hate how cold his face got in the winter.

Knock, knock, knock.

The sound made Cornelius jerk around to see who was banging on his window.

Jack grinned at him. "Ready to check this place out?"

Tucking his phone away, Cornelius joined Jack and Bridget on the sidewalk. He glanced up at the Wild Rose Inn. "This is a nice place, little B. Good choice for a wedding venue."

"Thanks. We walked by and I saw the plants in the garden and thought this was perfect." She stared at the landscape before them with a smile. While others saw wintering plants, Bridget could name every one of them. "When everything blooms in early June, it will be a flower explosion. I wish I could have that at home, but my plants serve functions. I have to choose based on our products, not on pretty."

Jack wrapped his arm around her waist. "You can have both at our new place."

"Ugh, stop being so handsy," Sarah called as she walked up. "You two are way too in love."

Cornelius had to admit that he agreed with his ex.

"Jealous much?" Bridget teased her sister, but Cornelius caught the way Sarah's smile wavered.

Was she jealous? He knew he sure was. This was the kind of relationship he wanted, what he thought he'd had with Sarah before she'd broken his heart. Seeing it day in and day out wore away at him, but at the same time, Cornelius also dreaded when they moved into their new house. He'd be even more alone than he was now.

"Okay, okay," Bridget said. "Let's go in and get started."

An hour later they'd decided to hold the ceremony at the northern side of the yard. Instead of having rows of chairs for viewing, they would have guests sit at tables to watch. The walkway would meander around through the set-up and this way there wouldn't be a need to move furniture around or go elsewhere for the reception.

"What happens if it rains?" he asked.

"It won't rain," Sarah declared.

He cocked a brow. "This is Oregon. It *might* rain."

"Not on my sister's wedding day, it won't." Sarah crossed her arms and glared.

He held his hands up in surrender. "Okay. If you say so." Fighting with Sarah was not on his list of to dos today.

The owner of the inn stepped closer. "I have a large tent that can be used if needed. The sides roll up so the flowers are still visible."

"Thanks, Jane." Bridget looked between both of them. "See? Covered no matter what."

Cornelius nodded and glanced back at Jane. She was so unobtrusive, he'd forgotten she was there. If he was honest, he'd forgotten her name until Bridge had said it. Jane seemed nice. He glanced at her left hand — no ring, pretty enough.

He wondered how long she'd been in town. Old Mrs. Dalton had run the inn for years. Why wasn't she out here helping? Maybe Jane had been hired to manage things since Mrs. Dalton was getting up in years. Whatever the reason, maybe she could be the answer he was looking for. True, he wasn't knocked out by her, but sometimes chemistry took time to build. That was what dating was for, right?

"I think we're all done here for now." Jack thanked Jane and took Bridget's hand in his. "We couldn't be happier with everything you have here."

Bridget spoke up. "I know you do the baking for breakfasts here, but I wondered if you might also make cakes?"

Jane's lips parted in surprise. "You mean like a wedding cake?" Bridget nodded and Jane blew out a breath. "Oh, I don't know. I've never tried something that intricate before."

"We wouldn't need anything super fancy. Maybe two or three tiers. Very simple decorations. I'm thinking smooth icing with fresh flowers instead of designs. We can provide the flowers so you'd have just the cake to worry about."

"Maybe. Let me think about it and practice a little."

Bridget grinned. "Thank you."

Cornelius trailed after his friend and his fiancée. Sarah had gone ahead of them. He took the opportunity to hang back with the inn helper. With a side-glance he cleared his throat. "So, um, Jane?"

She looked up with a polite smile. "Yes, did you have a question? Need something?"

They walked back into the house and he paused by the welcome desk. "I wondered if we, that is, if you would want to grab dinner sometime?"

Her skin flushed pink and Cornelius found himself charmed. With the color in her cheeks, she looked quite fetching.

"Like a...date?"

One side of his mouth kicked up. "Yeah, like a date."

She peered up at him with her fingers knotted together. "I'd like that. Yes."

"Good. How does Thursday work for you? At Moonlit Treetop Bar?"

Jane nodded. "I could be there at six-thirty."

Cornelius smiled, but there was a small rock in his stomach. It wasn't as if he hadn't dated before now, but nothing with intent. This felt different. Maybe it was having Sarah back in town, but something in his mind had decided the time had come to move on for real. Now to find out if the rest of him—in particular his heart—could follow suit. "Cool, see you then."

He took one step back and bumped into something. Or someone. He twisted and caught the person before realizing it was Sarah. His body ignited at the feel of her so close and his hands on her upper arms. "Are you all right?"

She avoided eye contact and pulled away. "I'm fine." With that, she brushed past him and raced out of the building like it was on fire.

Cornelius realized she'd heard his exchange with Jane. *Oh, shit.* Now how was he going to act when he saw her again? There was no claim on him and no reason he couldn't and shouldn't date, but deep in his heart, it stung with betrayal. *No.* He deserved to move on and find contentment with another.

Chapter Nine

Two days later and Sarah still felt like she was going to vomit. This was ridiculous. She was a grown woman and had broken up with Cornelius years ago. She'd dated and moved on. *He'd* dated and moved on. So why was him asking out the B&B owner throwing her off so much? "Get a grip," she told herself then focused back on the localized online advertisement she was working on for Three Sisters…and Evergreen Espresso…and the antique shop. Then she would look for more new jobs back in Seattle. Yes, she had a plan in place.

Seattle was safe, away from Cornelius and the constant reminder of all she'd lost with him — no Gran and her well-meaning but unhelpful comments about Sarah's lack of a love life. Plus no Bridget and Jack and their in-so-much-love and perfection together. The last part Sarah felt sick with guilt about, but her jealousy and annoyance at her little sister's happiness was there all the same. She couldn't help how she felt. Emotions were uncontrollable.

Exhaling, Sarah closed her eyes to try to push away her petty and unkind sentiments. She was happy for Bridget. Truly, she loved that her sibling had found someone special who cared and loved Bridget the way she deserved. Jack was a great future brother-in-law. He was kind and helpful and Bridget was his entire world. Sarah couldn't have asked for a better person for her little sister.

Yet here she was, envious as hell. Sarah hadn't had time to let loneliness in before now, to see what she'd been missing until it was right in front of her eyes. Yep, getting back to Seattle and a full-time job was a must. This discovered discontentment needed to take a hike—and maybe fall off a cliff while at it.

The door chimed and in walked a plain woman with brown hair and eyes. Familiar, but hard to place, nothing to distinguish her or mark her as special. Sarah couldn't even remember her name. There was one thing about this woman that Sarah did recall.

Corey had asked her out. Cornelius. He wasn't Corey to her anymore.

Inside, Sarah winced at her mean, vindictive thoughts. This woman was probably a lovely person and she wasn't as unremarkable as Sarah's emotions wished. Didn't Sarah want Cornelius to be happy? Could she begrudge him that because there were still unresolved feelings on her end? Her stomach rolled. She was so petty and hated that about herself.

Plastering on a smile, Sarah greeted her. "Hey, there. It's nice to see you again, um…"

"Jane," the other woman supplied with a brief, tight lift of her lips. "Nice to see you, too, Sarah."

Well wasn't that just great. *Jane* had remembered Sarah's name. It wasn't as if Jane was a difficult name.

"What brings you in? Bridget is in the back, if you want me to get her?" Sarah stood from the stool and moved around the dark wood counter.

"No, no. I'm not here for anything wedding related. I thought I'd check out the store. Wild Rose could always use new decorative items and I love to support local shops." Jane moved to a shelf with their spring scented candles. "These are so pretty."

"Aren't they? Bridget is so creative to add the dried flower petals into the wax."

"Do you also help make the products?"

Sarah leveled a stare at Jane. "I do. My cousin Becca also does. It's a family business and has been for generations — since before the Wildes came to Fallbank over two hundred years ago before the town was founded. How long have you been in Fallbank?"

"Oh." Jane rubbed the back of her neck. "About three years. I took over the inn for my aunt."

"I remember Mrs. Dalton. She was a lovely lady. Always fun to visit Wild Rose for Halloween trick or treating. She decked out the house for all occasions. Funny, I don't recall seeing you around town much." Could Sarah be any more snide? She knew she should stop with her indirect snubbing of this poor woman. Jane had done nothing to deserve it. Yet the petty jealousy inside Sarah wouldn't stop. It wasn't as if Sarah was a native either. She'd lived in Connecticut until her parents had passed. She needed to get ahold of herself. "Sorry." Sarah cleared her throat. "Was there anything else I can do for you?"

"Maybe some hand cream. With all of my baking, it takes a toll."

"That's right. You're going to make Bridget's wedding cake." One more endearing quality to add to Jane's list.

"I *might* make her cake. I focus on breakfast foods. You know, bed and breakfast. Pastries I can do. Cakes, we'll have to see." Jane shrugged and looked at the floor.

"Right. Here, let me show you what we have." In an act of contrition for her cattiness, Sarah did her best to be kinder. Thankfully, Bridget walked out from the back to save her.

"Jane." Bridget grinned. "How delightful to see you. What brings you in?"

Jane held up the candles. "I thought a few items for the Wild Rose might be nice to have on display. Help our local stores and showcase their items."

"How sweet of you. Thank you."

Sarah spoke up, her marketing senses never one to miss an opportunity. "You could also put business cards or a sign to display where they came from in case guests are interested."

Jane nodded. "Wonderful idea, I'd be happy to." She looked to Bridget. "Would you mind?"

"Not at all." Bridget hesitated. "Some people in town... They don't always welcome the Wildes. Old rumors about witches. I don't want this to impact your business."

With pursed lips, Jane took all of the cards on display. "I've heard the rumors. People are so ignorant sometimes, aren't they? Sarah was just showing me your hand cream. I understand you make it yourselves."

Bridget flushed, but smiled. "We do."

The two wandered over to where the lotions were displayed, chatting. Sarah felt her jealousy give way to the pain of acceptance. Jane was nice. She didn't bat an eye when Bridget mentioned their family reputation. She wanted to help local stores. She hadn't even reacted to Sarah's snobby remark about Jane not living in Fallbank for very long. Hell, Sarah didn't live here anymore, either. Sarah couldn't begrudge Jane accepting a date with Cornelius or him asking her out. Her Corey—Cornelius—deserved happiness and maybe Jane could give him that. God knew Sarah couldn't, not with the weight of what he didn't know lying between them.

"Oh, look at these wooden animals. How cute! I have the perfect place for the goose and the swan at the inn. Did one of you make them?" Jane smiled at the two of them.

Sarah felt her nausea level rise. "Cornelius made those. Right, Bridge?"

Bridget nodded. "He sure did. My fiancé Jack tinkers with woodworking and when he was roommates with Cornelius, they did some of it together. They still do, but since most of the equipment is at Cornelius' place for now, Jack doesn't do as much. Once our house is completed, we'll shift things there."

"How fun. I didn't realize Cornelius was so good with his hands." Jane flushed. "I mean, you know." She held up the wooden goose. "Working with his hands."

Bridget laughed. "We know what you mean. Cornelius is also one of the co-owners at TLC and does a lot of hands-on logging work, too."

"Do you know him well? I suppose you must, given that he'll be best man at your wedding." Jane placed the two figures on the counter next to the candles and lotion.

"He lives next door to us and Sarah —"

"I graduated high school with him," Sarah interrupted her sister. "We were the same year in school." She threw a keep-your-mouth-shut look to her sibling. Jane didn't need the sordid history of their failed relationship or that Cornelius lived next door to his ex — even if temporary.

"Gotcha," Jane said. "How nice to have a long-time friend close by. He seems very sweet. And those glasses of his are adorable. Very Clark Kent-Superman vibe."

Sarah forced a laugh from her lips. "Yeah." How many times had she had the same thought? Cornelius' glasses were sexy and she'd never hidden the fact that they turned her on when they'd been together…not that she felt the same way now. And she would not be jealous or begrudge Jane a chance at happiness with Cornelius. Maybe if she repeated that enough in her head, it would become true.

An awkward silence descended and Bridget cleared her throat. "Should I ring you up or did you want to look around more?"

"This is all I need today." Jane smiled, but it didn't quite seem to reach her eyes from Sarah's perspective.

Bridget ran everything through the system and Jane departed with a wave. Then she spun and pinned Sarah with an exasperated stare. "What was that?"

"What?"

"The thing with Jane. And Cornelius. And you."

"I don't know what you're talking about." Sarah shrugged and turned back to her computer, but her sister pushed the lid shut. "Rude." She glared at her sibling.

Bridget folded her arms. "I learned from the best. Tell me what's up."

"Fine." Sarah huffed. "I overheard Cornelius ask her out and she doesn't need our old history making things weird. It's all old news anyway." The more she said it, the more she would believe it. Right?

Her sister walked around the counter and hugged an arm around Sarah's shoulders. "Are you okay with this?"

With one brow lifted, Sarah said, "Of course. Like I said, old history." Now if she could convince her heart of the words coming out of her mouth.

* * * *

When Thursday rolled around, Cornelius found himself nervous and sitting at a table at Moonlit Treetop Bar. Jane should arrive at any moment and he jiggled one foot as he alternated staring at the door and looking anywhere but the entrance. What if this was a total bust? What if he and Jane had nothing to talk about? What if everything went great and this was the first date to the rest of their lives together? What if she was bonkers and turned into a stalker?

Okay, the last one seemed unlikely, but he never knew what could happen. What if, what if, what if... He was driving himself nuts with all the scenarios imagined in his brain. He needed to calm down. Why was he freaking out over this date? He'd gone out on other ones. This was no different than those. Except it was. Sort of. With Sarah back in town for who knew how long, dating seemed fraught with danger. He didn't want to run into Sarah while taking out another woman, but it was a small town.

And even before Sarah's return to Fallbank, he'd promised himself to get back out there. He needed an escort to Jack and Bridget's wedding. His mom was sick and it was time he stopped messing around and got serious about finding a partner. His parents wouldn't be around forever. Jane seemed nice. He needed to give her a chance for real.

The door opened and she walked in. From his vantage point, he watched as she smoothed her hair and adjusted her pink flowered dress. Then she bit her lip and shifted her gaze around the tables. Cornelius stood and waved. Her answering smile was pretty and his nerves eased.

As they both sat again, Cornelius sneaked a glance at Jane. Her dark hair had nice waves and the smattering of freckles across her cheeks and nose gave her a youthful appearance. When she looked his direction, he noticed her brown eyes. Odd, he hadn't remembered that her eyes were brown from meeting her before. If he were honest, he hadn't remembered much except that she was attractive enough and seemed nice. That impression still held true, but he didn't feel any kind of spark when their gazes connected.

It wasn't even five minutes in and he was already writing her off? No. Insta-chemistry didn't make or break a relationship. "So, how long have you been in Fallbank? It can't have been too long since we've not crossed paths before now."

Her cheeks turned pink. "I've, uh, lived here for three years. I took over for my aunt when she wanted to retire and sold me the inn."

Oh, shit. Three years? And he hadn't noticed? He choked out a laugh. "Wow, I guess that shows how little I pay attention to things around here."

"Well, I will admit to not getting out much. So there aren't too many who know me."

Cornelius lifted one side of his lips. "I guess we're remedying that tonight."

A smiling guy in a black graphic T-shirt with a baseball cap on backward approached the table. "Hey, there! Are you two playing trivia tonight?"

"Trivia?" Cornelius looked over at Jane. "I didn't know that was happening tonight."

Jane shrugged. "I've never participated before."

The man's grin grew wider. "Fantastic. It's pretty simple. We have six rounds with a break halfway through. You write your answers to each round on these slips of paper and this is your copy to keep track. Top three teams win prizes."

Cornelius arched one eyebrow to Jane. "You game?" Behind Jane's shoulder, the door opened and in walked three women and his best friend. Of course tonight would be the night the Wildes women and Jack would come out.

"Cornelius?"

He jerked his attention back to his date. "Uh, sorry, Jane. I missed that."

"I said, I'm game if you are."

"Cool. Let's do it, then." He accepted the sheets and a pen.

"Great. Come up with a team name and I'll circle back." He walked off to the next table and left them to their own devices.

"A name..." Cornelius winced. "Not my strongest suit."

"Same here," Jane replied. "Um..." She pursed her lips and stared off into space. "What about Trivia for Two?"

"Sure. Let's go with that." Cornelius watched her write the name down while trying to not be too obvious about checking out the group three tables over from him. The one with his best friend, his best friend's fiancée and her cousin...and Cornelius' ex-girlfriend. Not that he should care that they were here, or vice versa. So what if he was on a date? No big deal. He was allowed to take a woman out. They were cool to hang out without him. It didn't bruise his ego or make him wonder how often they got together without him.

The trivia host began speaking over the mic system and Cornelius pulled his attention back to the game and his date. And thank goodness they had decided to play trivia because the date might have been a disaster otherwise. Jane seemed shy unless asked a direct question. Cornelius found her sweet but quiet, and getting her out of her shell was a challenge. He also found his focus pulling over to the table with his friends, where Sarah cut surreptitious glances his way, too. It was hard not to compare the easy banter and rapport he and Sarah'd had from childhood against the strained conversation between him and Jane. Even with Sarah and his breakup and all of the awkwardness that brought, they still seemed to have a connection that couldn't be denied. They never lacked for something to talk about.

Somewhere between the round on Harry Houdini, because it was his birthday, and song clips that all had names to do with winter, he and Jane managed to hit a bit of a stride in conversation. He found out she was a middle child with four other siblings, had grown up outside of Tacoma, enjoyed baking and missed having late mornings since taking over the B&B for her aunt. He shared he was a native of Fallbank and an only child, preferred the outdoors to in and enjoyed eating baked goods. They came in fifth out of seventeen teams.

Sarah and her team, the Solstice Sisters, landed in third. Despite the game ending at eight-thirty PM, Jane begged off to head home.

"It's always an early morning for me. I have to get breakfast laid out by six or the guests can get testy. Sundays are my one 'sleep in' day and that means breakfast starts at seven. I prep most everything the day before, but some things have to be day of." Jane shrugged with a rueful smile. "I don't lead the most exciting life because of my inn."

"Nothing wrong with a quiet lifestyle. I'll see you to your car." Cornelius stood and waited for her to lead the way.

"Oh, I walked. Wild Rose is just a few blocks away." She tucked her long hair behind her ears.

"I'll walk you then. It's dark now and you shouldn't be alone." He threw a smile her way and hoped he wasn't coming off as stalkery or pushy. "That is, if you're comfortable with that."

Her voice was soft and pink tinted her cheeks. "That would be nice."

With that, he placed a hand on her lower back and they headed for the door. As they passed that table with Sarah, Bridget spotted them.

"Cornelius, Jane! Hi." Bridget rose from her chair with a grin. "How great to see you two!"

Jane smiled and Cornelius said hello. He edged a step or two more toward the door, hoping to escape without too much conversation given his ex was staring with a frosty expression. Most people wouldn't know, but the small, affable upward tilt of her lips was Sarah's polite mask when she wanted to scowl or glare. It was an interesting development. Was she jealous? That didn't make any sense. But…what would she be mad about? The whole thing didn't make sense.

Jane said, "Bridget, I think I can make your wedding cake." She twisted her lips to one side. "I think."

"That's amazing! I'm sure it'll be wonderful."

"Would you be able to come by for a tasting? I'd want your okay on it and to know what flavors you'd like." Jane looked at Jack then back to Bridget. "Maybe this weekend?"

Bridget looked at Jack. "Sure. Saturday afternoon at two?"

"Perfect. I'll have some options ready." Jane clasped her hands together. "We'll let you get back to your evening. We were heading out."

Goodbyes were exchanged and Cornelius followed Jane outside. The cool evening felt good on his heated skin. He wondered if that felt as awkward to her as it did to him. Probably not, given she didn't know the history between Sarah and him. The walk to the B&B was quiet and quick. They hadn't held hands, but Cornelius' fingers brushed Jane's a time or two. She didn't seem to mind, but Cornelius couldn't seem to find any kind of spark between them.

As they reached the large house, she opened a gate in the white picket fence and led them down a stone path at the back of the property to a small cottage. Then she turned to him. "This is me. I had fun tonight." Under the soft sconce light by the entry, her cheeks turned pink and she glanced away. "Thanks for asking me out."

Cornelius forced a smile. "Yeah, trivia was a good time. Maybe we can do this again?" God, but this was awkward. Jane was nice, but that was the problem. *Nice.* Not amazing or captivating or enchanting. No buzzy lightning feelings like he'd gotten with Sarah. It was always the issue with any woman he'd dated since her. *Give it a chance, Cor.*

Sometimes romance needed a chance to build. What was it they called it in books? Slow burn? Was that what this was? Hell if he knew. Cornelius made a mental note to look up "slow burn" before they had a second date.

"Sure, I'd like that." Jane's voice was so hopeful.

It gutted him. She was sweet and didn't deserve to be in the same headspace as an ex he couldn't seem to move on from. "What about dinner next week?" He forced himself to break through his hesitations.

She beamed at him and in that moment, Cornelius caught his breath. She was beautiful when she grinned. He'd seen her professional ones, but a real smile transformed her.

"Yes. Dinner sounds great."

A hard lump formed in his gut. "Cool. I'll call you and we can work out when." She might be pretty, but his heart was not in this. Too bad for it—his head refused defeat and pushed to keep moving forward.

Chapter Ten

Bridget hummed and held Jack's hand across the console of her car as she navigated the streets of Fallbank. Sarah looked out the car window at the freshly planted purple and blue flowers in the planters lining the sidewalks and quaint *Springtime in Fallbank* lamppost banners. The rain had moved on from this morning and patches of sunlight broke through the puffy clouds now dotting the sky. She had to admit, the town did a great job of refreshing the landscape with each season. The warm welcome feel of Fallbank was something she missed in Seattle. Seattle boasted plenty of entertainment, culture and architecture, but there was something magical about a small town.

Jack lifted his entwined hand with Bridget and pressed a kiss to her knuckles. She turned to him with the sappiest, loving look and beamed. Sarah pictured hearts streaming out of her sister's eyes.

Sarah glanced at Becca in the backset next to her and faked gagging. Becca's giggle and emphatic nod had chuckles bubbling up in Sarah. At least she had a partner in solidarity on the mushiness. Sarah loved it in romance books when the characters mooned over another but in real life it was obnoxious…or maybe that was her envy talking.

"What's so funny?" Bridget asked.

"Nothing," Sarah and Becca answered in unison. More laughter ensued and soon, the two were wiping tears and unable to control the wild hilarity gripping them.

Jack glanced back at them with a furrowed forehead. "No clue. They've lost it, I guess."

"Oookay," Bridget drawled. "I don't know what's so funny about cake tasting, but I can't wait."

Sarah gasped for breath and calmed her cackling. "Sorry. I don't know what got into us. You know how laughter is contagious and sometimes can't be stopped." She cleared her throat. "So what kind of flavors are you thinking? And why did the two of us need to tag along?"

She couldn't say spending time with Jane—the woman who'd gone out with Cornelius and Sarah wasn't jealous of at all—was the top of her list. Or listening to her sister and Jack sing Jane's praises with about her baking. A small, petty part of her wondered if Jane was going to bomb wedding cake making, yet she knew with all the other pastries and food making Jane did for the Wild Rose, it wasn't a strong possibility. Ugh, she hated feeling like this. She shouldn't dislike someone because of who they dated. Sarah had broken up with Cornelius years ago. They'd both dated others. Sarah knew this. It hadn't been an issue in the past. She also hadn't had to see it before.

Getting back to Seattle was becoming more pressing by the day. While the work she'd done for the couple of local businesses was fun, staying here and watching Cornelius and Jane fall in love was the worst. Her heart seemed hellbent on reminding her of all the ways she hadn't moved on from Cornelius. Trivia night had been a trial. Though she had pretended not to, she had watched the two of them like a hawk — every time he smiled or she laughed, their chatting back and forth, the way he brought her out of her shell...Cornelius' hand on her lower back as he guided them toward the door.

"Chocolate, for sure. We'll see what Jane pairs together with it," Bridget said, shaking Sarah from her thoughts.

Jack threw a grin her way. "Bridget and I thought it would be fun to do this all together. Since the wedding will be small and intimate, we wanted planning to include those closest to us."

A frown crossed Bridget's face. "Although Gran is stuck at the store. I wish she could have come, but with Arianna's upcoming mid-terms, she needed the weekend to study."

Becca piped up. "Gran is at her happy place and wanted us to be able to go. You know she doesn't mind running the store. Anything that makes her feel useful."

"You're right, but she'd be useful with cake tasting, too. Speaking of, we're here!" Bridget announced then bounded out of the car. Sarah blew out a sigh and shook her head. Her little sister was in love and getting married and freaking ecstatic. It was wonderful...for Bridget. Sarah, on the other hand, sucked in a breath and steeled herself. "Be pleasant. Be happy. Stuff your mouth with cake," she muttered to herself as she trailed behind them into the inn.

To her surprise, Cornelius was waiting for them in the foyer. "Hey." He waved to the group.

"We're all going to eat cake?" Sarah's question popped out before she could switch on her filter. "I mean, not that this won't be entertaining. Five people seems like a lot, that's all." *Awkward much? Way to dump all over your sister's excitement.*

Bridget threw a sassy look her sister's way. "We wanted the three of you with us. We're family."

Sarah couldn't argue that, so she found herself trudging along into a sitting area where Jane had a tray of tiny squares of different cake options. "Hi. Come on in and make yourselves comfortable." Jane peeked over at Cornelius and smiled in his direction.

Sarah refused to look at him to see his response. Instead, she glanced over at the different varieties of baked goods in front of her. All were cut into perfect squares with soft white frosting that had white scrollwork piped across it. The result was a subtle, elegant and simple design, given the same color was used for all of the decorating. Nothing fussy or frilly, exactly like Bridget. Jane had hit the design on the nose.

"These look outstanding," Jack said as he settled next to Bridget. Becca followed, leaving Sarah and Cornelius on a second, shorter couch. His knee pressed against hers as he sat and Sarah held herself rigid. His scent of earth and fir tree filled her nose and her body reacted. Her insides turned gooey and wet warmth tingled between her thighs. He'd always turned her on so easily. She closed her eyes for a moment to clear her mind and cool her body. All she wanted was to eat cake and get the heck out of here. If she could also not see

Cornelius and Jane together, that would be an extra dose of spectacular-ness.

Jane handed around different flavor options for them all to try—lemon, raspberry, vanilla cream. The favorite, though, was a rich chocolate ganache with a whipped cream on top sandwiched between two layers of the most delicious chocolate cake that had ever been in Sarah's mouth. The decision hadn't been close, despite all of the options being tempting. The buttercream was silky and light, not too sweet and the perfect complement to all of the varieties. No doubts were left that Jane wouldn't bake the perfect, mouthwatering wedding cake.

Did she have to be so good at...everything? Jane already had a great B&B, was sweet, promoted local stores within her own and now made amazing, melt-in-the-mouth cakes, too? It wasn't fair. Couldn't she be bad at something?

Sarah winced at her unkind internal musings. She shoved another forkful of deliciousness into her face. God, what was wrong with her? Why was she so...so...*jealous* all the time? Had she wanted to break up with Cornelius in the first place? No, but there wasn't a choice. It had to have been done. And it was years ago. Why couldn't she get past it?

Because you still love him.

Sarah choked on her bite. Alarmed faces looked her way as she coughed.

"Are you okay?" Becca asked as she stood and hovered closer.

"F-fine." Sarah hacked. "Just trouble swallowing." She gulped in air with a shaky smile, then grabbed the glass of water in front of her and drained it. "All good now."

Jane hopped up. "Do you need more water? I'll get you more."

"No, no. It's not necessary." She stood. "I'm just going to duck into the bathroom."

Sarah raced off, and once inside the restroom, she pressed her hands onto the counter and stared at herself in the mirror. "What the hell?" she whispered. "No. I'm over him. I am not in love with Cornelius." *Care about him? Sure. Lingering romantic-ish type feelings? Check. Horny and want to jump his bones? Also yes. But love? Love* love*? Nope. No, no, no.* Yoga breathing for a moment, Sarah rolled her shoulders back and opened the door and was hit with the sight of Cornelius.

Crap. She was one-hundred percent still in love with him.

Cornelius waited for Sarah to say something or move, but she just peered up at him with her lips parted. "Sarah?" He furrowed his brow. "You okay?"

"H-hi," she stammered and blinked. Darting her eyes from side to side, she cleared her throat. "Um, sorry. Yeah... All good. What's up? Did I miss something?"

"No. I was waiting to, you know." He waved a hand toward the restroom. Why was she acting so odd? Why wouldn't she look at him again?

"Oh. Shit, right. I'm being so weird." Sarah edged around him and took off for the other room like her pants were on fire.

"O-kay," Cornelius muttered. Once he was done in the bathroom, he came back out to find Jane at the front desk, checking in a couple. As they walked toward the curved wooden staircase, she spotted him and smiled—a real grin that lit up her face.

He answered her expression and headed her way. "I guess we're all done? Those cakes were incredible, Jane."

As a blush crept across her cheeks, she answered, "Thanks, Cornelius."

"So, I'll see you tonight, then?" They'd landed on dinner together and while Cornelius couldn't say he was excited, he had promised himself to give this more of a chance. His father's words about seeing him settled echoed in his brain.

Jane came around the desk, nodding. "Yep. It's a date."

A laugh stuttered from his chest and he wished he could rid himself of this cumbersome sensation that they didn't fit together at all. Gathering his courage and attempting to psych himself up for tonight, he leaned in and kissed Jane's cheek. "See you then."

As he turned, he caught Sarah's gaze as she stared at the two of them. *Aw, dammit.* He'd done it yet again. Why did Sarah have to be around every time he and Jane did anything couple-like in the slightest? It was as if his subconscious wanted him to make an ass out of himself. It wasn't like he was trying to get a rise out of Sarah or make her jealous. He didn't want to rub anything in her face.

Sarah blinked several times then flashed a quick smile in their direction. "We're heading out." The rest of their group gathered in the foyer and said their goodbyes.

Cornelius gave one last glance to Jane and trailed behind the rest of his friends. He flexed his fingers, the urge to do something active hitting him hard. He needed to get out of his head for a little while. After reaching his house, Cornelius beelined it out to his garage to do some woodworking. The soothing repetition and creative outlet would give him a mental break. His pet project was the right choice to focus on.

"Knock, knock," Jack said as he stood by the open side door into the workspace. "Mind if I join you?"

"Come on in." The relief Cornelius felt as his friend joined him was welcome. They could shoot the breeze and he could carve without pressure. But not on this particular figure. Cornelius didn't want Jack asking about it, so he began anew. He scooped up a fresh block of wood and started carving out chunks to get the rough shape of an animal. He'd start big and work his way down to tiny details as he coaxed a giraffe to life from the timber. Jack wouldn't have any reason to ask questions about a giraffe. Even if he did, there was no hidden meaning behind it to explain.

"You and Jane, huh?"

Cornelius almost screamed in frustration. Of course Jack would ask about his dating life. "Yeah. She's sweet. It's a second date, nothing serious."

"That's cool. I like her. She's nice. Glad you're getting back out there."

Cornelius nudged his glasses back up his nose and refrained from responding. He knew Jack was dancing around something, but he had no desire to pull it out of him.

"But…"

"There it is. But what?" He paused in his wood scraping.

"I wonder if she's who you want. You don't seem thrilled at the thought of going out with Jane."

"It's date number two, Jack. We're getting to know each other. These things take time."

Jack paused the sanding of his own woodworking piece, then looked Cornelius dead in the eyes. "Do they? I mean, when I met Bridget, the attraction was instant. And after talking with her before we'd ever gone out, I was picturing the two of us together—and not just in bed. In a relationship sense. Can you say the same?"

Cornelius huffed. "Not everyone has chemistry from the first moment. Plenty of people have to grow on one another. Build the foundation before the rest of it all. There's nothing wrong with that."

"You're right. There's not." Jack rubbed the back of his neck. "It's hard to picture for you, though. After everything you said about how you knew Sarah was the one from the start." Jack snuck a peek at Cornelius as he mentioned Sarah's name.

"So this is about Sarah. Not Jane." He set down his block and crossed his arms. "The fact is, Sarah broke things off and she doesn't want to give us another chance. I have to respect that. We ended a long time ago and there's no going back. With my mom's health, it made me realize I can't keep my life as it is. I don't want to. I want someone in my life. Companionship."

"I get it. I do. It's just that I don't see a spark between you and Jane. Companionship is nice, but it's not all-consuming love. There's a difference between being content and being happy. Comfortable versus challenging you to grow and be the best version of yourself. True partnership. The sense of being with the person who understands you and has your back and always supports you. The person who you can't wait to talk to. You want to spend every morning waking up to their smile and every night putting that smile on their face." Jack walked over and squeezed Cornelius' shoulder. "I'm not saying Jane isn't the one. Maybe she could be. I'm saying don't settle. Find what I have with Bridget, what you had once upon a time with Sarah. It can happen again for you. Don't let your parents get in your head where you wind up making a huge mistake and breaking more hearts by accident."

With a nod, Cornelius said, "You're right. I won't settle. But I also won't give up on someone so soon. Jane deserves a chance. *I* need to give myself a chance."

Chapter Eleven

By early April, Sarah had almost given up hope that any agency in Seattle was going to ever respond to her job applications. She'd checked every job site online and all the major and minor marketing firms in Seattle's webpages for new listings on an almost daily basis. She'd tapped out her networking options, too. There just weren't enough openings right now. At the moment, Sarah was focused on finishing an ad for TLC. Jack and Cornelius had gotten several leads from experienced loggers from the earlier job advertisement she'd done for them. Now that they'd been able to complete hiring, she was helping boost TLC's visibility for more contracts. She figured she could multitask while covering a shift at Three Sisters Apothecary. She was tweaking the design of a social media ad when an email alert popped up that made her squeal out loud.

"My goodness!" Gran spun around from her spot across the store where she had been dusting shelves and checking stock.

Sarah grinned like a loon. "Sorry, just excited." This news was what she needed to boost her optimism that things would start to go her way.

A sly smile crossed Gran's features. "Got a hot date lined up? Going to bring them to Bridget's wedding as your plus one?"

"Ha-ha, Gran." Sarah shook her head, but stretched her lips wide. "I got a response from a job application."

Gran frowned. "You mean for a position at an agency? Back in Seattle?"

"Yes, Gran." Sarah tilted her head as her expression faltered. "You know I've been waiting."

"Well, with all the work you've been doing around town I thought maybe you'd changed our mind and decided Fallbank was home again." Her grandmother shrugged. "There's lot of reasons to stay. After all, Bridget is getting married and she and Jack are moving. You could move into the house."

Sarah fought against rolling her eyes. "And live next door to my ex-boyfriend? Not happening."

"It was a suggestion."

She arched an eyebrow at Gran. "I'm going back to Seattle." Why didn't her family get it? Fallbank wasn't her home anymore.

Gran responded with a Look. "Don't get sassy with me. Wanting my grandchildren nearby isn't a bad thing."

"I'm not saying it is. I'm keeping your expectations in check. I don't want you to be upset when I move back."

The door chimed and Sarah turned to see the manager of a funky upcycled clothing store enter. "Hi, welcome to Three Sisters. Is there anything we can help with?"

The brunette crossed over to the counter. "Yes, I understand you did the recent marketing for Dori and Sam. Is that correct?"

"It is." Sarah nodded.

"Wonderful. I'm Vivica and I wondered if you could do the same for my shop? The clothing store on Fraiser Lane?"

The email response asking for a phone interview weighed in Sarah's mind. "I'm not sure…"

"I'll pay. Dori and Sam both told me you had reasonable rates and with no one in town having this kind of skill, I could use the help. Please?"

Vivica looked so eager, Sarah couldn't find it in her heart to say no. The money would be nice and it wasn't as if the job interview was tomorrow. Even if she did get the position, she had time to do this. "All right. Why don't we meet up tomorrow at your store so we can chat about what kind of campaign you're thinking?"

Vivica's eyes lit up. "Thank you. That's perfect. I'll see you then."

As she departed, Sarah toyed with a lock of her blonde hair. So many people around town seemed to need her assistance. Why had no one offered these services in Fallbank before?

Another ringing of the bell above the door brought her out of her thoughts and back to the present. Cornelius walking in had her standing straighter. "Hey."

"Hi, Sarah. Gran." He hugged her grandmother and a pang hit Sarah square in the chest. He had always treated Gran like family, even after they'd broken up. She adored him for that. She knew how much Gran liked Cornelius.

"What brings you in?" Sarah asked.

"Wedding planning." He nudged his glasses back up his nose.

Sarah melted a little on the inside. There was something so endearing about his glasses, a kind of sweetness that covered the heat he unleashed in the bedroom...not that she'd seen that side of him in quite some time. "What planning?"

"Bachelor and bachelorette parties. I've been instructed that they would like a joint one. At least for part of it."

"That sounds fun," Gran said.

"No, it doesn't," Sarah replied. "Why do they want to do this together? It defeats the purpose of the 'one last night as a singleton' vibe these parties should have."

Cornelius shrugged. "I agree, but I'm just the messenger. They were thinking an overnight in Seattle. Jack wants to invite his sister and brother-in-law. We'd get rooms at the same hotel, separate dinners, but come back together afterward for the end of the night partying."

Sarah pursed her lips as she considered. "I suppose that could work. We could go to a club or two, try to get VIP reservations. I know a few places. The girls could do a spa day before the festivities."

"Good idea. The guys could play golf or maybe there'd be time to catch a fishing charter."

"Now, all that's left is picking the weekend." She reached for her phone and pulled up her calendar. They decided on the third weekend in April.

"I guess I should go." Cornelius rubbed a hand on the back of his neck. He looked down then back up at Sarah. "Thanks for all the work you did with getting the new guys recruited. Those ads helped."

Sarah gave him a soft smile. "Glad to do it. Anytime." She paused and reached for her computer. "I was just working on these mock-up designs for the campaign Jack asked for. Want to take a peek?"

As he leaned closer to examine what she'd come up with, Sarah couldn't help but shift into him. A small gap remained between them, but she could smell his earthy, woodsy scent and feel the heat from his body. He bit his lower lip as he studied her screen. Her body flooded with memory and hunger for him. She knew what he could do with that mouth. How incredible he was at kissing...and more than just her mouth. Once upon a time, he'd known how to light up her body until she burst into a thousand sparkling stars. It was a sensation no one else had come close to creating with her.

Being back in Fallbank, this close to Cornelius, reawakened all the passion and feelings long since locked away. Her body tingled and she throbbed between her thighs. Then he turned to her with a smile bright enough to make the rain outside disappear and that throbbing blossomed into an aching slickness. Her nipples pebbled and Sarah swallowed hard. *Oh, boy.* She needed a spicy book and her vibrator tonight. She *needed* to rein herself in.

He caught her gaze and held it. Did he feel the same intense attraction, too?

"This is...good. Great. Sarah. Um, I mean, great job, Sarah."

"Thanks," she mumbled and broke eye contact. Embarrassed heat filled her cheeks and she glanced at Gran who was watching with avid curiosity. Ugh, she didn't need that. Gran wouldn't meddle, but she would make her opinions known. Sarah suppressed a sigh and turned back to Cornelius. "I'll send these over to you and Jack."

"Cool. I guess I'll head out then."

"See you." She watched him go, then as soon as the door closed, said to Gran, "Don't."

"Don't what?" Gran asked.

Sarah saw through Gran's faux-innocent expression. "Don't say anything about Cornelius. He's dating Jane. There's nothing going on between us."

"All I was thinking about was Vivica and the new marketing job you have. Seems like Fallbank could use someone with your skillset. I heard there's a vacant office for rent half a block over on Waterfall Lane. I wasn't going to comment on you and Cornelius at all. If you're the one reading into things, then maybe you should look closer at your own feelings."

Sarah sighed. "There's nothing there."

Gran threw a Look at her. "Uh-huh. You can only ignore things for so long. But I'm not getting in between you two." She paused and went back about her work. "So long as you and he get back together."

* * * *

Cornelius' phone rang with an alert for a new FaceTime call from his mom. He swiped despite standing in the middle of a forest on a job site. They were on a break and he was the boss. Plus his mom had cancer, so there was no circumstance he wouldn't answer when she called. "Hey, Mom. How are you?"

Her pale and worn face filled the screen. She'd lost her hair and dark bags colored underneath her eyes, but her smile still burned like a thousand-watt light. If that ever failed, then he would full-blown worry.

"Hi, honey. I'm getting through it. How are you?"

"Staying busy. Work is going well." He flipped the camera to face out and panned the forest. "I'm on site."

"Oh, I didn't mean to interrupt you."

"Never too important for my best girl. What's up?"

"I just wanted to let you know the latest update. My doctor did another scan and no new growths. With the surgery successful at getting the whole tumor, I'm in a good place. Three more rounds of chemo to go."

Relief hit so hard, he staggered back and landed on a log. His whole body shook with alleviation. "That's amazing. I'm so happy." He crinkled his nose at the itchy sensation in it and blinked against the gathering moisture blurring his vision. "I'm freaking thrilled, Mama."

His mom swiped at her own eyes. "Me too, baby. Me too." A shaky laugh escaped her. "After all, I have to be around to hold my grandbabies."

"Ma…" Cornelius groaned.

"I know, I know. I don't want to pressure you. I do want you to be happy."

He nodded. "I get that. I've been seeing someone. Sort of." He'd been on another date with Jane and they had a third lined up for next Saturday.

"Why don't I sense more excitement from you?"

Jane and Cornelius were past the blundering, basic getting-to-know-you phase and working up to friendship—which was the real issue. Friendship. The feelings he had were platonic. Jane was nice. That was it. Nice. He didn't know if he should keep at it with her or cut his losses. He didn't want to lead her on and make her believe there was more between them, but surely she felt that. She hadn't turned him down when he'd asked her out, but at the same time they still hadn't even kissed. Of course, two dates didn't mean much. It was early. "We've been out twice. Still getting to know one another." He shrugged. "She's nice, but I don't know if there's a spark there yet. Too soon to tell."

His mom tilted her head. "Hmm. Well, I hope there's clarity for you both in the near future." She flashed her grin again. "Enough about that. Tell me how things at TLC are going."

Thank God his mom intuited when not to push him. "Good! We've had a string of new interest coming in for us to clear some areas and also new avenues for selling the timber."

"Wonderful. What prompted this new influx?"

Cornelius stared into the blue eyes that were an exact match to his own. Did he want to tell his mom? Suppressing a sigh, he said. "We hired Sarah Wildes for marketing. She's done outstanding work. Sarah had to move back to Fallbank for the time being."

"Sarah? She's in Fallbank again? That's..." She pressed her lips together, but pink filled her cheeks.

This was why he hadn't wanted to mention Sarah. His mom still held out hope the two of them might get back together one day. She'd see this as the perfect opportunity. Cornelius could see the excitement in her features, the light in her eyes, the hint of a smile playing at the corners of her lips, the flush of her skin. At last this brought a little color back to her face. "Mom, don't. We're not—we're friends. Business partners. That's it."

"I didn't say anything," she protested, but her smile gave her away.

He used work as an excuse to hang up and halt the conversation he didn't want to have. "All right. I need to get back at it. The others will be wondering where I am. As the boss, I gotta set a good example."

His mom winked at him. "Thanks for indulging your mother."

"Never too busy for you, Mama. I love you."

"I love you, too. Take care of yourself. Make good choices."

He chuckled. "I will. Promise." He clicked the end button and tucked his phone in his pocket.

The following Saturday he found himself thinking about his mother's words. "*Make good choices.*" As Jane ambled alongside him toward the bowling alley, he wondered if he was making the correct ones. Jane had been so eager, so happy to see him when he'd picked her up at the Wild Rose. He wished he could say the same. Instead, he found himself digging deep for enthusiasm. He needed to get his head in the game or throw in the towel.

She asked him about his day and he responded on autopilot. He was mid-sentence when he glanced up the street as Three Sisters Apothecary was coming up. He always seemed to know when it was close by. As he looked, Sarah stepped out and locked the door behind her. As she turned, their gazes caught. She froze. He paused in mid-step and mid-thought. Despite the distance between them, he felt her pull. Her blonde hair was like a bright beacon calling to him. He ached to move toward her.

"Cornelius?" Jane asked. "Are you okay?"

He shook his head and jerked his attention to Jane. *His date*. "Yeah. I'm good. Sorry about that. I was thinking about something my mom said earlier. On the phone."

"Oh. All right." She still had her brow furrowed, so he drew his lips up to smile.

"Anyway, so we finished the job today which is ahead of schedule so the landowner will be happy. That means we can get this wood sold off sooner and get profits back to all of us."

Cornelius fought the urge to glance back and search for Sarah again. Instead, he and Jane continued on with their walk to the bowling alley. It turned out she wasn't the best bowler and Cornelius made an effort to be a bit goofier for her. Her laugh was nice and he enjoyed hearing it. At the end of the night—the completion of date three—he walked her back to the inn. As she stood in front of her little cottage looking up at him with hope in her eyes, he gathered his courage. Leaning in, he pressed his lips to hers. Jane softened into him, a sweet little hum coming from her throat. As he stepped back, she blinked up at him with the hint of a smile flirting at the edges of her lips.

"Would you... That is, do you... want to c-come in?" Her voice was low...timid.

He didn't know if she wanted him to go inside and was nervous or if she thought she needed to make the offer because he'd kissed her. Cornelius didn't want to make her uncomfortable and in all honesty, he didn't want to go in. Try as he might, he didn't feel anything when kissing Jane. "I have to be on a job site at six in the morning tomorrow. I'd better not."

She swallowed hard. "Okay. I understand." She fiddled with her keys and looked down. "This was fun. Thanks, Cornelius."

"Yeah, I had a good time." And he had, just not in a romantic sense. He needed to get his head sorted out. "Listen, Jack's bachelor party is next weekend, so I won't be around. How about I call you and we can do something after that?"

Jane nibbled on her lip, still looking unsure about his response. "Sounds good. Have fun." Her tone was shy all over again. Whatever progress he'd made in getting her out of her shell had been undone by his rejection of her offer. The sad part was that Cornelius didn't think he was bothered by the turn of events.

"I'll try." Cornelius laughed but knew he wasn't funny. "Night, Jane." He leaned in and kissed her cheek.

Jane lifted the corners of her mouth. "Good night."

Chapter Twelve

"Oh my God, that spot right there. Oh, yeah. That's so good." Sarah moaned.

"Oh, for crying out loud, Sarah. It's a massage, not sex. Quit it," Becca yelled. The laughter of Bridget and Allison, Jack's sister, filled the air.

"Sorry," Sarah mumbled, more for the masseuse than anyone else. "I just...um, have been stressed and the spot between my shoulders is tense." The warmth of the room, dim lighting and lavender scent in the air combined for the complete relaxing experience and Sarah was leaning all the way in.

"It's all good. I've heard way worse." The woman rubbing her back chuckled.

Sarah blew out a deep breath and let the magic of the massage therapist's hands loosen her body. For the past two weeks, she'd gone through three video interviews for different companies in Seattle. She was getting interest at last, but nothing was coming up with an actual offer yet. The frustration at how slow things were moving had built until she felt like screaming. It wasn't that she couldn't keep busy or money was tight. In fact, she'd taken on four more local businesses for marketing campaigns. Between that and the odd shift at Three Sisters, Sarah wasn't hurting for income.

Fallbank was considerably less expensive than Seattle and it also helped that she didn't have to pay rent. Gran and Gramps had paid off the house long before Bridget had taken it over. It made Sarah wonder what would happen to it after Bridget moved. Maybe Gran would move back in? Although her grandmother had said before how much she liked driving less, being downtown and her smaller living space.

While money wasn't a huge concern, Sarah had seen Cornelius with Jane twice more, once out for dinner and the other time they were walking through town. The sights caused her stomach to churn and hot jealousy swept through her each time. She needed to get her emotions under control. Cornelius seemed happy and she couldn't stop him, even if her heart pleaded for her to try.

After they wrapped up their massages, all four of them went to soak in the hot tub. Reclining her head, Sarah closed her eyes and let the heat from the water soak into her bones.

"Sarah, how're the interviews going?" Becca asked.

Sarah lifted her lids. "Good. Things move at a glacial pace in the corporate world. It'll be another week or two before I hear about anything. I'll have to go in for final interviews if anyone wants me." She sighed.

Bridget piped up, "But you're doing well in town. You've gotten a ton of clients by word of mouth. I'm amazed."

"I am, too. Who knew Fallbank was so desperate for marketing? The mayor's office reached out on Friday afternoon. They want to do some tourism creatives. They said if it went well, they would pass my information along to some of the other towns in the area." The ego boost that phone call had given her was still glowing within her.

Allison beamed. "How great! Way to kick ass. You must be excited. What do you think you'll end up doing? Coming back to Seattle or staying in Fallbank?"

Sarah jolted, causing small ripples in the water. "Seattle. I'm moving back to Seattle." Why would Allison think staying was an option?

"Okay. I was curious since you acted more excited about the local work than the opportunities with the big agencies." Allison scrunched her nose. "I didn't mean to read into anything."

Sarah waved a hand. "No big deal. My plan has always been to get back up here. It's taking longer than I anticipated, hence the freelance work."

Becca and Bridget exchanged a look. Becca said, "Options are never bad things to have."

Bridget nodded. "I've been grateful you're in town. With the wedding and house building stuff, you covering things at Three Sisters has saved me. I don't know how I would have gotten so much accomplished without you." She reached out at hand and Sarah squeezed it. Becca grabbed on, too.

Sarah loved the women in her life so much. The support they provided one another was immeasurable. "What are sisters for?"

Allison smacked a hand over her heart. "Aww, I've always wanted a sister! Brothers are big dorks who tease and dangle you upside down in front of your crushes."

They all laughed and Bridget added Allison's hand to their pile. "Well, now you have three of us."

For a moment, they grinned at one another. Then Becca splashed the water. "Enough of this mushy, emotional stuff. Time to get all sexied up and hit the town. We have celebrating to do!"

Several hours later, they were dressed to the nines, well fed and fast on their way to a future morning of hangovers. They entered the club with its pulsing music and shimmering lights, packed with beautiful people. Heat rolled in waves from the dance floor. Sarah looked to her little sister and saw the hint of apprehension on her face. Sarah was glad Jack had pulled strings and gotten them a VIP booth upstairs. Bridget would need breaks from the crowds, despite wanting to go out on the town for her bachelorette party. Sarah also knew Jack and his crew would be here soon and that would put Bridge at ease.

If only the same could be said for Sarah when the guys arrived. She had no idea what to expect with Cornelius. Would he flirt with other women? Dance? How serious were he and Jane? Could she handle seeing him in this setting? Their younger lives hadn't included much of a club life. Too young, too broke and too horny – and with the long distance – when they did get together, they spent it just the two of them. Tonight though, circumstances were a far cry from those days. How would he act here?

"Let's head up to the VIP section. I need a drink," Sarah shouted over the noise. They trooped up the stairs and were greeted by a hot, shirtless man. With a wide grin, he escorted them over to a massive curved booth covered in aubergine-colored crushed velvet with a low table in front of it. The position from the upper deck gave prime viewing of the writhing, grinding mass on the dance floor below.

"If you need anything at all, there are several of us circulating up here. Any of us are happy to help—just wave. We also have a bar in the direction"—he pointed to the left—"and restrooms are over there." He turned his hand to the right. "Anything I can start you all with?" They requested champagne, tequila shots and water.

"I'm going to hit the ladies' room," Sarah said, then headed to the bathroom, grateful again for the VIP status and not waiting in the lines downstairs. When she returned it was to find the girls laughing and the drinks delivered. Snatching up a shot, she raised it up. "To my baby sister and finding her true love! You and Jack are the perfect couple. Now to make this a night to remember in bits and pieces through a hazy fog of alcohol. Cheers!"

"Cheers!" Becca, Allison and Bridget echoed and they all downed their tequila.

"Let's go dance," Allison yelled, tugging at Bridget's hand. Trooping downstairs as a group, Sarah sighed and let the warmth of the alcohol loosen her muscles and her mind. She needed to get out of her head and enjoy celebrating her little sister.

* * * *

Cornelius slapped Jack on the back and barked a laugh at Hiro's last joke as the three of them entered the club. From the texts exchanged, the women were already here and Jack couldn't wait to get to Bridget.

They'd had a great dinner and gone ax throwing after, but as soon as the picture of a dancing, veil-wearing Bridget surrounded by a ring of men popped up, Jack couldn't be deterred from getting here. He'd raced over there so fast Cornelius almost thought the zombie apocalypse had started.

As they made their way in, Cornelius scanned the mass of people on the dance floor. The girls could be upstairs in the VIP section, but he had a hunch they would attempt to distract Bridget from Jack's absence. Familiarity struck him as he saw a woman with flowing blonde hair rocking her hips to the pulsing music. He traced his gaze over those locks down her back to an hourglass figure encased in a red dress that clung to her curves with a glittering material that fell to mid-thigh. She lifted her arms as she swayed and tossed her head back with laughter. His heart galloped in his chest while his dick hardened to attention. Damn, but Sarah looked breathtaking. He wanted to slide up behind and wrap her in his arms, to feel that gorgeous body pressed into his while he brushed kisses along her neck. Cornelius took a step, then another in her direction.

"Hey, there they are," Hiro said and pointed, not realizing Cornelius had already found them.

Shit. Cornelius shook his head. What was he doing? He was dating Jane. Sure, they weren't exclusive or even all that serious, but he didn't think she'd appreciate him fantasizing about his ex-girlfriend. He needed to get a hold of himself. Then Sarah turned, smiled and held her hand out to him.

Screw it. Dancing didn't mean anything. He could control himself. They weren't going to get back together, regardless. Their groups merged and Sarah was right there. She draped her arms around his neck as she moved with the music. He lifted his hands and placed them on her waist, holding her close.

"Corey, you're here! We never did thisss when we were kids." She winked and her body rubbed against his. "Shhhow me your moves, Superman."

His stomach clenched as all of his blood swam south. She had *winked* and called him *Superman*. It was his fucking kryptonite and she knew it. Sarah used to say his glasses were his cover for how he turned into a superhero in the bedroom. She was also slurring her words, which meant she was already several drinks in. He tightened his fingers as the heat from her soaked into his skin. The material of her dress was flimsy and if he'd wanted, he could shred it along the seams with ease.

"Sarah," he murmured, dipping his nose to inhale her scent. Peonies with a hint of sweet sweat filled his senses. Her soft hair tickled his cheek as she laid her head on his chest.

Tilting her face up, Sarah opened her mouth —

"Oh my God, Saraaah!" The female voice shook both of them apart as another woman bounded up. "I can't believe you're here."

"Tyneisha, hi!" Sarah lurched on her heels and Cornelius kept a hand on her lower back to steady her. "I'm so excited to see you. You have to meet everyone." She flung a hand at their group. "The couple over there looking at each other like they're about to go at it right here and now is my little sister, Bridget, and her fiancé, Jack." She pointed to Hiro and Allison who grinned at Sarah and her friend. "This is Hiro and Allison. Allison is Jack's sister."

Sarah patted a hand on Cornelius' chest. "This is Corey. No! Wait. You can't call him that. Cornelius, his name is Cornelius." She wobbled again and giggled.

Cornelius smiled and said hello while keeping an eye on a very tipsy Sarah. God, she was adorable like this.

Snatching Becca's hand, Sarah tugged her close. "This is my cousin, Becca."

Tyneisha looked Becca up and down with appreciation. In tailored black pants and a fitted button-up shirt that was opened enough to showcase the mounds of her cleavage, Becca looked sexy in an understated way. "Pleasure to meet you," Tyneisha said and bit the corner of her lower lip.

"Same to you," Becca answered as she kicked up her grin. "Want to dance or grab a drink?" She held her palm out and Sarah's friend slid hers into it.

"Yes, please."

The two of them wandered off, leaving Cornelius blinking. That was fast. Why couldn't he find that kind of instant chemistry with someone?

The lush softness of the female beside him pressed close again. *Oh yeah*, he thought as he looked down at his ex-girlfriend. *Because Sarah stole my heart and never gave it back*. Their chemistry was still off the charts given how he was responding to her tonight.

Another body stumbled into him, knocking both Sarah and Cornelius off-kilter and causing Sarah to laugh uproariously.

"Maybe we should sit down for a minute. Drink a little water?" Cornelius offered. He worried about how much she'd had to drink tonight and didn't want her to be hungover in the morning.

She giggled. "You might be right." He led them both upstairs, grasping Sarah's elbow to steady her and ensure she didn't trip. "Our booth is right over here."

She collapsed on the cushions and patted the space next to her.

Cornelius lowered to sit close and signaled a server. "A couple of waters would be great."

"And a Chivas and seven! It's his favorite."

"You got it," the woman in a short leather skirt and white cropped tank answered and headed to the bar.

"Corey," Sarah sighed and smooshed against him. Laying her head on his shoulder, she closed her eyes and a happy humming noise rose from her. "This is so nice."

His heart clenched inside his chest. Hearing that nickname on her lips was everything. She'd been the lone person who'd ever called him that and the sound of it still made his skin tingle and his nerves light up. Dragging a hand over his face, he looked down at her. Damn, he was in trouble. He should be thinking of Jane and feeling excited about her. Yet here he was, mooning over his ex because she was cuddly-drunk and used an old nickname.

The server returned with their drinks. Cornelius snatched up his scotch and Seven Up and downed it in three gulps.

Giggles met his ears. "Doesn't seem like you even tasted your drink, let alone enjoyed it."

He was too sober to make a stupid move with Sarah yet too buzzed to not feel... everything with her so close to him. The warmth of her soft body soaked through his clothes reminding him of memories he'd worked so hard to bury...like those of them without any barriers between them, skin to skin, lost to one another in their love and lust.

She blinked up at him, her eyes shimmering under the club lights. Her lips were so full and *right there.*

God, he was screwed. Knowing he had no one to blame but himself, he lowered his head to hers.

"Woo-hoo! I found them!" Bridget shouted as the rest of their group stumbled up the stairs and over to their booth. She spun to Jack. "I win! You have to do anything I say in bed for a week."

Jack flashed a sloppy grin. "Honeybee, I'll gladly do that anyway. I'm not seeing how I lose here." He leaned around her toward Cornelius. "I knew you were up here, I meant to lose this bet."

Bridget grabbed Jack's head and pulled him in for the kind of kiss Cornelius wanted to give to Sarah. Jack lifted Bridget up and Cornelius whipped his head away from watching his best friend push his next-door neighbor up against a column and dry-hump her.

"Get a room," Sarah yelled as she covered her eyes with her hands. "I don't want to see my little sister like this."

Cornelius shoved at his glasses and turned to help shield the view behind him. Allison and Hiro collapsed down into the semi-circle booth next to him. "Girl, same," Allison griped. "Except my brother. You know what I mean."

Cornelius looked over their crew as Becca and Sarah's friend joined them around the table. He was the sober-ish one here. His drink hadn't done anything and the few beers he'd had during dinner and ax throwing weren't coming close to getting him drunk. He was surrounded by couples — couples who were getting all kinds of frisky. Hiro had Allison smooshed into the cushions while they made out and Becca and Tyneisha had a heavy game of tonsil hockey happening. He looked at Sarah, who was staring at all the others with a bewildered expression. Then she smirked at

Cornelius. "Maybe we should do the same? When in Rome and all that?" She fluttered her lashes up at him.

Oh hell. He was in so much trouble. Cornelius jumped up. "I think we should head back to the hotel." He needed to get space from Sarah and the rest of the group.

"Good idea," Allison mumbled as her husband kissed across her collar bone. "We have a kid-free night and need to make the most of our room."

Like herding cats, Cornelius managed to wrangle them into a ride-share van to the hotel. When they arrived, Jack swept Bridget up to a suite he'd reserved as a surprise for them. Becca held Tyneisha's hand and threw a look at Sarah. "I'm stealing our room. You good?"

Sarah grinned and shot her two thumbs up. "Have fun, you two!"

Allison and Hiro stumbled toward the elevators, oblivious to anyone else.

And Cornelius was left with a swaying Sarah who beamed up at him. "I guess you can stay in my room." She was too out of it and he hoped she would fall asleep without propositioning him again. It wasn't that he didn't want to take her up on in, but not when she wasn't aware of what she was doing. He refused to take advantage of her. He opened the door to the room and ushered her inside.

"Oh, look at that bed! It's enormous." Sarah dove into the fluffy bedding and rolled around. "Wait, you were going to share a bed with Jack?" She cocked her head like a confused puppy.

He laughed and shook his head. "I knew Jack was getting a suite for him and Bridge. I thought it would just be me." *One bed. Right.* He scratched his neck. "I'll sleep on the...couch." He looked at the tiny sofa that would barely fit two adults sitting upright. It would do for one sleep. Maybe. He might need half a bottle of painkillers in the morning for his back, but he'd survive.

"That's silly! Like we haven't slept in the same bed before. Come on, it'll be like old times." She patted the space beside her.

"No, it won't be like old times," he mumbled.

Sarah ignored him and started wiggling out of the little red dress she wore and he flapped his hands at her. "No, no, no." He dug through his duffle bag and threw one of his T-shirts at her. "Go into the bathroom and change into that."

Her retreating footsteps and chuckles let him know she was at least following his request. Stripping, Cornelius switched into a pair of sweats and the other shirt he'd packed. Sarah emerged from the bathroom with his shirt hanging off one shoulder and the bottom edge flirting with her upper thighs. When she crawled onto the bed, the fabric gaped and gave him full view of her bare ass and the outlines of her breasts. Fuck, she wasn't wearing panties. He was hard in seconds. "Dammit." Averting his gaze, he willed his cock to calm down and shuffled to the opposite side of the bed. He climbed in and placed a pillow between himself and Sarah.

Ignoring it, she rolled onto her side and smooshed into the soft barrier, looking at him with big doe eyes. "Did you have fun tonight?"

He smiled. "I did. Hanging with the guys was fun." The urge to reach out and stroke his hand over her hair was almost unbearable.

She stuck out her lower lip. "What about with the girls?"

"Them, too. You should get some sleep." She needed to stop being so damn alluring. It wasn't as if she was trying to seduce him. It came natural between the two of them.

Sarah shook her head. "Not tired. Tipsy, but not sleepy. Wanna watch a movie?" She flopped onto her back.

Maybe that would get her to stop looking at him and get him to stop feeling tempted to kiss her and explore the gorgeous body underneath a very thin layer of fabric.

He flipped on the TV and she snuggled into the pillows and fluffy duvet. She stuck her nose into her chest and yanked up the collar of the shirt. "This smells just like you." She sighed and closed her eyes. "Like home."

Her words gutted him. What was he supposed to say to that admission? That she'd been his home, too? His safe place? Why had she burned it all to the ground? Instead, he held his tongue and clicked through the options, landing on a rom-com.

Twenty minutes later he peeked over and found Sarah smiling with slow, lazy blinks at the movie. His tense muscles relaxed a little. She'd fall asleep soon. Ten minutes later, she grabbed the pillow between them and rolled over, then scooted back until she curved into him.

Huffing out a breath, he turned off the television and closed his eyes in an attempt to overlook that the ex-love of his life was sleeping right next to him.

Chapter Thirteen

Bright sunlight hit Sarah's eyes as she squinted awake. Strong arms wrapped around her doused her in warmth, while slow and steady breaths matched her own and the woodsy scent of Cornelius filled her lungs. Closing her eyes, she allowed herself one moment to revel in the delight of having Corey in bed with her. Then she locked down the violent feelings demanding to be recognized within her and slid out of his embrace and the sheets. Cool air hit her skin, making her wince. A wave of dizziness hit and Sarah reached a hand out to the wall. Amazingly, she didn't have a headache and her stomach held just a hint of nausea. Not bad for how much she'd drunk last night. After a quick trip to the restroom, Sarah came out and peered around. She could sit on the uncomfortable-looking tiny couch, the harsh-looking desk chair or get back into bed. Not being a glutton for punishment, she chose the soft mattress and warm blankets. She wasn't a masochist, after all.

Lying back down, she closed her eyes and tried to fall back asleep, but instead watched Corey. He was peaceful in his dreams, no frowns or creases showing stress or unhappiness. It'd been a while since she'd seen him so at ease. After a few minutes, he fluttered his lids open and caught her staring.

"Morning," he said, his voice rough and low. The sound did delicious, dirty things to her body.

The air grew warm and sultry, filled with anticipation. She licked her lips. "Hi," she whispered, then she reached over him and snagged his glasses from the nightstand. He put them on when offered and lifted the corners of his lips. "Thanks."

They stared at each other for a long second. The tension between them stretched and snapped. Without speaking a word, they both reached for each other. In a heartbeat, she was flat on her back with Corey over her. His mouth crashed to hers and fireworks exploded. Their kiss was a burst of heat and desire and desperation. God, it had been since...their last kiss since she'd felt anything close to this hurricane of need and lust and love. No other had come close and she never wanted this to end. Her tongue met his in ways familiar and new. It was flying and falling all at once. *More.* She had to have more.

The shirt she wore bunched up at her waist as they pressed together. He rocked his hips and she parted her legs to nestle him against her heated core. A moan vibrated between their lips as he ground into her and she didn't know if it was from her or him. All she knew was that she was in Corey's arms kissing him and about to come from the hard ridge of his erection rubbing her through his sweatpants in the most perfect way.

Lifting her legs, she pushed at his sweats to get them down enough to allow his cock to spring free. Then he was gliding through her wetness and the head of his dick pushed over her clit and Sarah was lost. Arching into him, she threw her head back and moaned his name as ecstasy took her. Her body shook and shivered with her pleasure.

"Oh, fuck." He growled and jerked his hips away from her stomach and spilled onto the sheets. Panting, Corey rested his forehead to hers. "Sarie…"

The lenses of his glasses were fogged and she laughed. She ruffled her fingers through his hair, not wanting the moment to end. She knew when the buzz of their mutual orgasms faded that there would be awkwardness and questions. And neither of them had the answers. Even saying anything could crush this fragile aura.

Instead, she kissed him again. Soft and slow. Long and lingering. At last, when they parted their lips and tongues, Sarah wiggled from the bed and into the bathroom and snagged her phone on the way. She fired off an SOS text to Becca to see if her suitcase could be dropped at the room. She needed something to wear other than the dress from last night. "Becca is going to bring my bag over. Is that cool?" she yelled through the door.

"No problem," he called back to her.

When it arrived, Cornelius gave a quiet knock at the bathroom and slid it to her when she cracked the door open. After a fast shower and donning regular clothes, she emerged. "Hey."

Corey looked up at her. "Hey." An awkward pause rested in the air. "Uh, Jack messaged that he and Bridge are getting dressed. They want to grab breakfast somewhere."

"Cool." She watched as he took his turn in the bathroom and flopped down on the couch. Burying her face in her hands, she huffed. "What is wrong with you?" How did she figure this out with Corey in the limited time before they had to meet up with everyone and pretend they hadn't gotten one another off this morning? What did she want with Corey? Passion and sexual compatibility had never been the issue. The problem was her and her secret, one she still wasn't willing to tell him. She couldn't. He'd hate her. A tremble of fear shook her.

A knock on the door pulled Sarah from her spiraling thoughts. Springing up from the stiff cushions with relief that they could avoid the entire conversation, she opened it to a grinning Becca with Jack and Bridget in tow.

"Good morning," Becca said as they entered.

"Morning. Cor-nelius is changing the bathroom." She hoped none of them caught the way she'd tripped over his name, almost calling him Corey. She needed to get her head sorted out and didn't want them asking questions about the two of them in a one-bed hotel room last night. "Where's Tyneisha?" she asked Becca, going on the offense.

"She had to head home. Something about a standing brunch date with a friend. All good things. We had a great time together last night and are both happy leaving it as is."

Cornelius came out and Sarah relaxed at his appearance. They wouldn't interrogate her with him here. *Right?*

"Breakfast," she announced. "I know a great place we can walk to." She led the way and put her thoughts and feelings and what-ifs into a box and locked it away in her mind. This weekend was for Bridget and Jack and she didn't want to mess with it. Safer to avoid Cornelius and what happened until later...much later. Maybe never.

* * * *

Cornelius willed his phone to chime in response to the text he'd sent to Hop when he'd gotten home from Seattle last night. A quick glance told him his mental telepathy hadn't worked. Hop must not be able to respond or didn't want to.

He clicked open the thread and reread his message.

Cornelius: Are there any exceptions to your no break-up-make-up rule?

He didn't know why he felt like he needed Hop's permission to try again with Sarah. Maybe because his friend had been so adamant about it and Cornelius had been at an impressionable age where it had stuck with him.

Memories of Sarah in his arms, kissing him, coming for him replayed in his head. Forget what Hop thought—he was going for it. His heart knew who it wanted and that was Sarah. Now to persuade her to want the same.

Sarah had managed to avoid Cornelius for four days before he at last ran her down. How she managed to dodge him while living next door was impressive, but Cornelius knew she'd be at the dress shop for final fittings. And those were scheduled for today. He couldn't stop thinking about last weekend.

The two of them, in bed, together…where the hell had that come from? For years, they had skirted the edge of being friends and denying any attraction between them. Sarah was meticulous about not touching him. He was adamant about giving her the space she wanted. He didn't want her uncomfortable or feeling pressured in any way. Cornelius kept in mind that if he wanted her to visit, to come back to Fallbank where he had even a chance to see her, he had to ensure their relationship stayed friendly.

Yet that hotel room with its one bed had taken those boundaries between them and annihilated those walls to dust. For that moment, it was as if they hadn't skipped a beat. The taste of her lips, the feel of her skin, knowing how to tease pleasure from her body — all of it was as familiar and easy as breathing. And now his brain had those memories playing on repeat. His body was desperate for another round. His will to hold by the don't-get-back-together-with-your-ex rule was weakening by the minute.

He needed to talk to Sarah — and Jane. He'd talk to Sarah first, then Jane. Clarity on what was happening with his ex-girlfriend was paramount for him, even if the outcome wouldn't change him breaking things off with Jane. He and Jane had gone on four dates and kissed twice. No sparks. No desire. No urge to continue dating her and see where things went. She was sweet and pretty and worthy of someone's attention, but if his heart had been reluctant before, it was dead set against her now. Friends was a good place for him and Jane. She had to feel the same, right? This couldn't be one-sided.

His phone chimed and broke his intense thoughts. A quick glance showed a new text from Becca's older brother.

Hop: Nope. I don't have exceptions. Did you date someone I don't know about that you want to get back with?

Cornelius: You know her.

Hop: You mean my cousin? Sarah?

Cornelius had to chuckle under his breath. Who else would Hop think he was talking about?

Cornelius: Of course I mean Sarah. There's never been anyone else for me.

Hop: Well, shit. Why didn't you say so? No question that you and she belong together. Go get her back, dumbass!

This time he guffawed out loud. He should have known Hop wouldn't mean to not go after Sarah. They were family, after all. He tapped a quick reply then tucked his phone into his back pocket. A lightness filled him that wasn't there before. It seemed all Cornelius needed was his friend's permission and a hot-and-heavy make-out session with Sarah to get his head on right. He nodded to himself as he waited outside the store.

There was a light breeze, but early May was turning warm. The garden boxes lining the main streets of downtown had bright color flowers and lush green plants in them, making the town feel cheery and vibrant. Spring was making itself right at home in Fallbank. The grass was getting greener and the trees were starting to bud to life. The nagging rain seemed to be easing off and giving way to more peeks of sunshine. Given a few more weeks by the time the wedding came around, the wild flowers would be in full bloom. He smiled. Bridget would love it and Sarah would look amazing in her pale blue bridesmaid dress with the splash of colors as the backdrop.

The door swung open and Sarah, Bridget, and Becca stepped out, laughing together. The sight of the three of them had a grin spreading across his cheeks. The family resemblance was unmistakable. They were bonded together tighter than sisters. Now if he could convince Sarah to stay in Fallbank...and give him another chance. Rules were meant to be broken.

"Cornelius," Bridget exclaimed with a smile when she caught sight of him. "What are you doing here?"

He nodded to all of them then settled his gaze on the blonde who had of late taken up residence in his mind. "I need to speak to Sarah for a few minutes." He winked at Bridget. "Wedding party stuff."

Becca cocked one brow. "And you don't need me? The other bridesmaid?"

He felt heat flush up his neck. "I, uh... Sarah and I have already started this project, so I thought it might be easiest kept simple. Just the two of us."

Sarah fidgeted with the ring on her right hand. "Now's not a great time-"

"It'll just take a couple of minutes," he interrupted. Determination to not let her sneak away again gripped him tight. "Promise you'll be back with the girls in no time."

"We'll leave her with you and catch up at Three Sisters. Sound good, Sare-bear?" Bridget asked, then grabbed Becca's arm and tugged her down the street.

"Thanks, little B," Cornelius called after them.

"What's up, Cornelius?" Sarah looked around at anything but him. Two people walked by with curious looks as he and his ex loitered on the sidewalk.

On impulse, he snagged her hand and led them around the corner to a small alley between stores, out of direct sight from prying eyes of townsfolk. "Have you been avoiding me?"

"Why would you think that? What would there be to avoid?"

He placed two fingers under her chin and tilted her face up to him. Her green eyes drowned in uncertainty and he wanted to take that away. "Sarah. We need to talk about Seattle. About what happened between us."

She swallowed. "It was nothing. We got caught up in the moment is all."

"Nothing?" he echoed. "You're kidding me, right? I don't know about you, but I don't just…" — he struggled for the right words — "dry-hump women to orgasm." God, that felt so weird and juvenile to say and it didn't quite fit what they'd done, but there wasn't any other phrase that worked. "Stop pretending this wasn't something more." Cornelius shoved his glasses up his nose and ran a hand through his hair. How could she not be feeling the same way as he did?

With red cheeks, Sarah chewed her lower lip for a second. "I'll concede that it isn't something I'd do on the regular, but it doesn't change anything. We aren't meant to be together. It was a one-time event."

"A one-time event?" His pulse pounded and heat rushed through his limbs. The muscles of his body tensed as everything inside him screamed to prove her wrong, to show her how right they were together and that their connection wasn't a fluke.

She blinked, but held his gaze. "Yeah. I'm not even sure we could replicate the chemistry from last weekend."

"Is that so?" She did not just say that to him. There was no way Sarah believed that—none. She felt their pull, even if she wanted to deny it. "You're lying."

"I'm not." She tilted her chin up in defiance.

"Okay, then." He ground his molars together, stepped closer into her space and put one hand on the brick wall behind her. Leaning in to close the gap between them to a few mere inches, he growled. "Prove it."

Her mouth dropped open. "What?"

He pressed closer, feeling the heat rolling off her body. He stopped short of touching her and glanced at her pulse fluttering at her neck. "You heard me. Show me that we don't have a bond."

She licked her lips, but said nothing.

"Kiss me, Sarah. Show me there aren't feelings between us."

Cornelius closed the distance from him to her, the softness of her curves yielding to the hardness of him. Bringing his head closer, he watched for any sign that she didn't want this. Gave her the chance to say no or pull away. Instead, she lifted on her toes closer to him. When their lips met, he moved with deliberate slowness. Light brushes to tease turned to gentle pressure of his mouth on hers morphed into slow slides of their tongues along one another. She gripped his shirt before gliding her hands up to fist in his hair.

He groaned and delved deeper into the kiss, shifting his hands to grab her hips and align their bodies fully. The flame burning between them flared and became an inferno. Their chemistry bloomed into a wild tangle of desire and need, both of them lost in one another. He rocked into the cradle of her thighs and a whimper vibrated from her throat. When at last they came up for air, her panting breaths mingled with his. And the lustful look in her eyes let Cornelius know Sarah was as swept up as he was. There was no denying that there was still emotion present, but it was stronger than ever.

Cornelius rested his forehead to hers and laughed when he noticed his glasses had fogged over.

"I guess we did get a little heated," Sarah joked.

"I know we need to talk, but..." He dipped to capture her mouth again.

Sarah had melted into him again when—

"Oh! I'm sor—Cornelius?" A familiar voice jolted him from the intimate bubble they'd created. "Sarah?" This time Jane spoke more softly.

Fuck. Cornelius jerked back from Sarah and flashed a guilty wince at Jane standing at the corner of the dress store and the alley. He rubbed the back of his neck, embarrassed heat radiating from it. "Jane, I...can explain."

Jane crossed her arms around her waist and darted her brown eyes to the side. "I'm pretty sure I understand." Her voice was sad and dejected. "I should go." Turning on her heel, she walked off at a brisk clip.

"Shit," Cornelius muttered, then looked at Sarah. Her expression gave nothing away. "I need to talk to Jane, but this isn't over." He slid an arm around her waist. "We'll talk, yeah?"

The softness in her green eyes melted his insides. "Yeah."

With that, Cornelius stole one last claim of her lips before chasing after Jane. He caught up with her as she was turning onto the side path to the inn, the one that lead to the door she and her staff used. It was lined with tulips and daffodils that were a refreshing burst of color. It was a stark contrast to the woman huddled in on herself rushing up the brick-lined walkway. "Jane! Please wait."

She glanced over her shoulder.

He felt sick to his stomach at the wetness glittering in her eyes. He'd clearly misjudged her investment in their dating. "I'm sorry. I... This should have gone down in a different way and that's on me."

Jane stopped and allowed him to catch up. She looked down and fiddled with the corner of the cardigan she wore. "It's fine. We weren't serious or exclusive. It was a surprise, is all." Her voice trembled, but no more tears fell down her cheeks.

"It isn't okay. I messed up big time. I wanted to give us a chance, but the connection I'm looking for...it wasn't there on my side." He sighed and adjusted his glasses. "I should have said something sooner and I..." He couldn't bring himself to regret what had happened with him and Sarah, even though the guilt was there. Yet he should have owned up to his lack of feelings with Jane before now. "I'm so sorry, Jane."

She swiped at her face, brushing away the dampness. Then she inhaled and let it out. "It's fine. I'm more embarrassed than anything."

He shook his head. "You have nothing to be embarrassed about. *I'm* the one who should be ashamed."

"Well, like I said, we weren't exclusive or anything. I think I knew things weren't going to work out long term."

"Still doesn't excuse my actions. Sarah and I... We have a history together. We used to date." *That was putting it mildly.* "There's unresolved feelings on both sides and with her back in town, it bubbled up and overflowed."

"I get it. I didn't know about your past, but I could sense something when she was around." She paused and gifted him with a small smile. "I hope things work out for you two. Seems like there's strong feelings there."

"Thank you, Jane. I don't deserve your kindness or forgiveness, but I'm grateful."

This time when she turned, he didn't stop her from walking inside the inn. A twinge of guilt lingered, but the predominant emotion he felt was satisfaction...which should give him more remorse, but he didn't. What did spark was excitement at seizing a new opportunity with Sarah.

Chapter Fourteen

Before walking into Three Sisters Apothecary, Sarah licked her lips. The taste of Cornelius lingered there and she couldn't deny the bolt of lust that landed straight at her core. Ugh, what was she doing? Twice now she'd lost all control with Corey and didn't know what that meant. They still hadn't talked and her plan of avoiding him until the wedding had gone up in flames. After the second make-out session, not discussing what this...*thing* between them was had become moot. She knew there was no way he'd let the needed conversation go and be "just friends" again. Did she want to go back to being friends? *No*, her heart told her. But...he'd never understand why she broke up with him...wouldn't forgive her. She was sure of it.

And the added complication of Jane and being the other woman in the scenario here was not sitting well with her. She knew things between them were casual, yet Sarah couldn't shake the icky sensation left behind.

Sarah yanked the store entry open and came face to face with her cousin and grandmother. "Oh, hey."

"Hey?" Becca said with a shit-eating grin. "That's all you have to say?"

"Yes." She crossed her arms. Show no weakness was her motto.

Gran chuckled and nudged Becca out of the way. "We can grill her when we get to the house." Her grandma grabbed a box filled with ribbons and tulle and shimmery fabrics. Tonight they'd planned to do dry runs of what the centerpieces, bouquets and boutonnières would look like for the wedding. The flowers would come from Bridget and Becca's gardens and Sarah had already sketched out ideas along with an entire online mood board.

"Where'd Bridge go?" she asked and peered around for her little sister. If she was around, Sarah could keep Bridget talking about wedding planning and not Sarah's boy troubles.

"Some house thing popped up. Jack called and picked her up so they could go check it out at the building site," Gran answered.

"I hope everything's okay." Sarah frowned and wondered if she should send a text to her sister.

"I'm sure it's fine." Gran smiled. "House building is always an adventure."

Having no experience of her own, Sarah couldn't argue with that. They loaded into cars and headed over to the house. The fading sunlight painted the town in soft shadows backlit by oranges, pinks and yellows in the sky. The fir trees swayed with the gentle breeze outside the car windows. Sarah smiled at the familiar stores and Victorian-style houses painted in a multitude of rainbow colors in the neighborhood she had grown up in. Once inside the house, Candle greeted them with meows for food.

After feeding both the cat and all of them, they settled into the living room with roses, dahlias, dwarf bunchberries and lupines in buckets surrounding them, plus a variety of fern leaves, madrone and western hemlock branches for filler. The box of adornments was now empty and laid out across the coffee table. Sarah pulled out her laptop and brought up her wedding mood board. "I was thinking something like this for the reception."

The picture was of flowers and leaves woven into a long rope that would span the length of each table. The arrangement could be placed on top of the different textiles for a layering effect that would add to the overall whimsical, woodland feel. "We could take inspiration from this to make matching flowers for the wedding party. We can use the same fabrics to wrap the stems in for the bridesmaids and a bow to add for the groomsmen. What do you think?"

Gran threw her a Look. "I think we're going to talk about what Cornelius wanted with you and why you were so flushed and flustered when you got to the shop after."

"Gran!" Sarah exclaimed in betrayal. How could her grandmother ambush her like this?

The older woman shrugged with an unapologetic expression. "What? I did say we would get answers when at the house. Here we are. Fess up, young lady. Am I getting my would-be grandson back? I saw the way you two looked at each other. Almost enough for you to wind up pregnant."

A wave of pain struck Sarah like an arrow to the chest. She gaped at her waiting family. "I...I don't know."

Becca arched a brow. "How do you not know? What is going on with you two?"

Sarah threw her hands in the air. "I wish I could tell you." She looked down at the flowers and plucked a few of each for weaving together. "We had a...moment at the bachelorette weekend." Sarah was so conflicted on how to feel.

"I knew it!" Becca exclaimed. Gran nudged and shushed her.

"Then back at the dress shop, we had another. He wanted to talk, but Jane interrupted us. She saw us kissing." Sarah dropped the stems and rested her face in her hands. "I'm such a jerk. I can't believe I made out with Corey — twice — while he had a girlfriend."

"Doesn't sound like she was his girlfriend to me," Becca muttered.

Sarah threw her a glare. "They were dating, or whatever. I'm still a jerk." She'd known he was seeing Jane and still acted like she'd had some kind of claim over Corey.

Becca shook her head. "No. If anyone is, it's Cornelius. He's the one dating Jane, not you. He should have checked himself."

Gran put a hand on Sarah's shoulder. "Your cousin is right. Don't beat yourself up for something that isn't on you. Cornelius will need to make things right between him and Jane. And you."

Exhaling, Sarah fussed with the centerpiece stuff again. She didn't feel any less guilty. Jane was sweet and didn't deserve what she and Corey had done. "Can we focus on something else? I'm confused and would rather think about anything else at the moment." She hated this "other woman" sensation. Love triangles were one of her least favorite tropes in romance books and now Sarah felt like she was in one.

"Sure." Becca grabbed up her own stack of blooms. "Let's time this to see how long it'll take to create one, so we know how long we'll need to get enough of these for all the tables."

The front door opened and Bridget and Jack walked in. "Hi. We're back."

Sarah lifted her lips in a wane smile. Her sister glowed with happiness while her own heart was bruised and in limbo. But Sarah couldn't find it in her to begrudge Bridget her excitement. "How's the house?"

"Oh, fine. We had to make a shift in the cabinet layout, but nothing too major." Her sister shrugged.

Jack pressed a kiss to his fiancée's cheek. "I'm going to shower. I ran cables for the yarder today and feel grimy. I'll leave you all to…things." He waved to the general chaos of flowers in the room. "A pleasure to see you all."

They said goodbyes and Bridget asked, "What'd I miss?"

Sarah turned her laptop to show the mood board designs. Pointing at the inspiration picture, she said, "We're working to make a test one of these. What do you think?"

A grin spread across her sister's face. "I love it. That's perfect." She threw her arms around Sarah's shoulders. "You're the best, Sare-Bear."

"I know." At least she could get one thing correct in her life.

Becca snorted and shook her head while Gran chuckled. Then her grandmother tugged all three of them into a hug. "You girls. I'm so glad I have you here."

Warmth blossomed in Sarah's chest. She loved having this time with her family. She'd missed them while in Seattle and would miss them when she went back. *If* she went back. Maybe she could make a life in Fallbank? Maybe if Corey... No, she wouldn't make her decisions based on him, on a possibility of a relationship with him. She didn't know where they stood, but whatever choices she made, they had to be for her and no one else.

A knock sounded on the front door and Becca went to investigate. Gran and Bridge chatted about bouquets on the couch. A murmur of voices carried as Sarah focused on her project and footsteps came closer. She glanced up and found Becca smirking with Corey shuffling along behind. His gaze caught hers and the room fell away.

Cornelius couldn't look away from Sarah's green eyes. They captivated him. All he wanted was to go to her, fall on his knees and kiss her breathless. From the heat in her stare, he wagered she felt the same. A cough broke the connection and pulled Cornelius back to his surroundings. His ears grew warm and he adjusted his glasses.

"Cornelius, what brings you by?" Gran asked with a smile.

Rubbing his neck, he answered, "I was hoping I could chat with Sarah."

"Again?" Becca grinned.

"More wedding party stuff?" Bridget chimed in. Her expression was mischievous as she looked between the two of them. They all knew something was up and loved embarrassing the two of them.

Sarah stood and threw her family a scowl, then grabbed his hand and tugged him back out the door onto the front porch. She spun to face him, eyes flashing.

Danger. Make no sudden moves.

She was in her head about the two of them. Instead, he channeled his best boyish grin and said, "Hi, Sarie."

She rounded her eyes at him. "Don't 'Sarie' me. What are you doing here?"

"Finishing our conversation. You agreed we'd talk about us." God, why was she so hot when she was mad? He wanted to kiss her again and was holding back by a thread of control.

She crossed her arms, but instead of intimidating him, all he could focus on was how that pushed her tits up more. She had a fantastic body and her breasts were a particular favorite of his. Cornelius licked his lips.

"Eyes up here." Sarah snapped her fingers at him. "Cornelius, we can't do this."

Resisting the urge to shake sense into her, he sighed. "I know you're scared. I am, too."

"I'm not scared. I refuse to be the other woman. The one who breaks up couples." Her chin wobbled.

"You didn't," he interrupted. He couldn't stand the thought of Sarah hating on herself. "Jane and I weren't going to go the distance. Even if you weren't back in Fallbank, we wouldn't have worked out. I knew that before this past weekend. I wish I'd said something to her sooner and that's on me. But we've talked and Jane understands."

"She understands what?"

Time to make the leap. He stepped closer to Sarah. "That you and I are undeniable." He reached out and ran his palms up her arms, folding her in closer to him. "Try. That's all I'm asking. Just try being us again." He lowered his forehead to hers. Now that he'd come to terms with it, he had to convince her to give them a second chance. His need for her outweighed anything else. Cornelius wasn't sure he could survive without Sarah at this point.

"Corey..."

"Please, baby."

"Fuck it," Sarah whispered.

Then they were kissing. His Sarah was in his arms with her mouth on his and his heart was soaring. He couldn't get enough of her. After the weekend and their kisses this afternoon, and now Sarah's surrender to their connection? Adrenaline and excitement and lust and adoration burned like lava through his veins. He gripped her hips and yanked her soft, plush body against his. Sarah wrapped her arms around his neck, gave a little jump and wrapped her legs around his waist.

With a gasp, she pulled her face back. "Take me home. Your house. Now."

"Anything you wish, Sarie." He tasted her lips once more. "Hold tight to me." Without putting her down, Cornelius carried her down the sidewalk to his house, trading kisses the whole way. Once inside, he continued straight to his bedroom and kicked open the door. Falling toward the bed, he twisted so she landed on top of him. He didn't want to crush his girl with his heavy weight.

Sarah sat up and lifted her shirt up and over her head.

He groaned as he took in her full breasts encased in a pink lace bra. "So gorgeous." He traced his fingers up the dip of her waist, over her ribs, and caressed under the curve of her perfect chest. She sucked in a breath as he teased her nipples to tight peaks through the fabric.

Sarah rocked her hips over his erection and moaned. Sitting up, he kissed along her neck while he reached around to unclasp her bra. It fell away and he leaned back to look at her. She'd filled out over the years and her body was perfection, luscious, mind-breaking. He drank in her luminous skin and rounded breasts with peaked nipples begging for his touch, his kiss. On a strangled groan, he bent and lavished his attention on them until Sarah was writhing in his arms.

"Please, Corey." She tugged at his shirt.

He reached back and yanked the fabric over his head and tossed it to the ground.

She ran her hands over his shoulders and rounded her eyes. "Holy hell. Muscles *and* tattoos? Good God, you've gotten even more buff since college and that's saying something."

He couldn't stop his smirk. He wasn't bulky with muscles the way some of the other loggers were, but he was no slouch. His work and workout regime kept solid definition over his whole body, including washboard abs. The tattoos were also new, something he'd gotten into over the years. After the first one, he just kept adding. His back, shoulders and chest were sprinkled with art. Forest scenes, tribal art, even a few animals decorated his skin. Sarah dragged her fingertips over a forest-scape crossing his shoulder, to a wolf with its head thrown back in a howl on his right pec, down to a tribal knot on left ribs and up to his very first tattoo. The one that didn't quite match the others...the one covering his heart. Her movements froze.

"Corey?" She lifted her face to his, green eyes glowing in the soft light.

"You have to kiss a lot of frogs, right, princess?"

Sarah looked down, but not before he caught the tears glittering in her gaze. She bent and pressed her lips to the stylized outline of a frog sitting facing forward, the front arms curved to make a heart and the hind legs tucked in another behind those. At the top of the simple head outline was a tiara. His frog princess.

"I can't believe you have this." Her voice was hushed and she rested her palm over the design.

The inspiration came from their first kiss. She wanted to catch frogs to find her prince. He'd snatched up a large toad and held it up to her. Sarah kissed him instead, claiming him as her prince. In response, he'd appropriated her as his princess. During the darkest days of his loneliness, on the first anniversary of their break-up, Cornelius had gotten the tattoo, etching his pain and his love for her forever on his body.

"You were always my princess. No matter who else came along, no one could ever come close to you." Tears dripped down her cheeks and he brushed them away. "Don't cry, Sarie. It breaks my heart and I only ever want to see you happy." Cornelius captured her lips again, sliding his tongue into her mouth and tasting her. His princess wrapped her arms around him, pressing herself to him, skin to skin. Their kiss burned into a wildfire, sweeping them both into the tides of passion. The rest of their clothing was shed and when he joined his body with Sarah's, he couldn't help his own tears. He was home at last.

Chapter Fifteen

Sarah woke in the warm cocoon of Corey's arms. She blinked a few times and snuggled deeper into the big spoon of his body. The plush sheet and soft mattress cradled around them, giving a sense of another world surrounding them. The scents of the two of them mingled in the air. A contented sigh left her lungs as she relived last night in her mind. Their chemistry together was incendiary. It had always been that way, but now that they were adults with more life experience, the results were mind-altering, body-consuming, earth-shaking pleasure that scorched through both of them. She turned over in his embrace and cuddled into his chest. Inhaling, she savored the woodsy, earthy scent that was Corey. Everything about him appealed to all her senses. His smell, the way he touched her, his deep voice, the taste of his lips and skin and pleasure...not to mention he was hot as hell.

As she focused her vision on his chest, a low hum vibrated in her throat. The tattoos he had now were super sexy. She'd spent time last night worshiping them with her hands and mouth...among other areas of his body. Even now when her body was tender and sore from being well-loved last night she still wanted more. Wanted *him*.

Corey made a soft grunting noise and rolled onto his back. Sarah took advantage and claimed her place in the nook of his shoulder. She drifted her fingertips along the contours of his muscles and a satisfied smile overtook her expression. The ink over his heart caught her attention and a pang went through her. He'd tattooed her on his heart...after their break-up. She swallowed the lump of fear in her throat. What would he think if he found out her reason for ending things years ago? Would he forgive her? Could he?

"I can hear you overthinking. Stop it." He nuzzled the top of her head. "Whatever you're thinking about, let it go. It isn't important."

"What if it is? What if it changes this...thing between us?"

Eyes open, he shifted to peer down at her. Corey brushed her hair away from her cheek. "This *thing* between us? You mean a relationship? A real one? Being boyfriend and girlfriend again?"

Through the gap in his arm and the bed, she reached out and grabbed his glasses, settling them on his face.

With a small smile, he pressed his lips to hers. "Thanks, baby. Now quit avoiding the conversation."

With fake irritation, she narrowed her eyes at him. "Fine. Yes, us together. As a couple. Satisfied?"

His grin grew wider. "For now. Sort of." Corey chuckled and nudged one heavily muscled thigh through hers to press his hard erection against her hip.

Her insides turned liquid. God, she desired him like she'd never wanted anyone else. Everything he did turned her on. Giving into her body's demands, Sarah adjusted so that Corey was over her and nestled in the cradle of her hips. Arching up, she let him feel her wetness.

"Fuck," he moaned and dropped his forehead to hers, then kissed her so her toes curled.

She hitched a leg on his waist, opening herself to him, but he tore his mouth from hers.

"Not yet." His voice was gruff and dark.

Sarah whined as she shivered at the feel of him. "Corey…"

"In a minute, princess. We have more to this conversation. No distracting me." He rocked over her, their bodies rubbing together in delicious ways.

"You started it." She pouted, but lost her breath as he ground into her.

"Whatever you were thinking about, it doesn't matter." He nibbled and kissed and licked from her cheek down her neck. "You and me, right here and right now, is what's important. Being together again. Starting fresh."

"But—"

Corey kissed her again. "No buts. Just us. Yes?"

Worry edged at her consciousness, but he made it so hard to concentrate when he teased her into a frenzy like this. Her whole body was one pulsing mess of need. Lust was a drug in her veins and she wanted to drown in it.

"Sarie?" Corey bit the spot where her neck and shoulder met, sucking at the tender skin. At the same time, he notched his cock at her entrance.

"Yes," she keened and lifted her hips to welcome him inside. "Just us."

Then there was no more conversation, just whispered words designed to drive each other to heightened ecstasy.

* * * *

When she resurfaced again, Sarah took stock of his bedroom for the first time. He'd moved into the primary suite and his king-sized bed gave plenty of space for the two of them and their eagerness for one another. The walls were a pale, soothing mint that complemented his light wood furniture and dark green bedding. Light glinted off a small aquarium on a low table by the large window overlooking his backyard and the forest behind them. Sarah squinted at the tank. "Is that a fish tank?" She didn't see any movement of swimming.

Corey sat up with bright eyes and threw back the covers. "That's Lollihop and Jellygreen. I forgot you haven't met them."

"Lolli*hop* and Jelly*green*?" She blinked at him as he crossed to the side table. She snagged her lip between her teeth. Damn, he had a great butt. And given his comfort with walking around naked, he knew how good he looked, too.

"Come here." He held out a hand, beckoning her closer. With minimal self-consciousness, she slipped from the sheets and joined him.

Corey pointed to two small frogs about three inches in length. One was an olive green with small black spots and the other was a browner color with similar black spots. They had webbed feet and the brown one,

Lollihop, swam around while the green frog, Jellygreen, splayed out toward the top of the shallow water. There was gravel along the bottom with a few fake plants and several large uneven-shaped rocks with nooks in them. The tank was small, but longer than it was tall.

"You have frogs?" She stared back and forth from him to the amphibians.

His smile was luminous. "Yep. These are my girls, Lolli and Jelly. Jelly's doing the zen pose. They like to splay out like this when resting. They're African Dwarf frogs and I got them about five years ago. If I'm lucky and take excellent care of them, they should live another five more." He shifted the perforated lid and dipped one finger in. Both creatures swirled around him then darted off again. "They aren't frogs you can touch and hold much, but they keep me company."

Sarah reached over and squeezed his free hand. "This is amazing. How do you know they're girls?"

"The males are a little smaller and have glands behind their front legs, plus tiny nubby tails. And they make this buzzing noise to attract females."

"Typical men. Gotta show off for the ladies." She snorted, then gentled her expression. "This is so cool, Corey."

"Thanks." He wrapped an arm around her and dropped a kiss to the top of her head. "There's a teenager down the road who takes care of them when I go visit my parents. He's into reptiles."

She glanced up at him. "Can you teach me, too?"

"I'd like that, Sarie."

* * * *

Much later, once Sarah and Corey had been satisfied in bed and at breakfast, Sarah slipped home in the hopes that her arrival would go undetected. Tiptoeing inside and closing the door as quietly as she could, Sarah turned to sneak off to her room and catch up on her local marketing jobs.

"Hey there, big sis."

Sarah jumped at Bridget's voice. *Damn!* So much for not getting caught.

Pasting on a smile, Sarah found Bridget curled on the couch, petting Candle in her lap. "Hi, Bridge. What are you doing here? I thought you'd be at the shop."

Bridget flashed the most devious smile Sarah had ever seen on her little sister. Yeah, her sibling was enjoying tormenting her. Turnabout was fair play, Sarah guessed. Given how much teasing Sarah had done about Jack, this was karma coming back to kick her in the ass.

"Gran and Arianna are opening Three Sisters this morning. Did you have a good night?"

"Mmhmm."

Bridget arched one dark brow. "You abandoned me and my wedding flowers. You're my maid of honor. You better have more to say than 'mmhmm.'"

With a roll of her eyes, Sarah crossed her arms. "Yes. My night was fantastic. As was my morning."

"With Cornelius?"

Heat simmered along her nerves at the mere mention of his name. "Yes, with Corey."

Becca popped her head around the corner from the kitchen. "Halle-freaking-lujah!"

Sarah screeched in surprise.

"About time you two pulled your heads out of your asses and got back together. Are we making this wedding a double?" Her cousin waggled her brows at the two sisters.

"Hey," both Sarah and Bridget protested.

"I'm not sharing my wedding."

"We've been a couple again for less than twenty-four hours."

Becca laughed. "You two are way too easy to rile up." She focused those blue eyes on Sarah. "Spill the tea. What happened last night?"

Sarah flopped down on the couch, giving into their demands. "All right, twist my arm." She grinned and allowed the happiness bubbling inside her to be seen. "It started at the bachelorette weekend."

"I knew it," Bridget exclaimed. "You were acting all weird and jumpy."

Becca waved a hand as she sat on the floor across from them. "Old news. You told Gran and me that last night. Get to the good parts."

Her little sister pouted at being left out of the loop.

"We did some stuff that weekend and then made out again when he cornered me outside the dress shop yesterday," Sarah said to placate Bridget. "Then last night when he came over we talked and one thing led to another and we ended up back at his house."

"All. Night. Long." Becca cackled with glee. "Is he still as good in bed as he was when we were young 'uns?"

Sarah fanned a hand at her face. "Even better. Jesus, the man is a god in bed. I lost count of how many times he made me come."

"Hell yeah! Nothing like a night of great sex." Becca fistbumped her.

"But does this mean you two are back together? For real?"

Leave it to her cousin to focus on the physical aspects and her sibling on the feelings side. "Yes, we're in a relationship again." Sarah's voice was softer now. Inside, she was still a mess of emotions and trying to keep the negative ones at bay. Worry and anxiety gnawed at her, but her happiness and love for Corey were winning the battle...not that she was ready to proclaim her love to him. That wouldn't happen anytime soon. She was struggling with her past, but Corey was a weakness she never could get over. To be honest, Sarah didn't want to. If soulmates were real, he was hers without a doubt.

Bridget leaned forward with wide, eager eyes. "What now? Are you staying in Fallbank?"

"I don't know." Sarah shrugged. "We haven't gotten that far. This is new."

"No, it isn't," Becca interjected. "You two have a major history. You know what it's like to be with one another."

"Old-new, then. Or new-old. Whichever." She shook her head. "It's been over ten years since we broke up. We have to learn about one another again. Figure out if this — we — still work. I can't make huge life decisions because I got back with my ex-boyfriend."

"You got back with Cornelius?" Jack asked as he strolled out of the hallway.

"Jesus! Where did he come from?" Sarah glared at her sister. "Is there anyone else listening in I should know about?"

Bridget laughed. "It *is* Saturday. Jack isn't working, so he's here at home." She lifted her face for him to kiss her. Then she looked back at Sarah with a cocky grin. "Not my fault you can't remember what day it is and that Jack lives here. Must be your muddled sex brain."

Sarah rolled her eyes as Jack perked up. "You and Cornelius did the deed last night? I mean, I assumed so after my honeybee came to bed in a huff over your abandonment, but you never know."

Sarah buried her face in her hands as heat radiated from her cheeks. She did not need her almost brother-in-law having intimate details about her sex life. "Yes, if you must know," she mumbled.

Jack's smile was devilish. "I think I'll swing by my partner's house. Business to discuss."

Becca snorted. "Yeah, right. The business of him and Sarah getting it on."

He pretend-tipped an imaginary hat at them as he said goodbye, then headed out the door.

Sarah turned back to the girls. "Did you know Corey has two pet frogs?"

* * * *

"So, you and Sarah, huh?"

Jack's jovial voice boomed in the garage where Cornelius whittled away at his piece of woodworking. His mood was buoyant. He had his sweet Sarah back and his soul felt lighter than it had in years. He'd expected his friend to swing by when the news spread. Cornelius chuckled. "Hello to you, too."

Jack took up a perch on a bench and threw him an exasperated look. "Hi. Now—you and Sarah. Tell me what's up."

Cornelius focused on the repetitive motions of snicking the knife along the broadside of the block of wood he held. A wide grin spread across his face. "We're back together."

"And?"

"And what?" Cornelius side-eyed his friend. What else did he think needed explaining?

"Don't play dumb. I want to know what happened. What does it mean? Start talking."

Cornelius refused to look up. Inspiration had hit and he wanted to strike while the iron was hot, so to speak, on this project he'd been tinkering with over the past two months. "We've had a couple of interludes over the last week or so and as of yesterday we are back in a relationship." It felt outstanding to say that about him and Sarah. A giddy wave of excitement rushed over his skin. It was like he was twelve years old after his first kiss with Sarah all over again. This time he wouldn't mess it up. Not that he knew how he'd mucked it all up last time, but he knew it must've been him. He had to make sure he kept Sarah happy.

Jack clapped a hand on one of Cornelius' shoulders. "I'm ecstatic for you, man. About time the two of you stopped dancing around one another and started dancing with one another."

Cornelius beamed at his best friend. "Thanks. I'm still a little stunned, I think. I mean, last night and this morning were...mind-blowing. I can't say I don't have a few concerns. Worries. Whatever you want to call them. But I'm going into this with the goal of taking this one day at a time and not putting pressure on Sarah."

"How do you mean?"

"Well, we haven't talked about Sarah's plans for the future. She could get a job back in Seattle. She could stay here. Nothing clear yet. That's the kind of thing that drove me crazy last time around and I let Sarah feel my anxiety. It's what drove her away." He paused and considered for a moment. "I think."

"You don't know why she broke up with you before?" Jack's voice went up an octave. "You've never had the conversation about her reasons?"

Why was his best friend raining all over his parade? Couldn't he enjoy being back with the love of his life without analyzing and overthinking the whole thing? An echoing *ding* reverberated through the garage. *Yes, saved by the phone.*

He fished the device out of his pocket and saw a text from Hop. Sliding it open, he read the message.

Hop: Just got the word. Army leave secured. I'll be there for Bridget's wedding.

Cornelius: Awesome! How long will you be back in town? Hope we can grab some time to catch up in person.

Clicking the app shut, Cornelius lifted one corner of his mouth up. "Looks like Hop will make it back for the wedding."

"Hop?" Jack furrowed his brow.

"Oh yeah. I forget you've never met him. Seems like you've been around town for way longer than reality. Hop is Becca's older brother. Bridget and Sarah's cousin. He's in the Army and has been gone for a while. Good guy. Stoic, but dependable."

"Cool. Glad I'll get to meet him. Now stop stalling. You and Sarah still haven't talked out your shit?"

"I don't want to spook her. We'll talk about it when she's ready." Cornelius gave up on the woodworking project and stood with his arms crossed and facing Jack. "It's fine." His mood was destroyed and his creative motivation dried up.

Jack eyed Cornelius and cocked one brow. "Yeah, sure seems like it." He heaved a heavy sigh. "Look, all I'm saying is that honesty is the best policy. Take it from me, keeping secrets — or whatever you want to call this — between two people is never a good thing. It almost destroyed my chance with Bridget."

"Well, I'm not Bridget and I don't care. Whatever Sarah's reasons, I'm sure they were valid. I'm not going to force her to confess everything when she's skittish enough already. And whenever she does — because one day she will — I'll be okay with whatever she tells me. What matters to me is her and being with her. That's all." Cornelius glared at his partner and hoped Jack got the message to drop it.

"Strong words from someone who has no idea what happened. Has she ever given any indication?"

Cornelius ran a hand through his hair and tugged at the ends. If he had a dime for every time someone in this nosy town snooped for gossip on him and Sarah... But no, that wasn't what Jack was doing. He wasn't looking for scandalous details to spread around. His friend was coming from a place of love and loyalty, protecting him.

Cornelius shook his head. "No. She feels guilty, but hasn't ever given me an explanation. And I don't care. I'm taking this day by day because I know that's what Sarah needs. The point is that we're back together and that's what I want. All I've wanted for years now. I'm going to enjoy it and I'll be damned if I let something come between us now. I lived for over a decade without her. I've learned the meaning of gratitude and I'm so damn grateful to have Sarah back in my life again."

Jack pressed his lips into a thin line, but nodded. "Then I'm happy for you. I wish you both nothing but joy."

For some odd reason though, Cornelius didn't feel the same thrilling euphoria he'd had buzzing through him before Jack had come over. No matter. He'd meant the words he'd told Jack. Whatever the reason, he wouldn't let the past get in the way of his and Sarah's future. Picking up his project again, he focused on bringing the art out of the wood and taking his brain off the lingering doubts the conversation dredged up.

Chapter Sixteen

The sun shone bright on Sarah's drive over to Three Sisters Apothecary. Little pops of yellow, purple and red dotted the sides of the road as the first wildflowers of spring bloomed with the dark green of the thick fir trees behind them. With the wedding less than a month away, the signs of renewal were welcome. She'd doubted the weather and the vision Bridget had for the wedding, but her little sister was proving to be correct in her predictions.

After parking, Sarah walked over to the store with a smile playing on her lips. She'd spent the night with Corey again and she was counting the minutes until the day was done and they would meet up. He wanted to take her out to dinner tonight. "*A real date*," he'd called it. The thought of being in public together made her pulse race with anxiety and satisfaction. She knew the town would gossip over the two of them, yet she wanted to stake her claim, let the other women of Fallbank know Corey was off the market.

Humming as she crossed through the front door, Sarah waved to Gran. "Good morning." She made her way over to the heavy wooden counter that held the old-fashioned cash register and set up her laptop on the open space next to it.

Gran kissed Sarah's cheek as she walked by while dusting shelves. "Hello to my favorite oldest granddaughter. How are things?"

With a smile and shake of her head, Sarah answered, "Fine and dandy. It's a gorgeous day outside." She opened her email and took a sip from her travel coffee mug. Warm and welcome caffeine danced through her mouth and into her bloodstream. She locked onto an unread message and the liquid goodness soured in her stomach. On a soft inhale, Sarah clicked to find an offer as a finalist for a job interview at a medium-sized firm in Seattle, the one she'd had the phone consultation with a few weeks back. Before this past weekend, she'd have been ecstatic to receive this. Now, she didn't know how to feel.

"What's wrong? You've turned pale." Gran furrowed her brow and propped a hand on one hip. "Bad news?"

"I-don't-know-what-to-think news." Sarah raised her gaze up to Gran's. "It's an in-person interview request."

"That's great!"

"From a firm in Seattle."

Gran nodded with a neutral facial expression. "I see. Does this indecision have to do with you and a certain male in this town admitting their romantic feelings to one another?"

"Maybe." Sarah chewed on her lower lip as she processed her feelings. On one hand, she needed a job.

Steady income was a must. This opportunity was what she'd been after. The position was as a junior partner with her own team to lead, a chance to grow a business to a new level. On the other hand, the company was based in Seattle and while some remote work could be possible, it wouldn't be enough for her to live in Fallbank instead of Seattle. Corey couldn't up and move to Seattle, he was now co-owner of Timber Logging Company. The thought of leaving Corey after connecting with him again so recently had her recoiling in her seat. "It's so new. New-old or whatever. We're testing the waters to find out if what we had before is still between us now. I can't move back to Washington. It would ruin everything." Her heartbeat sped to a gallop the more she contemplated this.

Gran hummed, but said nothing.

Tilting her head back, Sarah heaved a sigh. "But I can't say no. I *need* a job. This is an amazing chance. How do I discount the potential answer to this?"

"Who says you can't go on an interview? Explore your options, then come back and talk about it with Cornelius. You might be surprised at what he says. Don't decide for him how he'll respond." Gran wrapped an arm around Sarah's shoulders and squeezed. "And don't cut yourself off from looking at possibilities. It's a conversation. The job might not get offered to you. If it doesn't, you've lost nothing. If it does, you have choices. You can say yes or no. That isn't a bad thing."

Sarah nodded. "You're right, Gran. Saying yes to a meeting doesn't obligate me to them. I'll think of it as an investigation. Fact-finding to make an informed decision."

As she replied back to say yes, Sarah felt better. Kind of. The enthusiasm she expected to have at the prospect of the job didn't materialize. Uncertainty still nagged at her. Did she tell Corey about this or wait to see what happened? There wasn't much reason to worry him if she didn't get the job offer, right? She could tell him she was meeting up with friends in the city. Sarah *would* do that, so it wasn't lying.

The bell above the door trilled as Corey sauntered in. Mmm, but she wished she could record him walking toward her and play it in slow motion whenever she needed a hit of serotonin. He looked good enough to eat. Smiling as if he could read her thoughts, he circled around the counter and kissed her long enough to have her pressing in for more. Cornelius leaned back with a satisfied waggle of his brows and a wink.

A beam of heat shot through her to land low in her stomach. "Hey, Corey. What brings you by?"

"I wanted to see you." He shrugged.

Sarah laughed. "You saw me this morning." With a glance at her watch, she said, "It was less than two hours ago. Don't you have work?"

"Yeah, I do. But there's a big storm coming in at the worksite, so we can't be out there today. I'm playing hooky. I figured if Jack can come up with whatever excuses he has for seeing Bridget during the day instead of being at the office, I could do the same." He pushed up the sleeves of his plaid shirt and rested his elbows on the polished wood.

Sarah eyed his well-defined forearms. Her mouth watered when she thought of those muscles flexing as he held her hips while driving into her. Shivers exploded across her skin.

A moaning sound dragged her back to the present, and she realized the sound came from her. Glancing away as she coughed to clear her throat, Sarah smiled. She didn't trust herself to speak yet.

He shifted over to dip his head close to her ear. "Judging by the lust in your eyes, you aren't mad to see me." After a quick nip of her earlobe, he pulled away.

She batted a palm at his shoulder. "Quit it," she grumbled. "Gran is right there."

"I think she's caught on to our adult activities," Cornelius stage-whispered.

"That I have," Gran chirped. "And my hearing is no worse for wear, despite my age."

Pressing her hands to her heated cheeks, Sarah shook her head. "Okay, okay. You're distracting me from the store. What's up?"

"I'm going to go visit my mom — and dad, for an extended weekend. Leave on Friday and come back Monday. I wondered if you wanted to join me?"

He looked so shy, yet eager and it broke her heart to say no. But she'd need to prep and travel to Seattle for her interview scheduled for Monday. "I would love to under normal circumstances, but..." Sarah cast around for an excuse. "With the wedding a few weeks away, leaving Bridget for a mini holiday may not be the best idea." She squeezed his hand. "I wish I could go. I'd love to see Clarissa and Boyd."

Cornelius nodded. "Checking on my mom is the main reason I'm going. Hope that's okay for me to duck out so close to the wedding...and other stuff."

She chuckled. "Other stuff. You're adorable. I get it. No biggie. I think I might see if I can meet up with a friend in Seattle while running a wedding errand for Bridge. She ordered a present for Jack and it's ready to be picked up." All of this was true. Sarah just left out the part about a job meeting taking place at the same time. Guilt pressed on her chest, but she was used to that sensation. After years of carrying her secret, Sarah was well acquainted with the plague of discomfort and warring with herself to tell the truth. And she would tell Cornelius, if an offer was given and decisions had to be made.

Repressing a sigh, Sarah bit her lip. "How is your mom doing? She's done with treatment?"

"This week is her last one. We're celebrating when I get there. Mom's in good spirits and the chemo hasn't been as brutal as she'd expected. It's the little things that keep her going."

"That's great news! Give her my best, will you?"

"Of course." Cornelius laced his fingers through hers. "Pick you up at seven for our date?"

With a grin and one firm nod, Sarah said, "Perfect. I can't wait."

Cornelius tasted her lips once more. "Same, princess. Same."

* * * *

Cornelius spent the entire week walking on clouds. His dinner date with Sarah had gone off without a hitch. They'd fallen back into their easy conversation and camaraderie. Every night they'd ended up at his place. Most of the nights, they'd torn at one another's clothes and fallen into bed together. Yet there'd been one night when he'd been too exhausted from work at a logging site for bedroom shenanigans. Instead, they'd curled up in comfy sweats with a bowl of fresh popcorn and streamed a movie while cuddling on the couch. It might not have ended up as physical as usual, but emotionally the night was spot-on for what he needed. A relaxing night with his girlfriend cuddled up next to him was perfect.

Sarah was also bonding with his pets. She had learned how to feed the frogs and helped change out the water once, too. He loved how often she would sit by the window and watch the girls swim around or burrow in their tank. He hadn't expected her to find them so fascinating, but was happy she did.

Now he was on a plane to visit his parents and stuff in as many mom hugs as he could into the next three and a half days. A quick cab ride later, Cornelius knocked on his parents' door to be greeted by his mother. She looked frail—too thin, too pale, no hair anywhere he could see—yet her smile was strong and her greeting cheerful. That alone eased a fraction of the worry lodged like a thick rope knot in his sternum.

"Hey, Mama." He dipped lower and folded his mother into a gentle hug.

She returned the gesture, then took his face between her palms. "My boy. I missed you."

"Same here." After depositing his bags in the guest room, he joined his parents in the living room.

"How's life treating you?" his dad asked.

"Can't complain and even if I could, I wouldn't. None of my stress compares to yours."

A soft snort left his mother. "As if we'd equate them. Everyone's worries are different, but no less valid." She eyed him the way every mother seemed to do, assessing their young for signs of truthfulness. "You do look lighter than the last time we video chatted. Dare I ask if this has anything to do with a girl?"

"It might," he teased. His parents didn't know the relationship development in his life yet. He had wanted to tell them in person and see his mother's reaction.

"One who lives back in Fallbank, now? Quite close to your own house?"

Heat stung the tips of his ears, but Cornelius smiled. "Yes, that's the one." He flicked his gaze up to meet hers. "Sarah and I are back together."

Clarissa clasped her hands together with a gasp of delight. Her smile lit up her face. "Oh, honey, I'm so happy for you two. This is the best news! You should have brought her with you to visit."

"I tried, but with the wedding coming up so soon, she needed to stay and help with things there." He wanted to promise next time she'd tag along, but also didn't want to get hopes up. Jack's concerns nagged at him despite the feeling of completion with Sarah. He was already in love with her again—not that he had ever stopped—but didn't want to jump too fast. He wouldn't risk scaring her off. The uncertainty of future plans hung over them like a dark cloud.

"Tell us everything. When did this happen? How did it happen?" His mother's elation pulled Cornelius back to the here and now. With a smile, he opened his mouth and filled his parents in.

Later in the evening, after his mom had retired to bed before the sun had even set, Cornelius and his father sat drinking beer on the back porch overlooking the water lapping soft and slow at the land while the sun melted into the water. Twilight was a touch chillier here than in Fallbank. The closeness of the ocean carried cooler temperatures with it. With a clear view of the horizon, the colors of the painted sky offered a view he didn't often get being inland from the Oregon coast. Yet the tall redwoods and firs growing around the rocks that lined the edge of the northern California coastline reminded him of home. "Why Eureka, Pops? I know you're from California, but southern Cal. So how'd you end up here?"

Boyd swigged his bottle. "Yep, raised as a SoCal surfer boy. Then I went to college in Oregon, met your mother and we settled in Fallbank because that's where she was from. It made her happy and that made me happy. When retirement came along, she offered to move back to my home state. But when we looked around all the sun and sand and surf, it didn't fit anymore. I love the ocean and being near it was important, but not the sunny palm tree beaches. Landing in Eureka was a way to take one more life adventure, get the salt water I craved and have the feel of home in Fallbank. Compromise."

Cornelius turned his dad's words over in his mind. He had to admit, when his parents had announced they were moving, and to California of all places, he'd thought they were crazy. Given time, he'd accepted his dad's desire to go back to his home state. Yet he couldn't figure out why choose a place similar enough to Oregon to make it seem silly that they had moved at all. Not that Cornelius had voiced his thoughts to them at the time. He'd been grateful for the house and having a bit of space to grow into his own. But it had been damn solitary.

"My turn," Boyd said. "Why Sarah? I know how enthusiastic your mother is, but going back to someone after you break up is not always the best idea." His father put a warm hand on Cornelius' shoulder and squeezed. "Not that I don't like her or don't want you to be happy. I just hope you aren't falling back on comfortable to appease your old mom and pops."

His father's concerns should have worried him, but Cornelius was too happy to be bothered. He kicked up one corner of his mouth. "Comfortable is not how I'd describe my relationship with Sarah. If I had to pick one word, I'd go with…fire. She and I burn when we're together. Yeah, we cuddle and are at ease with one another, but there's always an ember glowing and ready to incinerate us."

"That's good." His dad's voice was quiet, thoughtful. "I knew when I saw you two together as kids that she'd woven herself into the fabric of your soul." Boyd sucked in a breath. "When she ended things, the devastation I saw in you scared the hell out of me. I love that girl like my own, but I don't ever want to see the destruction she left in her wake inside you again. That was terrible." His dad sipped his beer and stared out at the ocean. "I know I told you we wanted to see you settled, but with the right person. I hope you know we don't ever want to see you fall on old habits because you can slip back into a relationship to make us satisfied."

Cornelius laughed as he pictured Sarah. His sword-wielding, take-no-prisoners, fierce and fighting princess. "That's not what this is. Being with Sarah again is like breathing fresh spring air and like drowning in a lake at the same time. We fit. That's not new and we both know it. That doesn't mean it's easy. She's holding back for some reason. Maybe because she doesn't know what next steps to make in her professional life and that impacts her personal life, and that makes me nervous. Whatever she decides, though, I'm supporting her. We'll figure whatever that looks like out. Once we both settle into our trust with one another given time, then we won't be sinking anymore. We'll float."

Chapter Seventeen

A car laid on its horn while following too close to the truck in front of it. Sarah cringed as the noise of Seattle assaulted her ears while she walked the three blocks to the marketing firm considering her for hire. When had she turned soft about city life? Rolling her shoulders back, Sarah shook off her annoyance and focused on the opportunity in front of her. This new firm had doubled their clients over the past two years and was making a name for itself with larger companies. She admired that they'd landed two athleisure companies run by and geared toward females. They had a diverse panel of chief officers and hoped their company culture reflected that, too.

As she strode into the lobby of the high rise, Sarah double-checked the floor the firm operated from on the display by the elevators. On the way up, she focused on taking cleansing breaths and settling her mind on the task at hand — sell herself as a kick-ass marketing designer and assess the company's fit for her as an employee.

The next few hours were spent with Sarah playing round robin with a panel of people interviewing her. The layout of the floor was open concept with a row of windowed offices along two walls and the space between wide open with community tables for groups, individual desks for standing or sitting and three conference rooms dotted throughout, also with glass walls all around. Inside one of these was where she was situated and her interview line-up came and went as scheduled.

It felt as if she were in a fishbowl given how others gawked as they passed by. The overall vibe was intended to produce a no-secrets, "we're all in this together" feel, yet Sarah couldn't shake the sensation of being on display instead. If she had to come in here each day, how would that be? Would the atmosphere build a family-like team vibe or would it foster competitiveness and cutthroat tactics to one-up each other?

The conversations flew by in a blur, given she met seven people in a three-hour time span. At the end, she was given a tour by Selena Juarez, a full partner and Creative Director for the agency. She was kind and congenial, answering questions while introducing Sarah to different team members. This would be her new boss, if Sarah took the job...if the position was offered to her.

As they rounded back to the elevators, the tall, lovely female offered a red-lipped smile to Sarah. "It was an absolute pleasure meeting you, Sarah. You gave impressive answers today and the quick feedback I was given from others has all been positive. Any additional questions I can answer for you?"

"Thank you, Selena. I've enjoyed meeting everyone here and learning more about the agency and role. My lingering questions are, what are next steps and when do you anticipate making a decision?" Sarah's stomach knotted as she thought about accepting the job, but shoved that aside. Right now, Sarah needed options and that all this was — potential. No reason to get ahead of herself and self-select out of the running or take that as a sign of excitement to say yes.

"We have one other person coming next week for interviews. Then last thing we'll do is confer to choose a candidate. You should hear from us within two-to-three weeks." She chuckled and winked. "You how HR can sometimes move slower than we'd like. I have confidence you'll hear good things from us soon, though."

Sarah shook Selena's hand, thanked her once more and headed back down to the lobby. All in all, this had gone well. The people Sarah would lead seemed competent and motivated to produce quality work. The leadership team she'd met appeared open to feedback and ideas. The culture resonated with her own values.

Why then did she walk out of the building with a sense of anticlimax? This should be her dream job, yet the eagerness she expected wasn't there. Sighing, Sarah ordered a ride share to meet Tyneisha for lunch before swinging by a shoe store to get the custom-made embellished slippers designed for Bridget to wear with her dress.

Tyneisha greeted her with a tight hug and big grin. "Sarah, I miss you! You have got to get back to the city."

They sat at an outdoor table at one of their favorite cafes in the business district. A rare day of spring sunshine meant Seattleites were out en masse. Budding trees lined the streets and flowers bloomed in pots outside stores and sky rises. Sipping a glass of wine, Sarah basked in the warm sunshine. A few hours' adjustment and she was feeling more at home again. She peeked at her friend. "I miss you, too. How's your new job going?"

Ty had landed a new gig two weeks ago, hence her exuberant celebrating at the bachelorette party. "Fabulous. I wish they had need of your skills, but I'll keep looking for a way to get you on board. We're work wives and I'm not looking to divorce."

Sarah laughed and nodded. "Can't argue with that."

"How was the interview?"

Sarah bobbed her head from side to side. "Good."

"Just good?"

"I mean, I thought I'd walk out more hyped than I am. Everyone comes off as nice. The work culture shows as a fit for me. But...I don't know? I can't say why." It baffled her.

Tyneisha arched one dark brow. "Does this have to do with your new boy?"

Scrunching her nose, Sarah giggled. "First off, he's a man. Second, he's new-old. We dated back in high school and part of college."

Her friend's eyes rounded as Ty said, "Oh, he's *the ex.* I didn't realize that from your texts."

"I don't know if I'd call him that—"

"Let's not play. You might have dated here and there, but nothing serious and you waxed on about this ex of yours like he was the chosen one who died."

"I did not," Sarah protested. "There was Hank and he was very sweet."

"You said he was shit in bed and broke up with him after six weeks because he couldn't find your clit no matter how many times you showed him."

"Fair." She paused and meandered back over her past dating life in her mind. "Gabriela and I could have gone the distance. She was outstanding in bed."

"And she was over-the-top paranoid about everything. Germs, safety, travel, walking down the sidewalk. You said she gave so many warnings, yet didn't come with her own red flag."

True. Gabriella had gotten suffocating with all of her ways to "stay safe" and finding danger lurking everywhere. "But she meant well."

"Still broke up with her. Then got drunk and whined about how hard it was to find someone to meet or beat the level of your ex." Ty crossed her arms and smirked. "I rest my case."

"Okay, fine. You have a point. Corey is the standard I held everyone else to and no one could reach it. The good news is I don't have to worry about that anymore because we're back together." Her grin was wide, but a small part of her trembled in fear. Things were so good right now. Was it the honeymoon phase? What would he think about her job situation? What if he-

Nope, not going there.

She refused to contemplate how he would react if he ever found out why she'd broken up with him in the first place.

Tyneisha reached across the table and squeezed her hand. "Look, I see how you light up when you talk about him. And God knows I saw the sparks between you that night at the club. But what happens in the future? When you get a job offer you want here, in Seattle?"

Did she have to go back to Seattle? The idea of not moving back was starting to have some merit. She already had five clients back in Fallbank. Freelance work was keeping her checking account happy. Living back home was keeping her and her family happy. Corey was keeping her lady parts and her heart happy. Why was she still pursuing options outside? Sarah chewed her lower lip. "What if I went out on my own?"

Ty blinked at her, then gulped her wine. "You mean start your own agency?"

"More like, boutique-style marketing. Freelance-ish, but have an office and whatnot without trying to become a giant conglomerate." Fallbank was affordable to rent a work space. There were plenty of small businesses in town and she could do remote campaigns, too. She winced. "I think my Gran is the one who suggested this a while ago and I dismissed the idea."

"Back before true love hooked its claws into you."

Sarah widened her eyes. Her friend sounded bitter. "Yikes. Methinks you doth protest too much. Or something like that. Ty, are *you* okay? I thought Becca said you two were good with a one-night thing?"

"Oh, for sure," Tyneisha answered with an emphatic nod. "I hold no ill will toward your cousin. She and I had a phenomenal time and I'm content to leave it at that. I sound jaded because love took my work wife away from me." Tears shimmered in her friend's deep brown eyes. "I miss my friend and I hate that you're three hours away. And you aren't coming back to Seattle. Admit it."

Now Sarah blinked at the stinging in her eyes. She felt the same way about Ty. Their friendship had started from their first day as interns together. It was hard to find another supportive and uplifting person in the corporate world. "I might not come back to Seattle. I haven't decided yet. This firm has a ton going for it and my entire adult life is here. I need to wait until I have an offer, whatever and whenever that might be. Then I can figure my shit out. If I don't move back here, though, you aren't getting rid of me. We're going to be friends forever."

"Promise?"

"I promise."

* * * *

Sweat ran down Cornelius' face as he yanked on the straps to secure the massive logs onto the back of the semi-truck. The day had been exhausting with him on tree-cutting duty then rounding things out with loading the haul. Despite the weariness in his bones, he hummed with anticipation. He and Sarah were going out again tonight. Wedding prep was in full force at the Wildes' house and they hadn't had much time together over the past week since his visit to his parents. Sarah was working hard at getting guest favors made and he was busy with his curio cabinet present for the happy couple. Today was Friday though, and he planned to take his girl out to spoil her tonight.

The vehicle rumbled off and his workers stood around awaiting orders. "Great job today. Finishing this commission means we're early with delivery for the customer. That'll have them coming back to us again. Appreciate the hustle and hard effort put in. Take the weekend to relax and meet me at the office on Monday at nine."

His team cheered at the late start next week, but given their dedication, it was worthwhile to reward their service to TLC in any way, big or small, that he could.

They dispersed and once back home, Cornelius showered, changed and walked over to pick up his date. Giddiness quaked in his stomach. He couldn't wait to see Sarah. Knocking, he waited.

Bridget opened the door and beamed. "Hey, Cornelius. Come on in."

Hugging her, he said, "Hi, little B. How's it going?"

She pushed her curls back from her face and huffed. "Planning a wedding and building a house are two things you shouldn't do at the same time. I don't know what I was thinking."

Jack walked up from behind and wrapped his arms around his fiancée. "You were thinking you love me and can't wait any longer than the bare minimum to get married and make babies with me."

Cornelius laughed, but choked it back when Bridget's face went dreamy.

"Mmm. That does sound perfect." She tilted her face up so Jack could kiss her. "Of course we could have eloped to make things easier."

Something twisted inside his chest as Cornelius watched the two of them. This was what he wanted with Sarah — the harmony, the planning, the future.

Babies. His mind pictured Sarah pregnant, then holding a child on her hip. He imagined cradling a newborn in his arms with a mix of their features. It shook him to the core. He hadn't allowed his brain to go this far since the first year of their break-up. It was too painful to contemplate. Now, however, the idea of a family with Sarah sent warmth from his ears to his toes. He wanted it so much a physical ache manifested in his ribs.

Sarah sauntered from the hallway, a smile playing on her lips. She caught sight of him and her eyes lit up. "Hey, handsome."

"Beautiful." He caught her mouth for a moment, delighting in the press of her lips and the heat of her breath.

"Aww, you two are so cute. Such couple goals." Bridget giggled.

"Wait a minute, what do they have that we don't?" Jack asked.

His girlfriend's sister turned to face her boyfriend. "Nothing," she stage whispered. "But I want to encourage them. It's obvious we're the better couple."

Sarah scoffed and side-eyed Bridget. "On that note, let's get out of here and leave the 'better couple' to themselves."

"Yes, please," Jack agreed and slid his tongue into Bridget's mouth.

Covering her eyes and muttering about things she didn't want to see, Sarah took Cornelius by the hand and led him out of the house. He helped her into his truck, eyeing the short blue dress she wore with appreciation before sliding in behind the wheel.

"Where are we going?" Sarah questioned as he drove toward town.

Lifting his lips into a crooked smile, he said, "It's a surprise." He'd thought about going to Portland or the steakhouse in town, but decided on another choice instead.

He parked in the takeaway spot outside the Thai restaurant. He knew she loved this kind of food and what her favorites were. Or at least what they had been before. Now that he considered, he should have asked instead of choosing for her. "Do you still like chicken panang curry?"

"My favorite. You remembered." Her gaze was soft and luminous.

"I try. I might not get everything correct, but it's not for lack of attempting. Sit tight and I'll be right back."

After retrieving their dinner, he set a course for a back road outside of town lines. Sarah watched with avid interest as he wound through the dark woods and up a rocky course along a small mountain. He watched with anticipation as her expression morphed when she figured out where they were going. He'd discovered this spot as a teen when he would go on job sites with his dad to start learning the logging business. Then he'd taken Sarah up there to share it with her. It was sacred to him.

They reached the summit and he backed into a spot at the edge of a ridge overlooking the valley below. In the moonlight, they could see the forest rising and falling with the topography and the lights of Fallbank nestled on the left corner. The daytime view was just as picturesque, but Cornelius craved the privacy the darkness would give them. Not that he expected anyone else to come by this secluded spot, but the stats were smaller at night.

Grabbing the food and hopping out, he came around and escorted Sarah to the back of his truck. Opening the tailgate, her low chuckle filled him with hope as she eyed the layers of blankets, pillows and oversized cushions he'd arranged. He placed the food midway up.

Glancing at her attire, Cornelius did the only thing he could think of. He swooped her up bridal style and laid her inside the truck bed. Laughing, Sarah wriggled up to the top before settling into the pallet he'd created. "Aren't you going to join me, big boy?"

Oh fuck, yes.

Moving with lightning speed, he jumped up and took his spot next to her. She grabbed his neck and hauled him down to her, kissing him with wild abandon. He slipped his tongue into the depths of her mouth in a rhythm he hoped to do with other parts of his anatomy and her body with all haste.

Reminding himself that he wanted to make this special for her, he pulled back. She sighed and opened her eyes. In the dim cab light he'd left on inside his truck, he could see her pupils were blown so large they almost eclipsed her irises. A thin ring of green was all that was left.

"Slow. Special. That's what I planned for tonight. Worshipping your body under the moonlight." He swallowed. "Are you hungry, princess?"

"Not for food. Not right now, at least." She brushed her lips along his, nipping at his lower lip. "I'm hungry for you. Fill me up, Corey. You always know how to make me so full."

Groaning out a curse, he pounced on her. Soft kisses, playful bites and soothing licks along her skin made her writhe beneath him. He peeled the silky fabric of her sapphire dress from her skin, followed by the tantalizing lingerie she hid underneath. His own clothes were shed with alacrity.

Cornelius whispered filthy things into her lush skin as he tasted his way down her collar bone, sucked at her breasts until she cried out, then down the soft curves of her stomach to her wet sweetness between her thighs. There he feasted until he'd lost her to pleasure twice and the flavor of her flooded down his throat.

Sarah grappled at him to tug Cornelius up. Unashamed of the evidence of her orgasms glistening on his chin, he hooked his arms around her knees, slid his tongue along hers and plunged his cock inside her body. Their mutual moans filled each other's mouths and vibrated the air. Then the flames burning between them raged into a wildfire and consumed them both.

After, they lay panting and tangled together. Cornelius pressed tiny kisses along Sarah's dewy, flushed skin. "Sarie. My Sarie." Love pulsed with every pump of his heart, yet he kept the words trapped inside him. They'd come so far from where they'd started again. But he still knew she was holding back. He couldn't figure out why—maybe until she sorted out what her future looked like. Nevertheless, he protected his heart. He'd all but served it up on a platter to her through gestures and other words, but not out loud. Speaking the words exposed him too much. Cornelius didn't want to deny his feelings, but he wouldn't take the chance of scaring Sarah away. Or making himself so vulnerable that she had the power to gut him all over again.

As if not saying "I love you" could keep that from happening.

His mind was right. If she left him now, he didn't know how he would survive, if he was honest with himself. Losing his Sarie, his frog princess, his true love, was incomprehensible to him, but a tiny ball of fear wouldn't stop thumping inside his chest. Shoving it down, he focused on the here and now, holding his love close where she couldn't be taken away.

Chapter Eighteen

Faint singing woke Sarah from her spot in Cornelius' bed. She smiled at the sounds of him in the shower and enjoyed the glowing contentment in her limbs. Last night had been utter perfection. That Cornelius had remembered that spot — *their spot*, from back when they were kids in love and lust brought a grin to her face that would not quit. She'd wondered where he was taking her last night, but when he had turned off onto the dirt road, her memory had unlocked and recognition shook her. Her insides had gone to mush and her lady parts had turned liquid.

It was where they'd lost their virginities together. They'd spent the following years escaping to hump like the little horndog teenagers they'd been at that location, out of sight from his parents and her grandparents. They'd slept out under the stars a few times, pretending to be at other friend's houses. Looking back, she wasn't sure they'd fooled anyone, but they'd been responsible enough teens and the adults in their lives had trusted them enough to claim ignorance.

Stretching, she basked in the well-loved ache in her muscles. They had gone at one another three times in the back of the truck, then twice more back at his house before giving in to sleep. She slipped a T-shirt of Corey's over her head and spent a few minutes communing with Lolli and Jelly. She'd taken to these tiny frogs with ease and loved being part of their care. The amphibians had gotten so used to her that now when she dunked a fingertip into the water, they would swim over to brush along her skin before taking off again. She loved it and them.

Sarah padded into the kitchen in search of the coffee wafting in the air. She'd finished up pouring when Corey's phone lit up with a video call from his mom. For a moment, she hesitated. He was still in the shower and it wasn't her place to answer his phone, but Clarissa was sick and Sarah wanted to know how she was recovering. Sarah knew the last round of chemo was complete, but imagined there was still work to do on the road to full remission.

Before she overthought the decision more, she grabbed up the phone and answered. "Hey, Clarissa."

Clarissa's face filled the screen and Sarah was taken aback for a moment. She hadn't braced for how ill his mother would look. Corey's reports were so positive that Sarah hadn't paused to think that Clarissa wouldn't look like the woman Sarah remembered. The sight of Clarissa with a scarf tied around her head and looking like she'd dropped twenty pounds was startling.

Then Clarissa smiled and the expression transformed her face into the person Sarah knew. "Sarah! Hi, sweetheart. How good to see you."

"It's wonderful to see you, too. Corey is in the shower at the moment, but I thought I'd say hello. Hope you don't mind." Embarrassment tingled under Sarah's skin. She and Corey were old enough to not hide that they were having sex, yet old habits died hard.

"Not at all. What a treat to get to catch up with you. How is everything?"

Sarah perched on a barstool at the island and rested the phone against a large bowl filled with fruit. "Things are good. I'm staying busy with some freelance work and a few regular shifts at Three Sisters. How are you feeling?"

"Much improved since chemo and radiation finished. I won't miss that at all. It'll take time for my body to recover, but each day I have a little more energy than before. My scans and tests are coming back with good results."

"That's wonderful news! I know Corey was so worried about you for a bit there. I was, too." She sipped her coffee. "I, uh, I wish I could have gone with him last weekend to visit you and Boyd. It's not the same without you two here."

Clarissa nodded. "We miss Fallbank, but Eureka is a wonderful home for our retirement. Of course, once Cornelius has children, I'll be hard-pressed not to want to have a little place up there to stay and be close by."

The thought of kids — with Corey — stuck in her brain. Sarah coughed to clear her mind and her tight throat.

Clarissa laughed. "I didn't mean to freak you out, sweetheart. Cornelius has plenty of time before that." She paused and pressed her lips together for a moment. "I know you and Cornelius are newly reunited." She flapped a hand in view of the camera. "And I love that for you both. I do. I just...worry. It gutted him when you two broke up before."

Sarah sucked in a breath as Clarissa's words slammed into her. A hard lump formed in her throat and she struggled to swallow around it. "Splitting up with Corey was the hardest thing I've ever done. Losing my parents is the one thing that compares."

"I know, Sarah," Clarissa murmured in a soothing tone. "It broke both of you and we all saw it. I don't think many people understood it either." Her gaze was soft and sympathetic. "Rehashing the past won't change it. That's not why I brought it up. All I ask is for you to be gentle with him."

Sarah opened her mouth, but his mom paused her.

"I don't want you to make assurances to me, because we can't predict the future and I never want either of you to stay in a situation that doesn't bring you happiness. Treat his heart with care. He does well hiding it, but Cornelius is more sensitive inside than most realize." She gifted Sarah a small smile. "You recognize that and it resonates with your own soul. Please, for his sake and yours, proceed with tenderness."

"I get what you're saying," Sarah replied. Her voice was subdued. "I never wanted to hurt him and trust that my intentions are pure."

"Thank you." Clarissa waved her fingers. "Enough heaviness. We need more lightness in life. Tell me how your freelance projects are going."

Sarah laughed and began filling her in on what she'd been doing the last few weeks. When she was in the middle of talking about her work on the epicycle clothing store, Corey joined her. He shuffled up from behind, leaning in to press his lips to the spot where her jaw met her neck and she shivered at the touch.

"Morning," he rumbled in a gruff, low voice. "Hey, Mama. How're you feeling?" He flashed a grin at her as he rested his chin on Sarah's shoulder.

The warmth from his chiseled chest soaked into her back and Sarah melted against him. Being in his arms was her safe place. Laughter from the phone brought her back to the present.

"I'll let you two go. Looks like Sarah is about to fall asleep. I'm sure you have better things to do today than entertain an old lady."

"You aren't old." Corey scoffed. Sarah shook her head in agreement with him. They ended the call and Corey nuzzled her temple. "There's the sidewalk fair downtown today, wanna go?"

Sarah glanced at the sunny weather outside. With one week until the wedding, she was eager for a break from the prep. "Sounds great. Let me get dressed."

Later as she and Corey strolled downtown hand in hand, Sarah was mindful of how at peace she felt. Despite the crowds, she wasn't annoyed by all the people like she had been when she was in Seattle. Happy greetings and chatting filled the air while vendors displayed their wares outside their shops. Bounce houses and snack kiosks with waiting lines dotted the street. Perhaps because the smaller community feel appealed to her maturity now, but she appreciated the charm of her hometown more than when she'd run off to Seattle for college.

They joined where Gran, Arianna and Bridget manned the array from Three Sisters Apothecary. "Hiya," Sarah announced. The sight of her sister wearing a witch hat adorned with spring flowers had a giggle leaving her chest. "Nice hat, sis."

"Thanks." Bridget preened before giving her attention to a customer. Sarah and Corey poked around and she nudged him when she spotted the wooden figures he'd made.

"Those are pretty great items. Wonder who made them?" she teased.

Cornelius blushed as someone scooped up a turtle and added it to their items for Arianna to ring up. "They're all right, I guess," he mumbled.

Sarah took pity on him and they both waved as they set back off along the road. "I can't believe Bridget is getting married next week and still working events for the store." Sarah sighed. "I should have volunteered for this so she could focus on other things."

Corey wrapped an arm around her shoulders and kissed the top of her head. "Little B is fine. She thrives on this kind of thing and I know from Jack that this is helping distract her from spinning out over the wedding and house. Jack is on duty for home building things this weekend and has a detailed list from her. She's in a good place."

Her guilt released as she snuggled closer to Corey. The couple came up on an empty shop window half hidden by the crowds. A small 'for lease' sign sat in one corner with a phone number written below. Her steps faltered as she looked over the storefront. It wasn't huge, more of an office space than anything retail…which was all she'd need if she were to open her own small marketing agency.

"You okay?" Corey asked, tilting his head at her.

"Yeah..." She dug her phone out of her purse. "I want to copy down this number." She typed it into her contacts and tucked the device back away.

He studied the empty space, then looked at her. His expression was neutral, reserved. "What did you want it for, princess?"

Emotions warred inside her. Was she contemplating this path because of Corey or because she didn't want to return to a large corporate marketing firm? Would Fallbank have enough business to support her? How much remote work would she need to do?

"Sarie?"

"Oh, um. I was thinking about finding out what the rent is." She trailed off, still lost in her thoughts, staring at through the window and trying to picture herself there. It wasn't difficult to envision.

He kept quiet and waited for her to continue.

"In case I wanted to open my own marketing business here. In Fallbank."

He bit his lip and nodded. "Do you want to do that? Have you thought about this much?"

"A bit. I've been kicking the idea around. I'm still exploring options in Seattle, but with the work I've done here, there's a foundation for it." She peered up at him and his blank expression. "What do you think?"

He kicked up one corner of his mouth. "It doesn't matter what I think. This is your decision, not mine. I don't want to control or dictate what you do with your life. I'll support you with whatever direction you go."

Why did that answer disappoint her? He wasn't forcing her onto one path or another, but did that mean he didn't care? Was he so unattached that she could move back to Seattle and that wouldn't upset him? He wouldn't miss her?

Corey stepped around to face her and took both of her hands in his. "I can see your beautiful brain whirling. It isn't because I don't want you here, Sarah. I...I want you to stay more than anything. But that's never been your dream. Even a few months ago, this wasn't on your radar. I don't want you to make such a massive career change—*life* change—if you aren't certain. And I don't want to be the reason you do this. I couldn't live with myself if you decided this because of me, *for* me. No matter what happens with your job choice, I'm not going anywhere. Okay?"

Struggling against tears, Sarah nodded. She sniffled, then a shaky laugh escaped her. In one speech, he'd put her fears at ease without her speaking them aloud. He knew her better than anyone else, could read her thoughts from her body language and facial expressions. Her heart squeezed inside her chest as a rush of love for him warmed her from head to heels. "Okay. I believe you." She smiled and lifted on her toes to brush her lips to his. "Thank you. For being more than I ever deserved."

He growled as he wrapped her in his arms. "You deserve the universe, princess."

She wasn't worthy of him, not after what she'd done, but her selfish heart still grabbed onto him and wouldn't let go.

* * * *

Cornelius whistled as he walked into the office the following Monday. He'd left Sarah warm and sleepy in his bed and looked forward to coming home to her that evening. Since their reunion, she'd spent almost every night at his place, claiming the space from her sister and

Jack was appreciated. He'd told her she would always be welcome.

Jack was already at his desk and he cocked a brow at Cornelius' buoyant mood. "I see you had a good night."

Cornelius' grin was wolfish. "It was excellent. And I don't see you complaining."

"Nope. I can't say I mind the extra alone time with Bridget, or the fact that it looks as if Sarah might be contemplating staying in Fallbank for good." Jack leaned back in his chair with his hands behind his head and feet kicked up on the table. "Plus I'm getting married in five days. Life couldn't be better."

Cornelius had to agree with his friend. The path he was on with Sarah was smooth and he could see well into the future with her. Hell, he was already daydreaming about when to propose. He knew it was fast, but they'd already lost twelve years. He wanted to jump in with abandon and move forward together. His heart was hers and always would be. Now he needed to sort out when to make his move.

He already knew he'd take her back to their place overlooking the town. And his mother had offered his grandmother's engagement ring if he wanted it. She'd told him back in high school the ring was his when he was ready, but last visit they'd sat down and looked at it. The band was etched with swirls and vines leading up where it split into two on each side to hold the oval center placement. Tiny circular diamonds lined each prong and terminated into an oblong basket that held a one-carat old European-cut sapphire with two round-cut half-carat diamonds on the top and bottom. He could picture it on Sarah's hand. Beautiful, unique, and a touch edgy. Just like his Sarie.

Given how the weekend had gone, he wished he'd brought it home with him. Still, he hadn't wanted to jinx things when Sarah hadn't yet settled on a job and where she was going to live.

Which led him to the conversation he needed to have with his business partner. "So, Jack. About the whole Sarah living here."

"Yeah?"

"What if she didn't? If she ended up back in Seattle?"

Jack dropped back to upright in his chair with a hard thump. "What? Why would that happen? That's not the plan, Cornelius. Bridget wants her sister here, so that's what I want. Is it not what you want?"

Holding up his hands, Cornelius said, "Nothing is set in stone. I want to have options. Potential plans in case she decides Washington is the best answer for her."

"But Bridget won't like that. She loves having her sister back in town. I want my honeybee happy." He pointed at Cornelius. "Fix this."

Cornelius laughed. "As if I could tell Sarah to do anything. All I'm saying is that she's contemplating Fallbank and what that looks like for her and her career. At the same time, I know there's things in the works in Seattle. That's where she built her entire adult life. Something kept her there for over a decade and I'm not going to stand in the way of her choices."

"Hold up." Jack shot to his feet with a glower. "What about us? As business partners?" He flapped a hand between them.

"Cool your jets, my dude. I'm not looking to run out on you and TLC." Cornelius held his hands out in a placating gesture. "I'm bringing this up so we can sort out what our options are."

"I don't like it. There is no alternative with you being in Seattle and me here. TLC is in Fallbank. I'm not going back to the city. Bridget would hate that. *I* would hate that."

"Not asking you to. But what about an expansion? Washington has plenty of logging opportunity. I could head up a branch of TLC from there. Hire a new crew. See what jobs or contracts are available. Use your connections to get going."

"I guess that's not a terrible thought." Jack crossed his arms. "I still don't like it."

Cornelius walked around and put a hand on his best friend's shoulder. "Not the top of my list, either. But I need the possibility. For me and Sarah. I… Shit, I can't lose her again." The pain that lashed his heart at the thought of not being with Sarah again almost made him double over. "I have to show her we can work no matter what life looks like."

Jack nodded. "I get that. It's not ideal, but I understand being willing to do whatever it takes to support the person you love more than anything in the world. Hell, I risked chopping off a leg to make a grand gesture to Bridget."

"I knew I'd get you to see reason." Cornelius joked. Then he rubbed his hands together. "Let's sit down and see what we can sketch out for a Washington branch of TLC."

Later, after many hours of spit-balling ideas with Jack, Cornelius drove home humming and feeling light. He couldn't say he loved the idea of moving to Seattle. He wasn't a city guy by any stretch of the imagination. It would mean longer commutes to work sites and the cost of living was way higher than Fallbank, but it was doable. He could sell the house and use that as a nest egg to start a life with Sarah up there. Maybe a compromise would be getting a house in the suburbs so he wouldn't have to drive quite so far. Maybe she could finagle a hybrid schedule of working from a home office a couple of days a week so the drive into downtown wouldn't be so taxing.

Whatever way it ended up, they had choices. They would figure out a way to be happy together no matter where that ended up. That was what mattered to him more than anything else. Hadn't his dad talked about compromise and committing to some sacrifices to make his partner satisfied? Cornelius could do that for Sarah. He'd move mountains if that was what it took.

The sun was lowering and painting the sky a dozen gorgeous reds, oranges, yellows and pinks when he pulled into the driveway. Cornelius walked in and found Sarah in the kitchen making tacos. "Mmm, looks delicious. Smells mouthwatering, too." He pressed a kiss to her neck and she tilted her head to smile up at him. "Good day today?"

Sarah nodded. "Yep. Bridget is vibrating with anticipation of the wedding, but all the details are done. She made me swear to lock myself in with her, Becca, and Gran on Thursday and Friday to complete the flower arrangements. Then we have a reprieve for the rehearsal dinner Friday night, then the wedding on Saturday. I'll be glad to relax from all the commotion when Sunday comes."

"I feel you on that. It's been so much wedding stuff that I forgot what life is like when it's not crazy. I guess I'll have to content myself with Jack and his sister's family for company while you're stolen away. Allison and Hiro are staying at the inn, but since they're coming in earlier than the rest of his family, we thought we'd cook out over here."

"Maybe I can persuade Bridge for us to have a joint pre-rehearsal-dinner dinner on Thursday." She turned around in his arms and pressed her lips to his for a brief moment. "We do have to eat at some point."

"I'll send Jack in. He can get her to take a break." Cornelius lifted the corners of his lips. "I like this plan." He glanced over at the taco prep his thoughtful girlfriend had prepared for them, then out the window to the sinking sun. "Feel like taking this to go?"

Sarah furrowed her brow at him. "Huh?"

He moved and pulled travel containers out from a cabinet. "That sunset is too pretty to miss. If we hurry, we can reach our place in time for the perfect view while we have dinner. You game?"

Her grin was wild and bright. "You're on."

Chapter Nineteen

"Ouch." Sarah hissed out a breath as a thorn jabbed her finger. She sucked on the injured pad for a moment, the taste of iron filling her mouth. Giving it a shake, she focused back on her task of creating a tenth flower arrangement for the guest tables. Arching her back, she sighed with relief that this was her last one.

"Someone talk about something or I'm going to start spiraling about all the things that are going to go wrong tomorrow," Bridget pleaded.

So far the day had gone well. Gran and Arianna had covered the store in the morning while Sarah and Bridget had gone to Becca's farm to cut fresh flowers and branches for all of the floral arrangements. In the afternoon, Gran and Becca had swapped places at the shop until things had slowed where Arianna could close without an extra set of hands. For the first time Sarah could remember, Three Sisters would be closed for two days in a row that weren't holidays.

Now all four of Wildes women were in the final stages of completing the table along with the altar arch that would frame the couple as they said their vows. Tomorrow would be bouquets and boutonnières, plus the cake topper, followed by manicures and pedicures before the rehearsal dinner. With how much her hands ached, Sarah was counting the hours until they were finished.

"Are you excited for the honeymoon, Bridget?" Becca asked.

Bridget scowled. "I'd be more thrilled if I knew where we were going. Jack still won't tell me. He won't even let me pack," she despaired.

Forcing down her laugh, Sarah furrowed her brows and nodded in sympathy. She didn't know where they were going, but Jack had enlisted her help to pack her little sister up for the vacation. She was under strict secrecy not to spill even one hint. All Sarah knew was it would be sunny and sandy.

"What if he thinks I'm going to walk around naked the whole time?"

Sarah burst out laughing. Jack had said to be minimal with clothing. "I promise you'll have things to wear."

A disgruntled grumble escaped her little sister. "Like you would know." Bridget froze, then jerked her head up to stare at Sarah. "You do know! He told you?"

"No, no, no. He didn't tell me, but Jack did enlist me to pack a few items for you." She pointed at Bridget. "Don't you dare tell him, either. You aren't supposed to know even that much."

"But...but..." Bridget pushed out her lower lip and sulked.

With an arched brow, Sarah said, "That look doesn't work on me. I'm not Jack."

"Okay. Let's change the subject." Gran intervened. "Becca, how was picking up Hop at the airport this morning?"

"No problem at all. Traffic from Portland was light." Becca beamed. "I'm so glad he's able to be here for the wedding. He hasn't been home in so long."

Sarah cocked her head to the side to think about when she'd last seen her older cousin. "He's been gone, what? Six years? Seven?"

Her cousin shook her head. "Last time he was in Fallbank was maybe ten years or so. He re-upped his enlistment with the Army and that extended things. Last time I saw him was three years ago at Christmas when Mom and Dad moved." She sighed. "I think his contract is ending again. I hope he stays this time."

"How long has he been in?" Bridget asked.

"Who even knows at this point? Let's see, he started at eighteen and he's thirty-five now. That would put him at seventeen years?"

Sarah blinked at that. She sometimes forgot how long he'd been gone. He'd left straight out of high school to join the military and now he was more like the long-lost relative coming home. She wondered how much he'd changed over the years. On occasion she'd text or call him, but more often than not, her updates were from Gran and Becca.

"I've been thinking about staying in Fallbank. On a permanent basis," Sarah blurted out. Where had that come from? Her brain had malfunctioned because she'd decided not to say anything until she made a final decision. She hadn't wanted to get her family's hopes up. Yet all this talk of missing Hop had brought to mind how much Sarah longed for all of them.

It felt as if the whole room froze. Sarah darted her gaze from one woman to the next to the next. Their stunned expressions held for a breath longer before all three of them broke out into excited exclamations.

"That's wonderful news!" Gran beamed.

"About time you came to your senses." Becca held out her fist for a bump.

Bridget bounced up and threw her arms around Sarah. "My sister's coming home! This is the best wedding present ever."

Laughter bubbled up from deep inside as Sarah clambered to stay upright under her sibling's onslaught. "I said I was contemplating it. Nothing for sure, yet." She wanted to keep expectation in check. She still had the position in Seattle she was waiting to hear back on. Plus the realtor handling the lease for the office space downtown hadn't called her back. They'd had initial conversations, but the agent was gathering details for Sarah. The space might not work out for what she wanted.

She bit her lip. Corey didn't know the depth that Sarah had gone to research options of owning her own small firm, being her own boss. That was a frightening concept—her entire livelihood and ability to support herself and any family she might have resting on her shoulders. No investors or big-name brands as clients to keep things going, no other colleagues to rely on in leaner months for her. Of course, that hadn't saved her when Jewel Creatives Agency had been bought out. She squeezed her eyes shut for a moment. The whole prospect was overwhelming.

Bridget flapped a hand. "Whatever. We have faith in where this is heading. You and Cornelius are too entwined to not be together and it isn't like he can up and move. TLC is here."

Frowning, Sarah shrugged. "This isn't about Corey. I need to sort out what I want to do with my career. With the freelance work I've picked up here, I can see the need for marketing in Fallbank. There's still digging to be done to figure out if I can get a small business loan and where I would set up an office, plus where to live."

Her cousin snort-laughed. "Like you wouldn't move in with Cornelius? Come on, Sarah. That's not a concern."

Gran held up a palm. "Girls, let's not ambush Sarah. The fabulous news is she's thinking about coming home on a permanent basis. Don't go overboard and scare her off."

"Thanks, Gran." Sarah hugged her grandmother. Being closer to the woman who'd taken her in when her parents had died was important to her. Gran was getting up there in age, despite being spry as ever. "Let's finish this up and get over to Corey's house for celebrating Bridge and Jack."

* * * *

Cornelius had his grill heated, drinks iced and a crowd of six — soon to be ten, gathered in his backyard. The weather was pleasant and warm without edging into hot. In some kind of miracle, rain was not in the forecast for the next seven days and Cornelius couldn't help smiling. It seemed Bridget did know what she was doing when she'd chosen the date — no precipitation predicted and the landscape was bursting with wildflowers and gardens at peak bloom. The yard at the Wild Rose Inn would be a spectacular backdrop for the wedding.

Hop stood off in a corner of the porch, leaning against the railing and nursing a beer. After flipping the burger patties, Cornelius closed the lid and walked over to his old friend. Despite being a few years older, he and Hop had bonded over being the two males when the Wildes females got together. Hop would be on driving and babysitting duty while Cornelius tagged along to be in Sarah's orbit. Their friendship was one thing that stayed around post break-up.

"How're you doing, man?" Cornelius slapped his friend on the shoulder, then mimicked Hop's stance.

"I'm back, so there's that." Hop sipped his beer.

Cornelius side-eyed his friend at the lack of enthusiasm displayed for coming home, particularly after leaving a dangerous part of the world. "Any reason you don't seem at all happy about being state-side? Or seeing your family?"

His friend sighed and ran a hand over his short buzzed hair. "I am happy to see my family. The wedding will be nice, I'm sure. I'm not certain where I go from here. My contract is up, but I could renew. It's not like I have some place to go or someone to come back to."

"You have here. Home. Fallbank. Gran and Becca, your cousins. Me. I know your parents moved, but that doesn't mean you don't have a home. And hell, if you need a job, come work for me. TLC could use your muscle."

"Maybe." Hop finished his beer. "I'll think about it."

"The offer stands," Cornelius said as he heard the gate to the yard open accompanied by female voices.

Jack's twin nieces raced in that direction. "Auntie Bridget," they screamed and clutched around her waist. Laughing, she hugged the girls as the group melded into the gathering.

Gran and Becca beelined for Hop and Cornelius found his way to Sarah, wrapping her up in his arms. "Hey, princess. How'd all the wedding prep go? You surviving?"

She melted into his body with a happy humming noise. "We finished the flowers for the tables and altar arch. Just the bouquets and boutonnières left. Ugh. I love my sister and I'm thrilled she's getting married, but all of this wedding stuff is ridiculous. So much effort for one day out of your lives."

"I don't know. There are some aspects that are appealing."

She stepped back, took his hand and led him over to the cooler. After grabbing a bottle, she popped the lid and sipped her beer. "Sure, the dress and the cake, the tuxes. But all the rest?" She waved a hand. "I'd rather have my focus on the person I'm saying my vows to and less stress about guests and food options and flowers."

"So eloping is more your style?" He hadn't thought too hard about the actual wedding of him and Sarah. More so, what life being married to her would be like. When brought to his attention, he realized a *wedding*-wedding didn't entice him either. His Sarie was right. The focus should be more on the promises of marriage than a big party. He liked the relaxed, laidback vibe, like what they had going on tonight.

Sarah smiled. "Yeah, I guess so."

"Good to know." He winked at her. "Now I gotta go check on the grill." He patted her behind as she stood there gaping at him like a fish.

Once everything was cooked and laid out buffet-style, Cornelius whistled to get the attention of everyone. "Thank you all for being here tonight. I know the real festivities don't start until tomorrow, but this impromptu pre-wedding-rehearsal-rehearsal dinner means a lot. The people gathered in this yard have become family to me. Some for more years than others, but the length of time is inconsequential. I'm honored to have each of you in my life and I hope that this is the first of many more nights like this one.

"When I first met Jack, I wasn't sure if he was going to make it out here in the wilderness of Oregon. I'm happy to see the pretty city boy stuck it out. When I introduced him to Bridget, I could see the sparks from the first moment. I couldn't be more thrilled for the two of them to get married. It isn't every day you see someone find their soulmate, but that's what Bridget and Jack are — soulmates. There's no doubt in my mind they will go the distance to lead full, joyful lives together." He lifted his drink. "To Jack and Bridget!"

"To Jack and Bridget," the crowd echoed and cheered.

"Now, let's eat," Cornelius called out. As the mass headed for the food, Sarah sidled up to him.

"Who knew you were such an orator?" She beamed at him and snuggled closer. "That was a beautiful speech, Corey."

The tips of his ears grew warm. "Nah, it was no big deal. Speaking the truth from the heart is easy."

She nodded and looked out at her family and their friends. "I told my family I might stay in Fallbank." She glanced up at him, but he kept his expression neutral. "This afternoon, while we worked on the floral arrangements."

"How did they take that news?" He tugged her closer by weaving an arm around her waist. Inside he was soaring with excitement. True, he had a backup plan should Sarah decide to go with the Seattle choice. But if he were honest, a life with her in Fallbank was the best dream he could imagine. He didn't want her to know that, though. Cornelius wanted Sarah to have control of her path and make the best choice for her. He would follow, no matter what.

"They were…ecstatic. Over the moon happy."

"And how did you feel telling them?"

"Lighter, more confident about the option. I could see that life with more clarity." She paused and worried her lower lip. "Made me want that life."

Overwhelmed, Cornelius hugged Sarah tight. Closing his eyes, he rested his cheek on the top of her head and allowed himself to feel the rush of euphoria sweeping through his body. "You know I'll follow you anywhere, right? You decide and I'm all in." He breathed against the tightness in his chest. "But staying would be wonderful. As long as you're with me."

"Yeah?" She adjusted to rest her chin on his chest so she could look up at him.

"Yeah. I don't want to be without you and I want you to feel supported in whatever you do in life. I go where you go." He was all in and didn't need her to be scared off again because of distance. Cornelius couldn't envision his future without Sarah. He'd never wanted to, and now that they had their second chance, he wasn't throwing away his shot. She revealed her hesitation in the tightness of her shoulders and the tense edge around her eyes. "You don't have to commit to anything. Telling someone a possibility does not obligate you. Even if you make a choice, you can always change your mind. Don't stress about it. Enjoy the next few days celebrating Bridget and Jack. Think about the rest after."

Cornelius loved the way her body relaxed into his. Her soft smile and affection glowing in her eyes made his heart soar. If he could keep reassuring her that they would be okay, her confidence in them would continue to grow. He just needed a little more time to build the relationship up before proposing—and eloping. He was so down for that. Anything to make Sarah his wife faster.

C h a p t e r   T w e n t y

The day before her little sister's wedding Sarah woke up with a smile and a sexy man cuddled up to her. Last night floated back to her in warm waves. The party had been fun and freeing. She and Corey were in sync and their talk about future plans had gotten her hot and horny.

But he still doesn't know why you broke up with him in the first place.

She shoved the guilty thought aside and tried to keep her mind in the moment. It wasn't difficult, given the hard bulge pressing into her backside. Someone was excited this morning and she wasn't about to argue. Turning over, Sarah slipped her arms around Corey's neck and one leg over his hip. She kissed along Corey's throat and he pulled her tight, rubbing their aligned bodies together and creating delicious friction. Within moments she was panting and wet. "Corey, don't tease me."

"Never," he growled then rolled her onto her back. He thrust home and they both moaned. "So good, princess." He tangled his tongue with hers as they loved one another. Her climax barreled down on her. This wouldn't take long at all.

"More, please," she begged.

With a groan, he laced his fingers with hers and lifted them above her head. She hooked her ankles around his waist and he drove deeper, harder into her. "God, Sarie. You take me so well. Be a good girl and come on my cock."

"Corey," she keened out as her body shook and shivered with release. With a shout, he joined her in pleasure. After catching her breath, she chuckled at him. Her Corey gave off hot nerd vibes with his glasses and plaid shirts, but in bed he was anything but. He said dirty things and did even filthier acts. They'd been wild and explorative as teens and time hadn't dimmed their insatiable thirst for one another. This morning's sexcapdes had been tame compared to last night. Her wrists were a bit tender from the silk necktie he'd knotted around her hands and attached to the headboard. He'd had each foot anchored too. And he'd utilized a few other tools, too...not that she was complaining. Any lingering soreness was well worth the pleasure she'd been treated to. "Good morning."

Corey grunted into her skin as he lay on top of her. He wrapped his arms around her shoulders and canted to the right so they were both on their sides, bodies still joined. A phone chimed and Sarah grimaced. "That's one of the family wondering when I'll be over." She pressed her lips to his shoulder. "More flower duty and then getting our nails done."

"Don't want you to go." Corey pouted and strengthened his hold.

"I know. I don't either." She sighed. "But we both have a busy next two days. How about we stay naked and in bed all day Sunday?"

"Promise?"

She laughed and kissed his nose. "Promise."

He relented and let her scoot from bed to shower. Then she made the short walk over to her sister's house. Wearing a tiny frown, she thought about her stuff still over here. Maybe she could bring up the idea with Corey to move her things to his place and stop pretending they had separate living spaces. Her phone rang and Sarah pulled it from the back pocket of her shorts. She halted as her old landlord's name popped up on the screen. With a swipe, she answered. "Hello?"

"Hey, Sarah. It's Phil, your old landlord. I have news for you."

"Oh?" Please don't let it be what she thought this might be.

"Your apartment is fixed. Everything is good as new. I can't believe how fast we got things turned around."

Her heart dropped at the announcement. "That's great. I...didn't expect this so soon."

"I wanted to let you it's available and yours if you want it again. You could move back in as early as mid-June."

"Wow," she croaked and swallowed to relieve her dry throat. "Do you need an answer right now?"

A nervous chuckle came across. "No, I can wait a few days. If you want."

"Yes, please. It's that I lost my job and I'm waiting to hear back on some opportunities. I don't know how fast

I'll know." Sweat broke out along the nape of her neck. She wasn't ready to make this decision. Sarah still hadn't heard on the job she'd interviewed for and the realtor in town was still looking into a few leasing questions. "Plus my sister is getting married tomorrow."

"I understand. Sorry to hear about your job. Terrible news. Um, I can't hold on for too long though. Would two weeks work?"

"That would be so kind of you. Yes, you'll hear back from me within that time. I appreciate this so much, Phil."

"Sure thing, Sarah. You were one of my best tenants. I'll wait to hear from you."

They disconnected the call and Sarah rubbed her forehead as she contemplated the news. It came down to a job more than anything else. She had no reason or income to support going back to her old place at this time. Inhaling, she shoved aside the information until later. Now was not the time to debate what to do. Her focus needed to be on Bridget's wedding. With her stress level decreasing, she walked into the house with a smile pasted across her face.

"Happy almost wedding day," Sarah called as she entered the house. She found the rest of her clan inside the living room with buckets of flowers and spools of ribbons strewn about. Candle batted at a reel of sky-blue lace and chased it across the carpet.

Bridget looked up with a murderous scowl. "You're late. Sit. We have work to do."

What the hell had happened to her sweet little sister? With wide eyes, Sarah glanced at Gran, Becca, and Allison. All three looked as startled as Sarah felt.

"She's stressed out," Becca mouthed.

Nodding, Sarah took a seat and grabbed up blooms. "What's still on the list?"

Her sister shoved a wad of silk at her. "Bridesmaid bouquets."

Sarah rested her hand over Bridget's and waited until her sister met her gaze. "Hey, Bridgie. It's all good. Everything is going to be perfect. You don't need to worry. I've got this."

For a strangled moment, no one moved. Then Bridget threw her arms around Sarah with a sob. "Thanks, Sare-bear. Sorry for snapping. I'm kind of freaking out."

Squeezing her sibling tight, Sarah made soothing noises. "No apologies needed. Your wedding is a big deal and I'm not going to let anything go wrong. I'm sorry I was late, but my focus is here." She sat back and wiped away the tears on Bridget's cheeks. "Now let's get these flowers arranged so we can move to the relaxation part of the day. You know I can get these done in no time."

"You better. Otherwise I'm demoting you from maid of honor." Bridget laughed and just like that, the cloud in the room broke and her sunshiny sister was back.

* * * *

Two hours later, they were finished with all the bouquets and boutonnières and everyone wore a smile. After clearing up the remnants of ribbons and plant pieces, they piled into cars to drive over to the nail salon. Allison's husband met them to drop off the twins and Sarah's heart clenched at the sight of the two girls' exuberance at being included in the festivities. They danced around Bridget and over to their mother before squealing and picking out the sparkliest polish they could find.

Watching them made Sarah yearn for something she hadn't wished for in years. The thought of having a child of her own was an idea Sarah had delayed and shoved aside and put on the back burner to her career. And she'd been at complete peace with it, too. Yet now, with Corey in her life again and all of her plans of her life in Seattle in shambles, she found her mind open to more. Paths of possibilities that had seemed hazy and far off were now bright with untapped potential. Did she want this? Was this option something she could let herself desire? What if Corey —

Her phone rang and tore Sarah's thoughts back to the present. When she glanced at the number, her heart caught in her throat. Gesturing at it, she stepped outside the salon and answered. "Hello?"

"Hi, Sarah. This is Selena at Pateli and Schultz Marketing. Do you have a few minutes to chat?"

Nervous tingles broke out along her arms. "Of course. It's great to hear from you."

"I'm calling to offer you the position with us. We were all so impressed with you and your work and would love to have you join our team."

It took Sarah a heartbeat to respond. "How great. Thank you." She winced at her lackluster answer, but instead of being elated as she should be, Sarah felt more scared than anything else. How had things changed so drastically in the span of a few months?

Selena continued to describe the offer and generous salary to entice her to say yes. All the while, Sarah listened but also freaked out in her mind. Her old apartment and a prime job in Seattle were offered to her on the same day. *Is this a manifestation? A sign from the universe?*

Did she believe in that kind of thing? Her little sister would see this as the world telling her what she should do. Yet Sarah hesitated. Her time back in Fallbank had altered her mindset and now she was torn. She'd loved her life in Seattle. She'd been fulfilled and happy… right? Or had she lied to herself to keep from wanting something different?

"What do you think, Sarah?" Selena asked with a thread of anticipation in her voice.

"I'm so flattered." She paused and swallowed. "The offer is incredible. I, um, I do need a little time to think about it. My sister is getting married and my brain is scattered, to be honest. Could I have two weeks to decide?"

"No problem. I didn't expect an answer right away. Let's plan to reconnect in two weeks, unless you make a decision sooner?"

"Sounds great," Sarah answered on autopilot at this point. Her cousin was watching from the window and Sarah schooled her face. *No need to send anyone into a panic.*

"If you have any questions for me at all, feel free to call. I look forward to hearing from you, Sarah. We're so excited at the prospect of you joining us."

"Thank you again, Selena. I'll be in touch." She hung up and stared at her phone for a second. Shoving her phone into her purse and her turmoil deep down inside, Sarah walked back into the nail shop. Her family was already in chairs with one saved in between Bridget and Gran for her. It sat there like a beacon, calling her to join them. *Like a sign from the universe.*

What the hell was she going to do now?

* * * *

Cornelius straightened his pale blue tie in the mirror as his best friend bounced on the balls of his feet behind him. "Nervous?"

Jack shook his head and smoothed his beard. "Ready. I want to go drag the officiant to Bridget's room and get married already."

Hiro chuckled from his spot on a chair by the window. "You've got a little time, my dude. There's another hour before we line up."

A grumble left Jack as he stomped over to a dark wood vanity and snatched up a small tub that Cornelius recognized as a Three Sisters' product—one that Jack had already used twice today.

"Whoa there, buddy." Cornelius yanked Jack to a halt. "No more beard conditioner. You don't want to end up looking like an oily rat."

"Bridget made this just for me. It's my 'signature scent' or something like that. I want her to know I love it and her. She'll be able to smell if I didn't use it."

Hop stared his soon-to-be-cousin down. "The whole town will be able to smell if you used it if you put any more on. You don't need extra. I'm well versed in all things Three Sisters. Trust me, you're good."

Jack relented and paced across the room. "What's taking so long? We're all set to go. I want to get married."

Laughter erupted from all of the men in the room. Hop, Jack's father and Jack's brother-in-law all guffawed alongside Cornelius.

John, Jack's father, clapped him on the back. "The ladies aren't finished. They take longer than we do, especially on occasions like this. Bridget wants to look as beautiful as she can for you."

Jack glowered at his father. "She's always beautiful and nothing is going to change that. And I'd bet all the money I have she's done prepping. Bridget isn't high maintenance."

Cornelius stepped over to save John from getting murdered by his son. Jack's father had a bad habit of saying the wrong thing and paired with his old-fashioned ideas, it tended to strain their relationship. "Hey, Jack. Didn't you say you had something for Bridget? Need it delivered?"

"I do. Get it? I do?" Jack laughed at his joke as he walked over to a vanity. Pulling out a small box with a card attached, he turned to hand it over. "Can you make sure this gets to my honeybee?"

Cornelius resisted rolling his eyes at the seriousness Jack held. "I can do that. Promise." Leaning in, he murmured, "Don't kill your father."

With that, Cornelius departed and made his way down a set of stairs and to a corner suite that the B&B offered. He knocked and a muffled voice answered.

"Who is it?"

"Cornelius. I have something for Bridget for Jack."

The door cracked open and his princess slipped through. "Hey, handsome."

The sight of her in what he'd been told was a Grecian boho-style dress made him salivate. It was the same goddamn dress she'd worn that day at the shop when Cornelius had gotten fitted for his tux. The urge to fall to his knees and delve underneath the flowing skirt to worship her between her thighs was almost unbearable. "Fuck, Sarie. You look...breathtaking. I don't have words for what you do to me."

Her smile was luminous. Unable to stop himself, Cornelius leaned in and pressed his lips to her swanlike neck. With her silky blonde hair twisted up onto her head, it gave him easy access. And this way he wouldn't muss her make-up. He made a mental note to kiss off the red lipstick she wore after the ceremony.

Her sigh brushed his cheek. "Corey."

His control snapped at the lust in her voice. With the hand holding the present he leaned against the wall, trapping his fucking hot girlfriend in between. He slipped his free hand around her, letting his palm stroke her exposed skin at her back. He traced his mouth along the line of her neck to her shoulders and down to the V and the spectacular display of her breasts. Humming, he licked along her lush cleavage and Sarah let out a breathy moan and pressed her hips to his.

The door next to them jerked open. "Oh, for God's sake. Knock it off, you two." Becca glared with her arms crossed over the sky-blue pantsuit she wore.

With a sheepish half-grin, Cornelius backed away. "Sorry. Can't help myself when it comes to my princess."

Becca rolled her eyes, then pinned her cousin with a stare. "Bridget will unalive you if you mess up your hair, make-up or dress. Now get back in here. No one at this inn wants to see you going at it in the hallway."

Embarrassment flushed his already heated skin and Cornelius nudged his glasses up on his nose. "Right. Um, can one of you give this to Bridget?" He held out the small package and card.

Becca snatched it along with Sarah's wrist, dragging her back into the room.

"Bye, Corey," Sarah called.

"Bye, Sarie. I love you!" he shouted as the handle snicked shut. Then he slapped a hand over his mouth. Shit. Had he just told Sarah he loved her? What was he thinking? She didn't have time to respond. Did he want her to? What if she didn't feel the same? Maybe this was the better way to go. Give her time to think and sort through her feelings without any pressure or expectation.

Sure, she'd done well with his admission that he would go anywhere she went, but that was all still hypothetical in her mind. There were no feelings exchanged in that conversation. Cornelius believed they were on the same emotional page, but he couldn't be certain until she told him.

Vowing not to bring up the L-word again until she addressed it, he turned to head back to the groom's room. The door swung open behind him and he spun around. His heart banged inside his chest with hope.

Sonia, Jack's mom, stepped out with a shallow box of flowers to pin to the tuxes. "Oh, good. You're still here. I thought I'd come along to see if we can get these on all of you and then John and I can head down."

Given how close Jack had been to snapping at his father when Cornelius had left, he smiled and held out his hands. "May I carry that for you?"

Before she could answer, Sarah raced out of the room and skidded to a stop. "I didn't expect you to still be here." She leaped at him, throwing her arms around his neck and kissed the hell out of him. Her lipstick was going to be a smeared mess on both of their faces, but he didn't care. His princess was in his arms and his brain was short-circuiting. She jumped back with a grin. "I love you, too."

He blinked and she'd disappeared into the room again. Jack's mom cleared her throat. Cornelius pivoted on his heel to face her, a goofy smile spread on his face. He held his hands out for the box of flowers again.

She handed it over, then tugged a handkerchief from the small clutch around her wrist. "May I?" She gestured toward his face. "You have a little lipstick. It's a mom instinct to clean you up."

They both laughed. "Thanks. That would be appreciated."

Sonia wiped away the evidence of Sarah's kiss attack with a gentle smile. "You two seem like a lovely couple. It's sweet to see Bridget's sister so happy."

"Thank you. Now, shall we?"

Chapter Twenty-One

They gathered in the back exit from the Wild Rose Inn as faint strains of music danced on the air from the speakers surrounding the garden around the building. Sarah looked at her baby sister with a heart filled to bursting with happiness. Bridget was ethereal in her wedding dress. The off-the-shoulder mermaid cut with delicate and simple lace flowers accented with a hint of tiny sequins for the perfect amount of flash looked incredible on her. With wildflowers woven into her half-up spiral curls, the overall effect was faerie-like.

A hard lump formed in Sarah's throat. She wished that her parents were here to see this. There were so many life moments their absence was challenging, but none had prepared her for this. Their tiny clan was expanding. Her sister was going to have a whole new family after today. The bittersweet sensation of gaining a brother while losing her sister had Sarah teetering on a tailspin.

"It's time." Jane spoke with a soft voice to direct them to move into line for the procession. Guilt flickered through Sarah at seeing Jane, but she didn't have time to dwell. Luna and Lilly danced down the path and around the corner to make a path of petals for the rest of them to follow. Allison was next, her knee-length flared dress swinging as she walked forward.

Then it was just the Wildes women left. Fighting back tears, Sarah clasped Bridget's hand in hers, then gathered Becca's and Gran's into a pile. All four of them squeezed fingers and palms together while exchanging watery grins.

"Love you, Bridgie. I can't wait to watch you marry your soulmate," Sarah told her. "I'm so proud of the strong woman you've grown into."

Becca nodded. "Jack is the luckiest man to have you."

"Don't make me cry." Her little sister sniffled and blinked. "I love all of you so much."

"We love you too, Bridget," Gran said then took a deep breath. "Now, let's go get you married."

With laughter and a group hug, Becca made her way to the front. Sarah winked at her baby sister and stepped onto the path. As she rounded the corner of the inn, the music grew louder and the guests came into view. Then she lifted her eyes to see Jack waiting in front of the wildflower arch backdrop and the officiant next to him on his right. On his left stood Corey.

They locked gazes and she couldn't look away. He was so damn handsome in his tux and dark blond hair tousled by the wind and those black frame glasses. With the bouquet in her hands and the lush garden setting popping with color around them, Sarah could imagine this was her wedding to Corey. When she reached her place at the front, she turned and kept looking at her love. That was what he was — her frog prince, her lover, her heart. The admission from him had been surprising, but the rightness of it had made her run after him. She couldn't leave him wondering. She might burn in hell for it, but there was no way she could give him up now. Corey completed her soul.

As the music changed to signal the bride's entrance, Sarah mouthed, "I love you" to him.

His eyes burned into hers as he placed one hand over his heart and told her, "I love you, too."

With a wink that made her heart flutter, Corey broke their connection and looked to where Bridget and Gran were walking arm in arm up the aisle. Sarah, on the other hand, watched Jack with avid interest. She loved watching the groom's expression when the bride came into view for the first time. Jack didn't let her down with his reaction. He staggered over one step to the side and lifted a hand toward Bridget. His expression screamed love for her sister. Unshed tears gathered in his eyes and he swallowed hard. When they reached the front, Jack stepped forward and kissed Gran's cheek. "Thank you for entrusting her care to me."

Gran shot him a Look. "Don't make me question it." They both laughed and she took her seat.

Sarah took Bridget's bouquet and her sister joined hands with Jack. Sarah tried to focus on the vows between them, the way Jack cradled Bridget's face as he swept away her happy tears with his thumbs. But Sarah's attention strayed to Corey over and over. Lucky for her, he did the same. Each time their gazes met, love pulsed through her blood, flushing her with warmth. When Jack and Bridget kissed at the end, it was all Sarah could do not to jump at Corey.

Swooping low, Jack scooped Bridget up in his arms with a beaming grin. With a delighted squeal, Bridget wrapped her arms around his neck and planted another kiss on her brand-new husband as he carried her down the path. Sarah watched them go and found herself swallowing back tears for what felt like the twentieth time that day. Who knew weddings made her so sentimental?

Corey caught her eye and laced his fingers through hers. Tucking her close to his side, they followed the happy couple. Hiro escorted Allison, then Becca and the twins held hands to join their group.

Later, after pictures and dinner and a sinfully decadent cake, Sarah took Corey's offered hand. He swept her out onto the dance floor and pulled her into him. There was no space between their bodies as they swayed to the music. She draped one arm around his neck as he slid an arm around her waist. Their clasped hands sat over his heart. Corey brushed his nose along her cheek before pressing his lips to her skin.

"Love you, my Sarie." He spoke into her skin with warm breath and soft words.

She snuggled deeper into his embrace. "Love you too. I always have."

"I know. We were each other's from the day we met."

She smiled at the truth of what he spoke. They had belonged together and to one another from the beginning. When she'd gone frog-prince hunting with him, she'd known she would kiss him, that he would discover how she felt about him. It had been one of the scariest moments of her life. The possibility that he might not return her love had made her cold with fear, yet the heat in his eyes — even at that young age — had bolstered her bravery and she'd planted her lips on his.

Their love story was better than any romance novel she'd ever read. It might not be angsty or gritty and dark or even as rom-com meet-cute as some books, but it was real. She wouldn't trade it for anything.

As she tilted her face to kiss him now, she vowed to come clean on her secret. They would weather her truth and come out stronger on the other side. Corey slid his tongue along hers and shivers broke out along her skin. Sarah held him closer, delving her fingers into his hair. When they came up for air, his glasses had fogged and she chuckled.

As soon as the newlyweds departed through a walkway lined with guests tossing wildflowers in the air, Corey grabbed Sarah's hand. "Let's go home, princess. I want to make love to you all night."

* * * *

The muffled sound of Sarah talking woke Cornelius up. He stretched his satiated muscles and exhaled satisfaction. He looked around the room that Sarah occupied in her childhood home. With Bridget and Cornelius having left for Seattle last night and onto their honeymoon today, Sarah had been tapped to house and cat-sit. While he preferred his own bed, he couldn't complain that last night had been one of the best of his life. He and Sarah had made love until the rainbow of dawn had broken across the sky. With a glance at his phone, he saw they'd had a mere few hours of sleep.

His girlfriend's voice reached him again and Cornelius realized she was on the phone. He shrugged on a shirt and a pair of sweats, then settled his glasses on his nose. As he stepped toward the door, a half-open box next to the closet caught his eye. Hanging over one corner was the sleeve of an old hoodie he'd once had, one that Sarah stole from him years ago. A smile crept across his face. He'd loved every time she'd worn it, like an unspoken claim that she was his and he was hers.

Stepping over to the tub, Cornelius kept an ear out for Sarah to wrap up her conversation while he peeked through the contents. He found letters and cards he'd given her through their years as a couple. He opened the one on top. It was dated in their senior year of high school, back when they would hide notes for the other to find as a surprise.

Princess, You are my favorite not-a-secret secret. I love that we're together and everyone knows it, but they don't know us. They don't know our hidden special place or that you sneak into my room at night or how I plan our future in my dreams. No one knows how you're my Sarie and I'm your Corey. Frog princess and prince. That you kissed me behind the bushes in your grandparents' yard and we still sneak off to make out there. My heart found its home the day I met you. One look in your gemstone eyes and I was bewitched by my Wildes witch. I love you. Now, and always.

The paper was soft and worn, like she'd unfolded and folded it a thousand times. The ink was faded in places, but still legible. Inspiration struck and he poked around for anything to write one. Cornelius found a Post It pad in the desk and snagged the neon purple paper. He scrawled a quick message, nothing long, but enough to make her smile when she found it. Then he tucked the square inside her pillow. When she laid her head on it, Sarah would hear the crinkle and discover it. Happiness buzzed within him.

He wandered back over to the box and dug out a frame with a collage of pictures of them — school dances and sports games, goofy ones, snapshots from hikes and trips to the beach. They'd made this together before she'd moved to Seattle for college. It'd hung on her wall above her bed in the dorm. At least it had before they'd broken up.

A chill struck at his heart when he thought back to the dark time just after she'd ended things...the depression and loneliness, hopeless and miserable, the sensation of being unwanted and unloved. It made him nauseous to think about, even today. He leaned over the box to place the frame back inside and a corner of black and white at the very bottom caught his gaze.

Cornelius tugged loose the shiny rectangle of photos. There were four pictures printed on the sheet — grainy, black and white images that didn't make sense at first. As he studied it, the meaning became clear. The date on the bottom confirmed his misgivings. This was why Sarah had broken up with him.

Fury scorched inside him. His pulse thrummed in his head as a wave of dizziness hit. *What the hell did she do?* The strip of pictures shook in his grip and Cornelius wanted to look away, but he couldn't. Each time he closed his eyes, his brain would hope he'd misinterpreted the photographs. But when he opened them, the story was the same. There was no mistaking. The only missing piece of the puzzle was, what happened next?

"Corey? Are you up?" Sarah called and her footsteps approached. "I have some news. Things I'd like to talk to you about." She walked in with a hesitant smile as she looked to the bed. Furrowing her brow when she saw it was empty, her expression cleared when she found him on the aubergine-colored tufted chair in front of the desk. "There you...are." Her voice trailed off when she saw the slip in his hand. Her skin paled to ashen and she gripped the doorframe. "I can explain," she whispered.

He cocked a brow. "Explain that you were pregnant?"

"I-I..."

"What happened, Sarah?" His voice bit out into the air, hard and cold. "How the fuck did you end up pregnant and where is the baby? Who was the father?"

She gasped and jerked back as if he'd slapped her. Her eyes clenched shut and her chin trembled.

"Oh, no. No, you don't. You don't get to play the victim here. Tell me!"

"You were the father," she shouted. "Of course it was yours. You think I slept around behind your back?"

Cornelius threw the offending ultrasound print out to the ground. "I don't know," he snapped back. "You never told me you were having a baby, so who can guess what else you hid from me?" He stood and clenched his fists. "For the last time, *what happened?*" The pain on her face should have gutted him, but the inferno burning him from the inside out overtook all other reactions.

She sagged against the wall and wetness fell from her eyes. "I had an abortion, all right? Condoms aren't foolproof. You accidentally got me pregnant sophomore year of college, and I terminated it."

Cornelius stared so long and hard that his eyes burned. He opened his mouth, then shut it. Opened it again. Shut it. Words failed him. Sarah had dealt with all of this on her own? Never breathed a word to him? "How...how could you not tell me? I would have..."

"Would have what?" Fire smoldered in her glare. "Tried to sweep in and save the day? Insisted that we get married, have me come back to Fallbank and give birth? Drop out of college and raise a baby together?" She scoffed and crossed her arms, all fight and ferocity now. "I wasn't ready for that! Not for any of it. Marriage, a baby... I couldn't! I couldn't throw away my entire future or yours. We were kids ourselves and not mature enough to be parents." She choked out her words. "It would have broken us, Corey."

"Well, you went ahead and did that anyway." He was livid that she hadn't talked to him about any of this. Hadn't *trusted* him enough to confide about this pregnancy. Why hadn't she had enough faith in him? "You should have told me. I deserved to know. Do you think I would have forced you into a marriage you weren't ready for? Into being a mother?" He shoved his hands into his hair and yanked. "I would never have taken your choice, Sarah!"

"I was scared! I panicked. My mind jumped to the worst conclusions and I took rash actions. I see that now, but back then? You have no idea how terrifying the whole situation was." Her entire body shook.

"Because you didn't tell me. You didn't trust me. How could you not trust me enough to share this? What did I ever do to make you think you couldn't confess this to me? I was half the reason you were in the damn predicament!"

"I know! I-I-I can't explain the fear, Corey. The overwhelming desperation. Try to put yourself in my shoes. All women are taught by society is that it's our fault if we get knocked up. That we're ruined goods and trapping some guy into marriage. That we have no other option but to have a baby and give up any other ambitions we might have. God forbid we want more out of life. That we take control of our bodies and determine what is best for us as an autonomous human being." Sarah shook her head and bit her lip. She closed her eyes.

"I couldn't face your parents or my grandparents. The people in town…they're already judgy assholes. I didn't want to add fuel to the fire, having the stigma of a shotgun wedding. A way to trap you. Or worse, the slut who killed a baby." Sobs broke from her chest. "I didn't know what to do, so I made the single choice I could stand. I picked me. My future. *And yours.* I ended the pregnancy and our relationship to give you a fresh start. I would carry this burden alone."

"So you were never going to tell me? This would have stayed a secret if I hadn't found the evidence? Why even keep that?" Cornelius was spiraling. The walls were too close and his lungs were tight. He struggled to breathe.

"I wanted to remember what I gave up. My penance and punishment. I lost the potential of a child. *Our* child. And I lost you." She moved closer to him and raised her hands, but didn't touch him. "You have to believe me, Corey. I had no plans to get back together with you, but… you were always the one. I wanted to tell you a thousand times over the years. I didn't know how. And I wasn't going to keep this a secret forever. I promised myself I would tell you before we made any decisions. So you could make your choice to stay with me or not with all of the information." She rested a hand on his chest. "Please, believe me."

He stepped back from her touch. "You want me to trust you when you didn't. Not when it mattered more than anything else in our lives. I can't, Sarah." Cornelius shook his head and walked toward the exit. "I just can't."

Chapter Twenty-Two

Corey stormed out and Sarah crumpled into a ball of tears. Her body rattled with the force of the cries ripped from her chest. She'd lost him. She'd known her abortion would break their relationship when she'd found out she was pregnant and her intuition was correct. Just not in the way she'd thought it would happen. She'd sabotaged them all those years ago and when Corey had convinced her to try again, she had faith in his promises that nothing would break them up this time. Sarah had been so desperate to be back with the one person her soul loved more than any other, she'd thrown away logic and intuition that told her that her past actions would always be their demise.

Now Sarah had to pay the price of her selfishness in not telling him all those years ago and not telling him now before they'd both gotten too attached again. Better to have him hate her and spare both of them this pain. It was too little, too late at this point. They would both choke and drown in the sorrow of their failed romance.

A quiet meow sounded as Candle took careful steps into the room and over to Sarah. The cat blinked at Sarah before rubbing her furry head along Sarah's chin. On a shuddering exhale, Sarah scooped the feline up and cuddled her close. The deep purr and rabbit-soft fur gave warm comfort to Sarah as she stroked the small animal's head and body. Tears still dripped from her face, but the heaving sobs had subsided for the moment. Sarah realized this was a small reprieve in the storm of emotions.

Support—Sarah needed support. She might not want it at the moment. Being around anyone right now sounded terrible, but she recognized her depression would need an anchor to keep her from crashing too hard. With wobbling, unstable steps, she made her way to the living room where her phone waited on the coffee table. Swiping it open, she sent off an emergency text to Gran and Becca.

Becca's response came through within moments.

Becca: I'm on my way. Bringing Gran with me.

A trickle of relief dripped through her and Sarah walked back to the bedroom. She collapsed in the middle of the mattress, closed her eyes and let the grief overtake her once more.

Later, she opened her eyes when Becca and Gran called out to her. Sarah had no idea how much time had passed. Every breath felt like an eternity despite the fact that her family had rushed to get here and couldn't have taken longer than twenty minutes.

Gran burst into the room, took in Sarah's prone form curled into a ball and hurried toward Sarah with open arms. "What happened, sweetheart? Whatever it is, it will be okay." She gathered Sarah into her arms and rocked side to side.

"I think I know what happened." Becca held up the ultrasound picture with her eyes so wide, the whites showed all the way around. "Are you pregnant?" she whispered.

"Not anymore," Sarah croaked.

Becca gasped and put a hand over her heart. "Oh, no…"

Gran shook her head. "She didn't miscarry and the pregnancy isn't recent. It's from back when she was in college. Isn't that right, honey?" All the while, Gran never stopped her soothing of Sarah in some form or fashion, be it gentle swaying, a strong hug or rubbing comforting circles on her back. Sarah sighed and sank deeper into her grandmother's consoling of her.

"H-how did you know?" Sarah gaped at her grandmother.

Gran's smile was sad. "I was joint on your credit cards and your health insurance was through me at the time. The statements came in the mail to you, but also here. It's not as if I thought you and Cornelius weren't having sex. I remember being young and in love with your grandfather. I never said anything because I was waiting for you to tell me first. It wasn't my place to question."

Sarah's voice was thin and weak. "I…I terminated it when I found out."

Becca pressed her lips together as a single wrinkle formed between her brows. "Okay?"

"Corey didn't know. Until this morning." Sarah swallowed to clear her throat. "He found the picture. I didn't have the chance to tell him."

Becca's expression morphed in a flash. She shifted from concerned to unbelieving in the span of a heartbeat, so fast that Sarah almost convinced herself the concern had been a figment of her imagination. "*You* didn't tell Cornelius? Ever? He learned about this today?" Becca shoved a hand through her hair. "Jesus Christ. I can't believe this. How could you not tell him?"

"Easy there. No one is blaming anyone for past choices." Gran held up a palm to keep Becca from exploding. "We're going to support Sarah through all of this." She hugged Sarah once more, then leaned back. "Why don't you tell us what happened?"

Sarah sniffled and closed her eyes in misery. Becca had every right to be irate with her. She was pissed at herself. She'd lied and hidden information from the love of her life and now everything had blown up in her face. "I got pregnant by accident sophomore year of college. Corey and I were always careful, but nothing is foolproof. I-I-I didn't know what to do. I was twenty years old and scared out of my mind. How could I become a mother? It would destroy all of my plans, and Corey's, too. He'd want to get married, but we were still just kids. Becoming parents seemed insane. So I got an abortion. And I never told anyone. Instead, I broke up with Corey, knowing this would rip us apart if he found out. He deserved someone better than me. I was selfish."

Gran scoffed. "That's not true—"

"It *feels* true. I've not once regretted my choice. It was the right thing to do. I stand by my decision. That doesn't change that my reasoning was all about how this would impact *my* life and *my* goals. Corey's too, and I chose for him. I didn't have enough faith in us that he wouldn't insist on getting married and having a baby. I should have trusted him. Now it's too late. He found the picture and when I told him, he blew up. I can't blame him, either. W-we're through. He broke things off and stormed out."

Sarah dissolved into a mess of snotty bawling again. Gran held her close and Becca joined them. She wrapped her arms around the two women and they all waited for Sarah to ride out this wave of pain. As she regained hold of her emotions again, Sarah sniffled. "Thank you both. For being here for me."

"We're always here for you." Becca squeezed Sarah tight. "You and Bridge are my sisters, even if we're technically cousins."

Gran nodded. "I would never abandon any of my grandchildren." She pulled Sarah to standing. "Why don't you go take a shower? It'll help you feel better. Becca and I will go make something to eat. This is hard, but you and Cornelius will get through it. Wait and see."

Sarah shook her head, but didn't argue. Fighting with Gran was a lost cause and wouldn't fix anything anyway. Instead she did as she was told and took a shower. Her heart bled like it had been shredded into ribbons and every muscle ached like a giant bruise. Each breath ushered a new wave of pain and Sarah saw no way out. Breaking up when they were in college had been crippling, but this time it was catastrophic. She hadn't anticipated this level of anguish and heartbreak. There didn't seem to be a way to right things with Corey. She hadn't trusted him and she couldn't blame him for feeling betrayed. She couldn't undo the wrongs of her past, all she could do was try to ease his suffering as much as she was able. The phone call from this morning swam through her head. Maybe giving as much as space as she could would be best for both of them. She'd never get over Corey, but distance helped her focus on outside things. It might give Corey the opportunity to find someone worthy of him.

* * * *

Rage pulsed through Cornelius as he slammed his ax through the log standing upright. It split with a loud *crack* and the two pieces fell to the sides. He grunted and stacked another to be divided in half. He'd been chopping wood for two hours out by the office and despite his muscles screaming in protest, the emotional storm inside him rampaged on.

How could Sarah not have told him she was pregnant? Why hadn't she trusted him? She had put herself through hell going through everything on her own, then had sacrificed their love out of some misplaced sense of honor? Sure, he could follow the logic she used — with the exception of why she'd jumped to that plan in the first place.

He'd hoped working out might help him understand, yet reason still eluded him. Either way, she'd made her choices for herself and him, and now their relationship was on the rocks all over again.

"Dammit," he shouted and tossed the ax to the ground. Exhaustion flooded his bones and he stumbled back onto a bench. He dropped his head into his hands and shoved his fingers into his hair. How were they supposed to work this out? Move forward together? His heart was bruised and his ego was battered. Her lack of trust slew him to the core. Cornelius needed time to sort out his feelings and find his path back to Sarah. Deep in his chest, he couldn't shake the innate certainty that he and Sarah were meant to be.

That said, forgiveness wouldn't come today, or even tomorrow. Letting go of this lie by omission would take time — time to cool down, to understand her thought process and come to terms with it all. His heart keened inside him, crying out to go back to Sarah. He knew she was crushed and hurting, too. It tore at him to know she was in pain, but so was he. If he wanted to help soothe her suffering, he had to fix his own.

A faded blue truck drove up and parked in the dirt lot off to the side of the building. His friend and Sarah's cousin climbed out. Hop raised a hand in greeting.

With a single nod, Cornelius acknowledged his presence. "Hop. What brings you by?" Still sweating and out of breath, Cornelius watched his friend to see how he would react. Should Cornelius brace himself for getting punched or chewed out?

Hop ambled over. "I talked to my sister. Figured since you weren't at your house, you'd be here. I'm sorry as hell about what happened between you and Sarah. That's a tough blow to take."

"Yeah. I can't say I ever saw that coming. She hid everything well." Cornelius jerked his head in the direction of the door. "Let's go inside." He opened the office and grabbed two bottles of water from the fridge. Handing one over, Cornelius chugged half of the other one down before dropping into his office chair. Hop took up the one across from Cornelius' desk.

"So what now?"

Cornelius shook his head. "Hell if I know. Shit, I can't believe she was pregnant, that she went through all of that turmoil alone. It kills me that she didn't have faith in me to support her in whatever decision she made."

For a long minute, his friend sat quiet and brooding. "I can't claim to have any clue what Sarah's motivations were or why she didn't tell you, but I do understand feeling like you just have yourself to rely on. Fear causes reactions that seem bizarre or wrong in retrospect, but in the moment, whatever choice you make strikes you as the single option available.

Hindsight is a gift and a curse. And not everyone is given it." Hop drank from his water. "What do you say we go somewhere we can find something stronger to drink?"

"God, yes," Cornelius agreed. The physical activity he'd done had helped with muscle exhaustion, but his mind was still too active. "A drink or several is what I need tonight. No more thinking."

A few hours later, Hop dropped a drunk Cornelius off at his home. Cornelius stumbled inside and collapsed face first into his bed. The smell of peonies from the nights of Sarah sleeping next to him filled his nose and a pained grunt escaped his chest. *Fuck. Why did our relationship have to get ruined?*

* * * *

In the morning, he dragged himself out of bed, wincing and cursing his overindulgence the night before. His head pounded as his stomach churned with threats to make him kneel at his toilet to atone for his actions. Grimacing as each step he took hurt, Cornelius managed to check on his pets, get himself showered and dressed before hauling off to the office where his crew expected him. Fighting the urge to vomit, he divvied up groups for the week's clearing sites before falling into his desk chair. Wallowing in misery, he tossed back a couple of painkillers along with an entire bottle of water. Getting rehydrated was his lone goal of the day.

Around lunchtime, his phone rang and Cornelius sprang into action. He fumbled his phone, but managed to see that his mother was calling—not Sarah. He hadn't given her a reason to call. Only reasons to not.

Swiping to answer, he closed his eyes and mumbled, "Hey, Mom."

"Cornelius? What's wrong? Why do you sound like you've been hit by a truck?"

Don't I wish.

"Sarah and I..." He pulled at the ends of his hair. "I don't know what. We broke up? Sort of."

"How do you 'sort of' break up?"

"She lied to me. The reason she dumped me the first time was because she was pregnant."

His mother's gasp filled the line.

"She ended it. The pregnancy, I mean."

"Oh, my." His mother's voice was soft and pained. "I can't imagine how hard that was. And to go through it alone? So heartbreaking. That poor girl."

Poor girl? What about him?

Incensed, he shoved his glasses into place on his nose and huffed. "What about me? She didn't have any faith in me at all. Zero trust after being there for her for years."

"Cornelius," his mother said in her gentle mama-is-about-to-school-you voice. "She was twenty years old. You were in Fallbank and she was in Seattle. It wasn't a lack of trust. She was isolated and afraid. She was looking out for your future and hers. Not to mention the guilt and self-loathing that must have been burning inside her to have her break things off with you."

Exasperation choked him. "She could have talked to me about this."

"Did you two ever talk about children? Before this happened?"

"Sure, in abstract. Not like we planned to have them anytime soon back then. We had other priorities."

"Had you discussed pregnancy scares before? What would happen if she did wind up pregnant before you were both ready?"

A memory he'd tucked so far away that he'd forgotten it existed surfaced in his mind... Being seventeen and starting their senior year of high school. Sarah had missed her period and come crying to him. He'd assured her she wouldn't be a single mother. He'd marry her and make things right. That they were going to end up in that place anyway, so what if they got there faster than expected? Luckily it was a false alarm.

His air left his lungs in a shaky *whoosh*. He didn't need to say anything. His mother could hear the unsaid words over the silence on the line.

"Mmhmm. So how would you react if you had your entire future dangling on the edge? And jump to the conclusion that you wouldn't be upset by her decision? You know she loves you. She didn't want you to hate her, so she let you go."

"But I wouldn't have hated her and she should have known that." His voice was as weak as his argument.

"Fear is a terrible motivator. The real questions are, will you let her past actions that can't be changed dictate your future with Sarah? Is this forgivable? Is there enough love between you two to move past this and build back your foundation stronger than it was?"

Like the petulant child he was, Cornelius pouted at her words. "I'm thirty-one years old. I hate it when you're all logical and right, Mama."

She laughed and the sound eased the ache in his soul. "I'll always be your mother. And here for you no matter what. Now, go talk things out with that sweet girl."

Cornelius hung up with his mom and worked on his plan to fix the fight with Sarah.

Chapter Twenty-Three

"You're going to move? To New York?" Becca stared at Sarah as if she'd grown three heads.

"It's an option. One I have to pursue." Sarah shoved her make-up bag into the small suitcase on her bed. It might be rash to leave hours after Corey had dumped her, but she had a chance and was seizing it. "I can't let my career die. I need a job." She needed to get the hell out of Fallbank. Corey had disappeared after their break-up and she wanted to be gone when he did return. Her heart couldn't take seeing him. Not this soon. Never might be too soon.

Becca crossed her arms and glared. "But I thought you said you were staying here and opening your own firm?"

Sarah paused and looked up at her cousin. "No. I said I was thinking about it. Investigating a lease for an office space. I never said it was for sure." And now it was off the table. She was either going back to Seattle and the agency there or to New York, to take a job with the company that had bought out her Seattle firm and let her go, then called her and offered her the job of her dreams with one catch — moving to the east coast offices.

"I think you're being too rash about this. You were in a good place. The family's back together. Even Hop is going to stay for a while... I think." Becca sighed. "This will break Gran's heart."

It was Sarah's turn to glower. "Don't you dare guilt me for thinking about my life. Choosing what I need to do to make a living. Are you going to berate me the entire time we drive to the airport? Because if so, I'm getting a ride-share."

Her cousin held up her hands in the universal sign for surrender. "Okay, that was out of line. You have every right to do what's best for you. I just think that's here. These past couple of months are the happiest I've seen you in years, Sarah. Don't lose that."

Too late. She'd lost Corey and with that her happiness, especially in Fallbank. She slumped onto the edge of the bed. "I wish I could tell you I'm going to be okay, but I'm not. I don't know how long it will take to get even a fraction of back to where I was when I lived in Seattle. What I do know is that I need distance right now. I can't be in town and see the pitying looks. Run into Corey while at dinner. *Live next door* to him."

She shook her head. "No. I can't." She swallowed back the tears threatening to fall again. The past few hours had been awful and filled with sobbing. Her heart begged to stay, to fight for him. Her head told her to run far and fast. The call for the job had come through right before Corey had found out and broken up with her. She'd wanted his opinion. It wasn't as if Sarah had been overjoyed for the chance, but now she was glad she hadn't turned it down on the spot. She'd had the prudence to at least consider things and hold her tongue on the phone.

Sarah looked up at Becca. "I need this. I'm not saying I will move, but I'm not saying I won't. I can't make any promises right now."

"Okay. I get that."

* * * *

Hours later, Sarah waited for her chance to exit the plane with her carryon at hand. This would be a quick trip to New York, but if things worked out, she'd be out here for much longer the next time, when she moved across the country. Her head and heart were a complete chaotic mess at war with one another. And she was exhausted from the turmoil. Sleep had eluded her on the flight and her mind whirled the entire time. She looked forward to grabbing a cab and getting to her hotel to sleep. The time change meant it was past midnight and she still had an hour before getting to her lodging in the city. A couple walked hand-in-hand in front of her and it took all her strength not to throw herself onto the ground and throw a toddler tantrum. What had she done in a past life to deserve this one? Orphaned at ten, given the perfect partner just to have their relationship blow up not once, but twice. How much suffering and loss could one person take?

When she checked in and struggled up to her room, Sarah fell onto the bed and curled into a ball. She didn't bother with washing her face or brushing her teeth. She closed her eyes and prayed for sleep.

The morning dawned bright and sunny. Sarah winced at the light streaming into her room and dragged herself into the shower. Once dressed, she claimed a cup of coffee from the hotel lobby and set out.

The humid heat smacked into her as soon as she stepped foot outside. "At least there's sun," she mumbled to herself. Glancing around like the tourist she was, Sarah sought out the direction she needed to go for her interview. Walking loosened her muscles and the busy, crowded streets fascinated her. There were so many more people than Seattle. Or maybe it was that the city itself was so small from a geography perspective that it turned everyone into sardines. Regardless, she was grateful for the distraction. It helped pull her mind to the here and now to get into the mindset she needed for her meetings.

The towering steel skyscraper Sarah stood outside was intimidating in a way she'd never experienced in Seattle. There were plenty of soaring buildings downtown there, yet here the vibe was different. Maybe it was the history that permeated everything — even new construction held an oldness that had seeped in from the ground.

Someone bumped into her and as Sarah turned to apologize, the pedestrian snarled at her. Rolling his eyes, the man snapped something about idiot tourists then walked on. She was taken aback by the interaction and left wondering why people felt the need to be so rude.

She shook off the irritated sensation left behind as she made her way up to the floor the firm operated from. She wished she'd realized how much the bustle and pulsing demand to go-go-go wasn't held to the outside. The need to hurry and cursory exchanges of words was the standard, not the exception. Her west-coast upbringing chafed at the urgency with which everyone moved. Even during interviews and learning about the company, if she spoke too long or took her time answering, she felt the impatience. The Human

Resources team made her an offer at the end of the day. The salary and benefits package was generous and Sarah couldn't say there wasn't some inkling of temptation. Yet when she asked for two weeks to decide, they'd countered with one week and that left her feeling dissatisfied.

Too unsettled to go straight back to her hotel for the evening, Sarah wandered the streets, thinking she'd grab a taxi to take her back. A trickle of happiness went through her at the prospect of getting lost. Along the way, she noticed how little green there was in the city and sought out a park.

Along her journey, she found a local bookstore and ducked inside. She'd hoped this would be the mood boost she was looking for. After all, a new stack of romance books could lift anyone's spirits. Making a lap around the store, she couldn't locate the shelf she was looking for. Sarah looped around twice more before admitting defeat and seeking out an employee.

"Excuse me," she asked a younger man with a name tag on. "Could you direct me to the romance book section? I can't find it."

A single twist of his lips and raise of his eyebrows was his patronizing nonverbal response. He waited for a long moment, then said, "We don't have that kind of section at this store. Is there a real book I can help you find?"

Asshole.

Sarah pinned her most saccharine smile on her face. "No, I'm good. I only read from the top- grossing genre that amasses more than a billion dollars in annual sales. Why would I read any of those other, lesser genres that can't even compete?"

She stomped out of the shop, fuming over the jerky attitude that guy had thrown at her. After a few more blocks of walking and working up a sweat, she stumbled upon a small fenced-in green space. "Perfect," she said and sauntered in.

The pathway was crushed gravel and the crunching noise her shoes made was pleasant to her ears. Surrounded by trees, flowers and grass, Sarah released the tension in her body. Birds chirped and squirrels chased one another through branches. A sense of home seeped into her bones. Rounding a corner, she jerked to a stop. The sight of a woman in a wedding dress arrested her. A photographer knelt and snapped pictures as she moved through a grassy plot. The gown's voluminous skirts swayed and sparkled in the late afternoon light.

Sarah's heart pounded. It was a sign—the surrounding, the feeling of home and the wedding dress modeled in front of her. She knew where she belonged...and with whom. Corey might not forgive her right away, but he deserved for her to try. When things got tough with him, she'd run away again. She'd spent too many years in a place that allowed her to pretend she wasn't still bleeding out inside, that she wasn't desolate and yearning for human connection, that her job fulfilled in enough to make life worthwhile. It was time to make changes for the better, not worse. And to prove to Corey that she was with him for better or worse.

Sarah was a fan of romance novels. She had an e-reader packed with them. One thing they'd taught her was that when love grew challenging, a grand gesture was the solution. Staring at the woman in the exquisitely fussy gown in front of her, Sarah saw her plan come to life. She spun around and raced back to the street and hailed a cab. Her flight back wasn't until tomorrow morning, but she needed to get to the airport. Maybe there was a last plane out that she could grab a seat on.

As she sat in the cab, Sarah pulled out her phone and made three phone calls. The first to the firm she'd left an hour earlier. The second to the agency in Seattle. And the third to the realtor in Fallbank.

* * * *

Cornelius walked into Three Sisters on a mission — find out where the hell Sarah went. He hadn't seen her at the house since their fight and the desperation was wearing on him. The bell above the door jingled as an alert to his entrance and Gran bustled through the door leading to the stock room.

"Hello, Cornelius. What brings you in today?" She smiled, but held back from her normal joyful hug for him.

He steeled his nerves and adjusted his glasses. "Hi, Esmerelda, I'm looking for Sarah. Do you know where she is?"

"Why would you want that information? Last I heard from my granddaughter, you weren't wanting to talk to her at all." She cocked a hip and despite the upturn of her lips, she was giving him her best Look. Her eyes held an anger he hadn't seen since his teenage years when he and Sarah would get caught past curfew.

Clearing his throat, he attempted to speak without betraying the fear Gran was putting in him. "I was a bit rash and upset last time she and I spoke." He paused, unsure of how much Sarah had shared with her grandmother and didn't want to betray her past actions just in case. "I'm hoping to fix that. Apologize for how I reacted."

Gran pursed her lips and took a few steps closer. "How do you plan to make this up to her? I won't have her devastated like I found her last time." She crossed her arms and full-out glared. "Do you know what she looked like when I showed up at her house? In a ball on the floor bawling her eyes out. She could barely speak." The older woman who looked like she wouldn't hurt a bee, poked a finger at his chest. Hard. "After what she confessed to you! How could you walk away from her?"

"I-I-I wasn't thinking. We were both caught up in too many emotions and I freaked out." His emotional dam burst. The pain of losing Sarah — twice now — of picturing her sobbing on the floor of her house, having to shoulder the burden of accidentally getting pregnant and walking into a clinic alone. All of it crashed through him and he broke down. Tears fell from his eyes. Cornelius yanked his glasses off and swiped at the wetness.

Gran wrapped her arms around him and he cried on her shoulder. "Oh, honey. I'm sorry." She rubbed his back in soothing circles. "I know how much you two love one another, but I have to protect my grandchild, too. It'll be okay."

"I didn't know. She never let on. At all. I would have supported her. If she'd told me, I wouldn't have forced her into anything." His pain poured out of him. "I can't imagine how scared and alone Sarah felt going through all of this by herself. I thought she and I were solid. That she'd tell me anything. It hurts that she felt like she couldn't."

"It's all right. Things will work out." Gran patted his back as Cornelius lifted his head and breathed deep to steady himself. "You two will fix your relationship. Just don't take twelve years this time. You're both mature enough now to sort it all out."

"Thanks, Gran." He sniffled, wiped at his cheeks once more then put his glasses back on. "I promise I'll never react like this again. Please help me find her so I can make it right?"

"She's in New York City."

"What? How... Why would she go there?"

Gran shook her head. "The company that bought out her Seattle firm wants to hire her to work in their east coast offices. She went for an interview."

He gaped at her. "When did they even have time? We fought yesterday. I slept at my office for one night!"

"They called her yesterday morning. She took a flight out yesterday afternoon. Sarah won't be back until for a couple of days at the earliest."

"Shit." Cornelius grimaced and looked at Gran. "Sorry." An idea formed in his head. "Okay. I can work with that. Yeah. It gives me time." He pressed a kiss to Gran's cheek and grinned. "Thanks, Gran. I have to go."

She chuckled. "As long as you mend the relationship with Sarah, that's all I want for you two."

With a buoyed sense of purpose, Cornelius raced out of the store and to his truck. Once home, he booked a flight to Eureka and called the neighborhood kid up the road to check on Lolli and Jelly. Throwing a quick bag together, he called Hop for a ride.

"What's going on, Cor?" Hop asked as Cornelius jumped into the car. "Where's the fire?"

Lifting one side of his mouth, Cornelius answered, "I'm making moves to my life, starting with a visit to my parents."

His friend side-eyed him while still balancing watching the road as he drove. "What are you doing? You aren't moving, are you?"

"I'm not sure." Cornelius turned the idea over in his mind. Moving to Seattle would be easier than New

York, but he'd do whatever it took to win back his Sarie. "That depends."

"On what? How can you move? You're half owner of Timber Logging Company."

Cornelius shrugged. "Yeah, but maybe I sell. Or become a silent partner and let Jack take over. Oh, by the way, while he's out on his honeymoon and I'm...busy, could you stand in?"

"Me?" Hop asked and threw Cornelius an are-you-crazy look. "Isn't there someone else who works for you that you'd rather tag in?"

"Julio can manage the crews, but I'd like if you could take care of the day-to-day office operations. You have the skillset for it and I trust you." He fished the keys to the office out of his pocket and tossed them in the empty drink holder. "Call if you have questions, but it should be straightforward. You worked at TLC in high school. We haven't changed that much."

Signs for the Portland airport appeared and Hop guided the car toward departures. "I don't know, Cornelius. This doesn't sound like the best of ideas."

"Sure it is." Cornelius said as he opened the car door. "You need a job anyway, right? For however long you're sticking around town, this can be yours." He shut the door before his friend could respond. With a wave, Cornelius loped off into the airport.

A short flight and ride-share later, Cornelius was walking into his parent's house. He was tired, but happy. He had a plan and a purpose. Time, for once, was on his side. He bid his mom and dad a good night, ignoring their questions about his spur-of-the-moment visit. Then he collapsed on the bed in the guest room and slept well with hope for him and Sarah dancing in his dreams.

Chapter Twenty-Four

Weary and blinking with sleep, Sarah opened her eyes as her flight landed back in Seattle after her whirlwind trip to New York. It was her second night in a row of little to no sleep, but this time she'd been on a plane home, back to where she belonged. The New York firm had understood her decision to run down their offer, and the conversation had been short. Over faster than she'd expected, which was the one perk of the east coast waste-no-time vibe, she guessed.

The second conversation with Selena at Pateli and Schultz Marketing took a little longer. Selena had negotiated hard to convince Sarah to join their agency, but Sarah's mind was made up. She knew where she belonged and with whom. Her goal was to make it happen. Living in Seattle for so long had given her the perspective she needed to understand that while a career at a big marketing firm was exciting for a while and even fulfilling in some aspects, she could attain the same accomplishment with her own small boutique business — maybe even more when it meant she could have closer relationships with clients and see the fruits of her success firsthand with the places in town.

Letting herself accept she was worthy of being loved and accepted by her family, no matter her past actions, had broken down the last of the walls she'd built. She wanted to be closer to her sister and cousins and Gran. She wanted a life with Corey...if he wanted one with her. She couldn't force that answer, but she would hope. And make a grand gesture to let him know how serious she was about him, that she did trust him.

Once home, she showered and drove into town, back to the wedding gown shop. Once there, Sarah paced until the owner unlocked the doors with a smile.

"Hi, can I help you?"

"Yes. I need to buy a dress."

Lana held open the door. "Come on in. You're Sarah, right? Your sister just got married?"

She nodded. "Yep, that's me. Thanks, Lana. I hope I'm not blowing up your appointment schedule."

Lana shook her head with a chuckle. "No, you're all good. My first appointment of the day isn't for an hour. And even if it was right now, I always account for walk-ins and have staff on hand." She tilted her head at Sarah. "What are you looking for?"

"A wedding dress." Sarah giggled as Lana widened her eyes. "And I need to walk out with it today. As soon as I can."

"Oh, wow. We can try for sure, but I can't make guarantees. Most of the time we order with the measurements needed and it takes a couple of months to get in. Then there's alterations. Very few come in and walk out with a gown the same day." Lana wrung her hands and her voice held a note of panic. "Not to mention it can take time to find the right dress for you."

"No worries on that concern. I already know which one I want." Sarah beelined to where she'd found the all-lace strapless gown when shopping here before. Heart stampeding in her chest, she whispered, "Please still be here. Please, please, please."

A rush of giddiness caught her as she spotted *the dress*. Beaming, she pulled it out and held the fabric up like a trophy. "Success!"

Lana laughed. "Well, for the first step. Let's get it on you and see if we can accomplish your goals."

Sarah shimmied over to the changing room. "Today is both our lucky days. You get to name whatever price you want for helping me and I get to make my dreams come true." She hoped, at least.

Hours later, Sarah stormed into Three Sisters. Her entire jubilant mood was in tatters. Her grandmother was behind the counter. On the verge of tears, Sarah swallowed hard. "Do you know where Corey is, by chance? I've been looking for him all over the place."

Gran furrowed her brows. "I don't. He's not at home?"

Sarah shook her head. "Or his office. I've checked. I've looked at all of the coffee shops, restaurants and bars in town that he likes to frequent. I can't find him."

"Find who?" Hop asked as he walked out from the back of the store.

She threw her cousin a half-hearted wave hello. "Corey. He's just gone."

"He's in Eureka visiting his parents. He'll be back in a couple days."

Both Sarah and Gran blinked in confusion at Hop. "How do you know?" Sarah questioned.

Her cousin shrugged. "I gave him a ride to the airport. He left yesterday night."

"But he…" Gran trailed off her thought and closed her mouth. Then she rounded on her granddaughter. "Why are you looking for him, anyway? I thought you were heartbroken over him."

Her tender heart stumbled in its rhythm. "I was. I am. But I understand his response. I didn't trust him enough and that's a hard betrayal to get past. I hoped to talk to him and change his mind." A new plan swirled in her mind. "Hop, what are you doing here? Can you run the store for a couple days so I can steal Gran away?"

Her cousin shook his head. "No way! I've never been in charge here. Besides, I'm covering for Cornelius at TLC while he's gone."

Gran spoke up. "I can call Becca and Arianna. I'm sure between the two of them, we'll be fine. If not, Three Sisters can handle a day of being closed."

"Bridget will flip! She already closed for two days for the wedding." Sarah shuddered to think of her baby sister's wrath at finding out Sarah had been the cause for Three Sisters missing another day of sales this month. "No way."

"It will be fine. What do you need me for?" Gran walked over to pick up her phone and started typing out a text.

"We're going to Eureka. I'm making my grand gesture and you have to join me. We leave in the morning."

Sarah went home and collapsed into bed. The exhaustion of the wedding, the blow-up with Corey and the less than twenty-four-hour trip to New York slammed into her like a freight train. She rolled onto the pillow and a crinkling noise vibrated under her ear. Raising up, she examined the pillow before sticking her hand inside the cloth case. Dragging out the slip of paper she grasped, her breath caught as she recognized Corey's handwriting.

You still feel like home.

The message was simple, but perfect. She knew he had to have left this before finding out about her pregnancy termination, but it gave her the hope she so needed. Holding the small square of neon-colored paper in her hand, Sarah fell into a deep sleep.

The next day, when Gran and Sarah were on the seven-minute ride from the Eureka airport to the house that Cornelius' parents owned, Gran asked, "Tell me what a grand gesture is again?"

Sarah smiled and smoothed her hands over the fabric covering her knees. Her nerves were out in full force as she dodged the questioning glances from the driver in the rearview mirror. "In romance novels, there's always a dark moment toward the end where the couple faces a crisis to their relationship. One of them goes out of their way to do something wild and thoughtful to prove their love and win back the other. That's what I'm doing here."

Gran eyed her and arched one brow. "Well, you've got the wild part of this checked off. Let's see how Cornelius feels about all of this." She paused. "And maybe I need to borrow some of these books. Sounds like fascinating reading."

As the car turned up the road to stop at the drive of the house, Sarah reached out to grab Gran's hand and squeezed. "Sure thing. I hope this works out as well in real life as it does in the novel."

* * * *

Cornelius eyed his latest woodworking project with criticism. He'd been working on this piece for over two months and it was his most important one to date. His freshly purchased eleven-piece set of wood carving hand tools sat waiting alongside the various grades of sandpaper he'd bought at the local hardware store today. Cornelius wanted this perfect for the use he had in mind.

A breeze filtered in from the water just a few yards away from where Cornelius worked on his parents' back porch. He traced his fingertips over the curves of the wood, testing for roughness and splinters. A small patch over the rounded stomach abraded and he reached for the convex gauge chisel and brushed it across the uneven spot. Then he grabbed the P400 grit sandpaper and rubbed with a hint of pressure. Another touch test left him satisfied.

The door opening behind him pulled Cornelius' attention and he turned his head. "Hey, Mom. Great timing, I need your unabused fingertips."

His mother laughed. "What on earth does that mean?" She came around and looked at the carving on the table. "Oh, this is darling. What beautiful work."

He grinned at the praise. "Thanks, Mama."

Her hair was slowly returning and with the sunlight's angle, made her head look like it was ringed in a fine layer of fuzz. Warmth filled Cornelius' chest. It was a much-appreciated sign that she was healing and growing stronger and healthier each day. Her treatments were complete and heavy monitoring would be ongoing for now. His relief was palpable. "I need you to check it for any spots that are uneven or bumpy and need smoothing. My hands are all calloused so I can't always pick up everything. This needs to be perfect."

She lifted the figure and took her time exploring every angle and inch of it. "You have such a talent for this, Cor. I'm amazed you've been doing woodworking for just a year. Remarkable." She handed it back to him with a lift of her lips. "It's perfect."

A glow of happiness expanded from the center of his ribs and spread through his limbs. Her proclamation meant he was ready. Well, almost. He needed one last item. "One last test. Do you have Grandma's engagement ring?"

His mother raised her blue eyes to him. "I do. Why do you ask?"

"I was hoping your offer to have it when I was ready still stands." The time was right, though he needed to win back the woman first.

A guarded expression overtook his mother's face. "It does. As long as you're certain about who you offer this heirloom to."

"I am." His stomach twisted into knots. He'd expected his mom to be the easy, soft one to convince of his decision. It turned out his father hadn't had concerns when they had chatted earlier in the morning. Now as the afternoon was melting into evening, Cornelius was set to take this last step and head back to Fallback for Sarah's arrival back from the east coast.

"Who do you plan to give this to?" Her tone gave nothing away.

"Sarah." His voice was strong and sure, just like his faith in his choice. "She's my soulmate, Mama. I messed up and should have stayed to hash things out when I found out about her abortion in college. You were right.

271

I'm willing to do whatever it takes to fix things between us."

Her grin was wide and dazzling. "I'm so happy for you, baby. I've been waiting for you to find the person you wanted to spend your life with." She reached out and hugged him tight.

A tightness grew in his throat and Cornelius swallowed to push it away. He would not be overwhelmed by his emotions again. Then he blinked and a tear ran down his cheek. "Dammit." He chuckled, then sniffed back the flood of feelings. "Stop making me cry, woman."

His mother's laugh vibrated through him. "Sorry, sweetie. I did my best to raise an emotionally balanced son who wasn't afraid to express himself." She leaned back and cupped his cheeks. "Looks like I succeeded." She pressed a kiss to his forehead, then stood. "Now, let's go get that ring."

Cornelius snatched up the wooden figure he'd carved and followed after her. She went into the primary bedroom, then shuffled through a drawer to pull out a small black velvet box. "Here it is."

Cornelius set down the figurine on the top of the dresser and with a steady hand, he plucked up the square and opened it. The ring was as he remembered. Elegant, sophisticated, timeless. The stones sparkled up at him. He lifted the cool metal and placed the band into the basket of the cradled arms he'd carved. It slipped in and sat like the offering it was intended to be.

"Oh, Cornelius. That is lovely." She looked up at him. "You've been thinking about this for while, huh? To have this ready now?"

"Yeah," he whispered. "Since she got back into town." He cut his eyes to the side at his mom. "Is that weird? Stalkery?"

His mother laughed. "No, honey. You went with your instincts. Plus you've given her all the space and time she needs."

"I'll be right back," he said then ran out to the room he slept in. Shuffling around in this duffle bag, he found the oak box, another creation of his. Walking back into his parent's room, he lifted the lid. A pillow of dark blue fabric filled the bottom. Cornelius placed the figurine holding the ring into the plush cushion. It rested as he'd imagined it. "There. Now, it's perfect."

"Who knew you were such a romantic?" His mother hugged him again. "I can't wait to hear the whole story of how you propose."

Cornelius knew it needed to be spectacular. With all the romance books Sarah read, the bar was sky high. He needed to step up. He opened his mouth to reply when the doorbell chimed through the house.

After a moment, his father yelled. "Cornelius, it's for you."

Drawing his brows together, he walked with his mother trailing after him. Who would be at the door for him at his parents' house? That didn't make any sense. He rounded the corner and spotted Gran standing in the entrance. "Wha..."

Gran grabbed his dad's arm and gestured to Cornelius' mother. "Why don't we give these two a few minutes to speak." She hustled the three of them out and onto the porch. She stepped forward and Sarah came into view.

The sight almost sent him to his knees. "Sarah," he croaked. She took a step closer and he braced himself up with one hand on the wall. She was a fucking *vision*.

Sarah was just inside the house and backlit by the sunlight. She wore flawless, natural make-up with the pop of her red lipstick. Her hair curled and shimmered around her bare shoulders. Her body was encased in the most exquisite wedding gown he'd ever pictured her wearing. The neckline dipped like a heart between her breasts and the white lace fabric clung to her curves all the way down until flaring into a short train at her feet.

Cornelius pressed a hand over his chest and rubbed. Inside, the sensation of his heart exploding made him lightheaded. "Princess..."

Sarah lifted her eyes to him. "Corey, I'm so sorry. Please, please forgive me. I'll do whatever it takes to put us back together. I promise I'll make things right." She pressed those red lips together, but he caught the tremble there. "I know I can't undo what I did and I stand by my decision, but I should have told you. I made decisions for you and I shouldn't have. I won't make that mistake again. And I'll never leave you. Please, give us one more chance." She walked closer until a handful of steps lay between them. Sarah beseeched him with those dark brown eyes of hers. They sparkled with unshed tears. "Will you marry me? I swear to make you happy every day for the rest of our lives."

"Sarie." He closed the distance between them, hauled her into his arms and kissed the hell out of her.

Chapter Twenty-Five

"Corey. My Corey," she murmured in the moments they paused for air as they kissed and kissed and *kissed*. Sarah wound her arms around his neck and held tight to him. She reveled in his hands holding her close so their bodies lined up without a millimeter of space between. She sighed into his hold and every worry and fear that had kept her from sleep and caused her muscles to ache with tension drained from her body.

"Wait!" Corey exclaimed then pulled back.

With wide, intense eyes, she gasped. What happened? Cold terror gripped her heart. He'd changed his mind. "Cor—"

"I'll be two seconds. Don't move." He held up one hand. Then he dipped in and stole a kiss before turning and running down the hall.

Leaving her to gape at his retreat. How was she supposed to react to this? What was this all about? "C-Corey?" she called after him.

"Stay there," he shouted from another room.

So she did. A few moments later, he emerged and came toward her with a box in his hands. He was an adorable mess. His hair was disheveled from her hands, faint smears of red lipstick were on his lips and skin and his glasses were still tilted. Her heart squeezed with love for this man...her perfect match who she didn't wish to spend even one more day apart from. He hadn't let her get the rest of her plan out before kissing her senseless. She opened her mouth but stopped when he shook his head.

"Sarie. My princess. You own me, heart and soul. I'm sorry I was such an idiot." She went to speak again, but he reached out and laced his fingers with hers. "I want you to know that I will never stop loving you, no matter what. And I know you trust me. You were scared and alone and I'm sorry I wasn't there. I should have gone with you to Seattle instead of staying back in Fallbank. I will follow you anywhere, Sarie. Seattle, New York, the moon! Wherever you want to be is where I want to be, as long as I'm with you."

She wept at his sweet declaration. "I love you, Corey. I want to marry you. And live in Fallbank. I turned down the job offers and I'm signing a lease for my own office."

He knelt down in front of her and held out the small wooden chest. Then he lifted the lid and took her breath away.

"I love you, Sarah Wildes, and I always will. Will you marry me, too?"

She stared down at the petite carving of a frog with a tiara on its head and curved arms holding a beautiful ring. "Oh, Corey," she breathed. "This is gorgeous." She flicked her gaze up to his. "You made this? For me?"

He nodded. "I started when you came back to Fallbank, before we got back together. You've held my heart since I was ten years old and I never want it back. You're my princess. Will you be my queen?"

Love and joy surged so strong in her veins that she threw herself at him, then thanked God for his quick reflexes. He lunged up and caught her with one arm and let their momentum stumble their bodies back to the wall. Holding the sharp corners of the wood away from them, he kissed her again. Heat licked along her skin as he licked into her mouth. Desire flared along her nerves as their tongues twined and lips slid along one another's. She moaned and arched against the hard length of his body, rubbing to try to ease the building ache of lust.

With a groan, Corey leaned back and rested his forehead to hers. "We have to slow down. Our families are right outside and I don't want to ruin this dress. Jesus, this dress, Sarie. You look like every fantasy come true. I want to worship every inch of you."

"Mmm, that sounds like heaven. Let's go with that plan." She tried to nudge him down the hall and he laughed.

Corey put a few inches of space between them and she whimpered. With a wink that made her lady bits flutter in anticipation, he lifted the ring out of the box, then set the holder on the ground. Grasping her left hand, he slipped the band down her ring finger, then kissed her warm skin.

"I want to marry you today," she blurted out.

He cocked his head. "Come again?"

"Now. Today. I want to get married. We've waited long enough and I don't want to spend another night not married to you."

"But, we can't—"

"Yes, we can." She flashed a tentative smile at him. "I called the courthouse and they will perform the ceremony this afternoon if we want. I just have to confirm with them."

Corey shouted with excitement and scooped her up into his arms—bridal style, of course. "We're getting married! Today!"

She full-on laughed as he hurried out to where his parents and Gran waited on the porch. She clung to the neck of her soon-to-be-husband as he burst outside.

"Let's go! We're getting married. Now. Right now." Corey's grin was so huge she couldn't help wondering if it hurt to smile so wide. Then she realized her expression mirrored his and that no pain would be felt today for either of them.

"What?" Clarissa said as she bounced her gaze back and forth from Corey to Sarah.

"We're going to the courthouse." Sarah laughed and nuzzled closer to Corey's neck. "But I think a quick change of your clothes might be nice."

He glanced down and flashed her a sheepish twist of his lips. "I'll be back in ten minutes." He pressed a kiss to her cheek, set her feet to the floor and dashed off inside. "Pops, I'm borrowing a suit."

Boyd cupped his hands around his mouth and yelled back, "Whatever you need, son."

Clarissa grabbed Sarah and squeezed her tight. "Oh my. I am *so* happy for you two. You and Cornelius somehow seem to be in sync at all times. You know he was here to get his grandmother's ring?"

Sarah held up her hand and wiggled her fingers. "He got to that part. After I proposed to him first."

Boyd's laugh boomed out. He scooped her up in a bear hug. "Couldn't ask for a better daughter-in-law. Knew you and our stubborn son would sort things out one day."

Clarissa slipped an arm around her husband's shoulders. "We should maybe try to clean ourselves up, too."

Gran walked over, smoothing out the dress she wore. "I will express my gratitude at getting a little hint of what was going to happen so I could prepare." She cocked one brow and nodded her head toward Sarah. "You should have seen the looks we got while leaving the airport after she changed into that. She got dressed in the bathroom next to baggage claim! I thought our driver was going to swallow his tongue."

Corey's parents laughed and ducked inside to freshen up. Sarah turned to her grandmother and they walked inside. Sarah ducked into the powder room to fix her make-up and reapply her lipstick. She loved how well Corey wore it after kissing him. When she exited, she wandered over to Gran. "Thank you for coming with me. I couldn't do this without you."

Gran flapped a hand in the air. "Psshh. Yes you could. You didn't need me to have the bravery to get what you wanted. You never have."

Sarah nodded with a smile. "Asking Corey to marry me, yes. But getting married without you here, no. There's no way I couldn't have you here with me for this." And she thanked her former company for the generous severance pay she hadn't had to dip into yet because two last-minute, same-day plane tickets had been hellaciously expensive.

"That is true. I would have had your hide if you'd eloped without me." Gran fixed Sarah with a Look.

"You do know Bridget and your cousins are going to riot when they hear you and Cornelius snuck off to a courthouse."

"A chance I'm willing to take." She lifted one corner of her lips as giddiness thrummed through her. "I'm not risking another day not being married to Corey. I'm done messing around when it comes to him."

"I couldn't agree more, my Sarie." Corey emerged from the hall looking devastating in a black suit that clung to his shoulders and arms. The pants shifted over his muscular thighs in ways that made Sarah spike with envy. He held out his hand and she placed hers in. "Shall we, my frog princess?"

"Yes." She beamed. "Let's go get married, my frog prince."

* * * *

Cornelius laced his fingers with Sarah's as they walked across the square to the courthouse. Along the way, a street vendor selling flowers caught his eye. He pressed a kiss to his wife's hand, then jogged over to purchase a bouquet of pink peonies and blue hydrangeas. When he returned to Sarah's side, he presented the blooms with a smile and pressed his lips to her blushing cheek.

"Already winning at being the best husband." She dipped her head and inhaled the soft scent.

"The smell of peonies always reminds me of you. I couldn't resist."

Then they walked up the steps and into the Victorian-style building to get married. The ceremony was short and sweet. Cornelius stared into Sarah's gorgeous brown eyes as he swore to love her for the rest of his life and she vowed the same. She managed to surprise him again when she produced a brand-new wedding band for him. He gaped as she slid the black tungsten-carbide band inlaid with a thin strip of dark oak onto his finger. She'd winked and smirked at his astonishment.

When they were pronounced wedded, Cornelius gathered his bride to him and kissed her long and slow. He relished the delightful way Sarah melted into his embrace and met each press and touch of his tongue with her own. When she nipped his lower lip, he chuckled and lifted his head with his glasses fogged up. His Sarie would always know how to heat him up.

Applause sounded in the judge's chambers and they grinned at the small gathering of family. Cornelius blinked away the stinging sensation in his eyes. He was ecstatic to have both of his parents present for this. A pang hit the middle of his chest and he snuggled Sarah closer. He hurt for her not having her mom and dad present, but was grateful Gran was with her. His Sarie deserved the world, and he would do whatever he needed to give her everything her heart desired.

"Let's take these newlyweds out to celebrate and then they can enjoy their wedding night," his father announced. "Come on, we did a little magic of our own and got reservations at the best restaurant in town and you have the turret suite at the pink mansion off Humboldt Bay."

After being seated at a large circular table in a corner, they celebrated with delicious food and Sarah's favorite dessert, crème brûlée, that Cornelius spoon-fed to his bride. He grew more and more aroused with every lick of her tongue and wrap of her lips around the spoon. Ready to be alone with Sarah, he began looking for ways to wrap up this meal when champagne was delivered for everyone.

Gran raised her glass. "A toast to the bride and groom. Sarah, you have always been my strong, independent granddaughter who recognized what she wanted in life and grabbed for it. You've never let anything hold you back and that's a characteristic I've always admired. You were ten years old when you met the boy you announced was your 'best friend.' At twelve, you walked into our kitchen and almost gave your grandfather a heart attack when you declared you would marry the boy next door." Esmeralda blinked away the wetness gleaming in her eyes. "And now you have. At long last." The table laughed at her words before she continued. "I couldn't be prouder of the woman you've become or the man you've chosen as your life partner. You two complement one another in ways not many can achieve. You're like planets orbiting around each other. It's beautiful to watch. Here's to a lifetime of happiness and love for the both of you."

His parents raised their glasses alongside Gran while Cornelius twined his arm through Sarah's before sipping from his glass. Leaning in to kiss her, Cornelius lingered over her lips until his father coughed loud enough to rattle the table.

"Save that for tonight, Cornelius. We're out in public. Be respectable."

His wife's cheeks flushed, but she shifted closer to whisper in his ear. "You can disrespect me anytime and anywhere, baby."

Cornelius clenched his jaw against a groan and adjusted his hardening cock under the table. "You are in such trouble when we get to the hotel," he murmured and Sarah winked.

"Promise, promises."

His restraint snapped. Launching to his feet, Cornelius gripped Sarah's hand in his. "This has been the best day of my life, getting to marry the woman of my dreams. I'm so grateful and lucky you three were here to witness our vows and celebrate with this outstanding meal." He looked at the gorgeous female beside him with a soft smile playing on her features. "But it's time for us to depart for the night."

"See you in a few days," Gran called as the two of them walked just fast enough to turn heads in the restaurant. Although, he conceded, that could also be his breathtaking Sarah in a wedding dress that looked custom designed for her that caused everyone to stare.

The hotel was less than a block from where they had eaten and the crisp night air cooled the heat burning between them to a simmer. Impressed by the urgency pulsing through his blood, Cornelius checked them in with expediency and had his princess inside the turret room in mere minutes.

Encircling her waist, he spun to press her back to the door and took her lips like a savage hellbent on conquering. He plunged his tongue along hers to taste the sweetness persisting from the creamy dessert and wine from dinner. It wasn't enough. He needed Sarah's rich, delectable flavor in his mouth. Falling to his knees, he hiked her dress up to her hips and pressed his face at the apex of her thighs. Her needy scent drove him wild and he yanked the silk thong barrier off her legs. Dragging one leg onto his shoulder, Cornelius feasted on his mouthwatering bride until she cried out his name and her essence danced along his tastebuds like the sweetest ambrosia.

Then he gathered her trembling body in his arms and turned to the massive four-poster bed where he spent the rest of the night pleasuring his queen until the sky lightened with pinks and pale yellows and they both fell into an exhausted sleep.

* * * *

Sarah luxuriated in the warmth of her husband's nude body beneath hers as he drifted his fingers up and down her spine. She was boneless and satiated as she lay draped over him. They'd spent the past two days and three nights locked away in their suite with room service deliveries as their single contact to the outside world. Neither of them had worn a stitch of clothing since stripping out of their wedding clothes and Sarah wasn't the least bit mad about it.

Cornelius had made love to her in every position and on every surface possible in the room. They'd made copious use of the dual-person soaking tub when her sore muscles protested. Sarah was already making a mental redesign of the bedroom at Corey's house to bring in a four-poster bed. His creative use of the poles had her addicted and she wanted to reenact those unorthodox sessions over and over. His ingenuity in the bedroom had expanded over the years and she was an eager participant in the sexcapades Cornelius offered.

"I don't want to leave," she mumbled. Sarah peeked her lids open enough to study Cornelius' handsome face. She eyed the short, scruffy beard growing in since he hadn't shaved in several days. Brushing her fingers along his sharp jaw, she said, "I like this. It's sexy. And feels amazing with your face in the middle of my legs."

Corey snickered and dipped his head to steal a kiss. "Then I'll keep it for you. Until you tell me otherwise."

With upturned lips, Sarah hummed with glee. Glasses and a beard. Who knew she'd find that so hot? Never before had her husband grown out his facial hair so she'd never considered the look on him. Now it was certain that she wanted him to keep it, at least for a while longer.

"But we do have to return to reality, my queen. As much as I'd love to spend the rest of my life naked and inside you, the world won't allow it." He kissed away her grumbled protests and shifted them to sitting upright. "But perhaps we have time for one more round..." As he tugged her to straddle him, they joined together and moved languidly until bliss overtook both their bodies.

A shower, fresh clothes and a ride share later, the couple were back at Cornelius' parents' — her new in-laws' — house. Gran was packed and saying her goodbyes for the three of them to catch their flight back to Oregon. Nervous tingles prickled along Sarah's skin. When they arrived home, they would have to face their friends and families to tell them of their elopement. Sarah winced at how Becca might react, but cringed when she thought of Bridget's response. Her little sister was going to rip Sarah a new one. It wouldn't be pretty or simple, but once Bridget recovered from her anger and hurt at missing their wedding, she would be thrilled.

At least, Sarah hoped so...

* * * *

A week later, Sarah paced outside the house that she had grown up in. Her little sister and new husband were due back from their honeymoon any minute. Stomach twisting in knots, Sarah chewed on her lower lip. She still couldn't predict how Bridget would react to finding out that she and Corey had eloped.

Becca had taken the news well. It helped that Hop had seen Sarah leaving the wedding dress shop with her gown and after coming by Three Sisters in search of Corey, connected the dots. Then he'd shared his suspicions with his sister. When Corey and Sarah stopped by the farm, Becca had taken one look at their joined hands, screeched a curse damning her brother about being right and run to sweep them into a massive hug. The memory of her cousin's happiness for them eased a bit of the anxiety-causing sweat breaking out under her arms.

A red truck swung onto the road and Sarah's heart tripled in speed. This was it. Her sister wouldn't hold a grudge forever. She wasn't the vindictive type...but Bridge was sensitive. She'd feel cheated to have missed their ceremony and gauging how long her feelings might be bruised was fuzzy for Sarah. Sarah hated that she would upset her baby sibling—it went against all of her protective instincts as the eldest child in particular after losing their parents.

The vehicle pulled into the drive and Bridget hopped out. "Sare-bear! We're back. I missed you." Her little sister ran around and threw her arms around Sarah.

"Hey, I thought I'd distracted you so no one else entered your thoughts except me." Jack climbed down with a welcoming smile. "I guess I need to work harder on my techniques."

Bridget blushed and giggled. "You did just fine, husband." She threw a wink at Jack. "I didn't want Sarah to feel slighted."

Sarah almost pretended to be injured, but decided not to. No reason to rile her sister up when there was delicate news to deliver. "How was the honeymoon?"

Her sister's dreamy expression said it all. "Wonderful." Bridget sighed. "Tahiti is stunning. The villa we had was on the water. On the actual water. Jack did fantastic in planning."

"Tahiti? That sounds amazing. Nice job, new brother."

Jack brushed off one shoulder with a smirk. "Anything to make my honeybee smile. Where's Cornelius? I figured he'd be with you."

Sarah's mouth dried. "Yeah, he's uh, inside. There's something I wanted to talk to you about me and him."

"Oh, no." Bridget covered her mouth and her eyes filled with tears. "Did you two break up again? You can't!"

"No, no, no." Sarah waved her hands as panic set in. "We didn't... I mean, we did but we're back together."

"Oh thank God. Don't scare me like that, Sarah." Bridget smacked at her sister's arm. "So what's up? I mean, it's not like you got married in the past two weeks." Her laughter died out as Sarah's guilty expression. "What?"

Swallowing down her nerves, Sarah licked her lips. "Yeah, we did. Corey and I eloped. Surprise?" She wiggled her fingers in an awkward jazz-hands gesture.

Her sister's face vacillated from happy to stunned to sad. "Are you serious?"

A wave of unease hit Sarah. Her sister was not sending signals that she was handling the news well.

Her mouth was too dry to form words. Instead, Sarah pressed her lips together and nodded.

"H-how?" Bridget wheezed. Jack hovered behind her, wrapping his arms around her in support. Sparkling tears dripped from Bridget's eyelashes.

"Well," Sarah said as her voice broke. She coughed and began again. "You see, we had a fight. A big one. The details aren't important now, but it was bad. And you know how there's always a grand gesture in romance novels?" Sarah shrugged her shoulders as her sister sniffled. "I made one of those. I bought a wedding dress, tracked down Corey, proposed and we went to the courthouse in Eureka for a civil ceremony."

"I missed my sister's wedding." Bridget's voice was small and shaky. A sob broke from her chest.

"Bridge, don't cry. I can't stand it. I'm sorry, so sorry." She grabbed her sibling into a tight hug. "I never meant to hurt you. But I couldn't lose Corey, not again. Please understand and forgive me."

She let Bridget release her emotions while Sarah held her. At some point, Cornelius came out in spite of Sarah's instructions to let her handle telling the news. In time, her baby sister's cries subsided.

Stepping back and leaning into her new husband, Bridget wiped at her cheeks. Blinking at Sarah and Corey, she asked, "You're married?"

A joyful laugh broke free from Sarah's chest. "We are."

Corey wrapped his arms around Sarah's waist from behind. "I'm sorry we rushed it, little B. We just couldn't wait any longer. You know how miserable we've both been more than anyone else. You've had to put up with my mopey ass living next door for years.

And I'm sure when you and Sarah visited, you picked up on her own hang-ups, too."

Bridget nodded, acknowledging the misery she'd witnessed in both of them for years. "That is true."

"Plus my mom has been sick." Sarah's husband's voice cracked. "Since we had my parents and Gran together, it seemed like the best chance. That or wait months more and neither of us wanted that. You can appreciate that, right? I mean, we'd already let twelve years go by."

"Holy cow, it's about time." Bridget's smile was shaky, but genuine. She pressed her clasped hands in front of her mouth with a shake of her head. "Thank God you two got it together!"

The tension burst and their group of four collapsed into a massive hug.

"Thank you, Bridge, for forgiving me for eloping. It killed me not to have you there." Sarah fought back her tears again. She was sick to death of crying.

"As long as you let me throw you two a celebratory party. I can't be left out of everything."

"You got it, baby sis."

Epilogue

Four months later

Cornelius whistled as he walked down Main Street from his parking spot to stand outside the quaint office of his wife's new work venture. Tucked between a second-life clothing shop and the hardware store that had been a staple in Fallbank for over sixty years, Magical Marketing shone with a modern chic vibe to entice customers inside. A half smile teased his mouth as Cornelius looked at the sign of a stylized frog wearing a tiara in the center of the agency's name proudly displayed over the door. It matched the tattoo over his heart.

His wife was an instant success with the local enterprises in Fallbank. The offering of a local boutique marketing firm had business owners and entrepreneurs showing up in droves. Requests from online contacts also flowed in at a steady rate, giving Sarah a very rewarding launch of her own agency.

He watched as his gorgeous bride drew with intensity on her tablet with a stylus pen. Sarah nibbled on her lower lip as she studied the mock-ups she was creating. A crisp breeze ruffled the hair at his nape and Cornelius flipped up the collar of his jacket. Autumn was setting in and he was looking forward to cuddling with Sarah in front of the fire as the weather grew colder.

Swinging the door open, he offered a grin to his Sarie and held up a brown paper bag. "Lunch? I know you ran out the door this morning in a hurry."

"Aw, thank you. I have the most thoughtful husband." She lifted up on her toes to kiss his cheek above the beard she still loved.

"I do what I can." He tossed a wink her way and began pulling out the food offerings.

Sarah snatched up the cup of carrot ginger soup with glee. After shoveling two mouthfuls in, she hummed in delight. "Just what I needed. My stomach has felt a touch off today."

"Are you okay?" Cornelius narrowed his eyes and studied her closer. She didn't look pale or sick, but he knew she hadn't slept well the night before either. "Do you need to go home and rest?"

She waved him off. "No, I'm good now. The soup hit the spot."

"If you're sure?" With assurances and a kiss, his bride of four months sent him on his way back to the offices of TLC. Two hours later a text popped up from Sarah and he snatched up his phone in haste. Maybe she had taken a turn and decided to head home and rest. He hated the thought of her being sick.

Instead a strange picture of a white stick displayed on the screen with the question, *how many lines do you see*? Peering at the image, he saw a tiny square with one pale pink line and what might be a second faint line. What the hell was this?

He typed back.

Corey: How many are there supposed to be?

Sarie: That depends on what you want the answer to be. How many do you see?

Corey: Two??

Sarie: Congratulations! You're going to be a daddy!

The speed with which he hit her number to call amazed him. "Are you serious?" he asked as soon as she picked up.

"I am." She laughed. "It dawned on me when you left that I was late, and given my queasiness, I thought I'd pick up a test. I meant to wait until we were home, but you know me. I'm impatient."

Cornelius jumped from his chair, beaming like the proud papa he would soon be. "I'm coming to get you and we're celebrating."

"Our special spot?"

"Our special spot, Portland, Seattle, Paris, the moon. Any place you want, Sarie. As long as I'm by your side, that's where I'll stay."

Wrighting the Wrongs:
The Wrong Brother
Maren Jenner

Coming October 2024

Excerpt

Leah

People are always asking how to get a guy, but I already know the secret.

Garlic.

Case in point, I started sautéing my green beans with freshly minced garlic minutes ago, and now it sounds like a herd of elephants above my head. I listen as the four Wrighting brothers thunder down the stairs, then they spill into the kitchen. It's a good-sized room until we all try to cram in it. They are not little.

All of them are at least three inches taller than my five foot nine frame and have varying degrees of muscle. Steven, the oldest, beats me to the microwave. I set my plate of chicken and mashed potatoes back on the counter then call out that I'm next.

While I'm waiting, I walk over to nudge Sebastian, my boyfriend. "Hey."

He doesn't even look up from his book.

"Sebastian!" I poke my head between him and the pages.

His hazel eyes widen as he registers my face. "Leah! Hi."

I grin back, and the microwave beeps. Steven removes his food, leaving the door wide open. Of course, his chili exploded everywhere, leaving a horrendous mess. Grumbling, I grab a paper towel and scoop out most of it, then pop in my chicken.

When I turn around again, Sebastian has pickles, cheese and mayonnaise on the counter. His eyes are glued to his book, though he holds a mayo slathered knife in his other hand, about to spread it all over a piece of still-wrapped cheese.

Without a single slice of bread nearby.

I sigh at the familiar sight. "Trying to make a sandwich?"

"Hmm?" He follows my pointed stare and frowns. "Oh."

Silas, the youngest and closest to my twenty-two years, passes me the bread as we exchange exasperated looks. The microwave beeps, and I bring my plate to the stove only to find half my green beans are missing.

I know exactly what happened. After living in this house with all of them for almost four years, I only have one complaint, and I can sum it up with one word.

Shawn.

I whirl around to find the bane of my existence with a bowl in his hands. And he's chewing. I storm up to him, snatching away the bowl.

"Those are mine!" I growl when I see only five beans left.

He shrugs, giving me his most infuriating smirk. "Sorry, thought they were fair game. If it helps, they were delicious."

Fury sears through me, a constant whenever he's around. "How many times do I have to tell you to ask before you just start eating?" I don't bother waiting for a response before I stomp back to scrape what's left of my beans onto my plate. Then I hurry to the table before anything else can go wrong.

I grew up with the Wrightings. Our parents are close and I had no siblings, so they became my family. Even Shawn. We haven't always hated each other—that came later—but our rivalry has always been there.

As the brothers file in to sit around the table, I marvel at their differences. Sure they all have brown hair, but the shade varies. Their noses are all the same, regal and straight, and there is a resemblance in their smiles.

Steven scrolls through his phone as he eats his chili. His hair and eyes are the darkest but his skin is the palest. Sebastian is the tallest of them, with close cropped hair, hazel eyes and glasses. Even he is tanner than Steven, since his love of plants often takes him outside. He absently sets his plate next to me then almost misses his chair because he's so focused on his book.

Silas keeps his dark brown curls on the longer side. His amber eyes and easy smile lends to the Golden Retriever air he exudes. His normal exuberance is missing today as he slumps in his seat with a couple cold slices of pizza. A sure sign he was out too late last night.

If I had to choose one brother to call the most attractive, I'd have to pick Shawn. *Reluctantly*. And I'd refuse to tell him because his ego doesn't need any more fuel. His green eyes, sandy brown hair and sculpted physique all combine into one delicious package that even I can't deny.

But looks definitely aren't everything. I glance over at my boyfriend—steady, dependable Sebastian. My heart may not flutter when I look at him and my stomach may not flip, but the safe routine of our relationship is exactly what I need right now.

Shawn takes the chair to my right, setting his heaping plate of casserole on the table. Comfortable silence fills the air as we all dig in, only to be broken when Sebastian bites into his sandwich.

Or tries to.

He pulls back, confused, and I hold back a snort at the still-wrapped piece of cheese with teeth marks impressed upon it. He sighs as everyone starts laughing, then he peels back the layers to actually unwrap the cheese.

Shawn shakes his head. "Sebastian, man, how many times do we have to tell you? You gotta pay attention when you're making food."

"Look who's talking," I say with a glare. "Paying attention is definitely important, especially to key details like who's food it actually is!"

"I said I was sorry," he huffs. "Yeesh."

"It doesn't change the fact that I no longer have a good chunk of my dinner." I stab at the last green beans on my plate, shoving them in my mouth. One thing Shawn and I agree on, the beans were delicious. Too bad I don't have more of them.

"It's not like you don't have other food."

I chew angrily, trying to resist retorting, but my tongue refuses to listen. "You know, if this was the first time, it'd be one thing. You do this all the time! Yester—"

"Seriously, guys," Steven says, setting down his phone. "I'm trying to eat."

Silas nods, and even Sebastian arches an eyebrow in agreement.

I sigh in resignation, not wanting to ruin everyone's dinner. "Sorry."

Shawn, however, says nothing, and it makes me feel better when Sebastian leans forward to address him. "You are in the wrong here, Shawn."

Shawn's lips press tighter together, then he bites out, "I said I'm sorry."

I bristle again, but Sebastian simply says, "Sometimes actions speak louder than words."

And Shawn deflates, all the fight whooshing out of him. "I'll do the dishes tonight, Lee."

My lips part at the offering, and I study him, making sure it's not some trick. But he is all sincerity, so I tentatively offer, "Thanks, Shawn. That'd be nice."

"So," he says, a hint of his smirk returning. "Am I forgiven?"

It's more of an olive branch than I want to give, but all the brothers are watching my reaction. I concentrate on cutting my next bite of chicken, dragging out the silence.

Except Shawn isn't done. "C'mon, Lee. Please?" And he juts out his lower lip, tilts his head slightly, then turns on the puppy dog eyes.

I hate that expression with every fiber of my being because I can't resist it. Oh, how I've tried. Today is no different, and I finally huff out, "Fine. You're forgiven."

His triumphant grin makes me want to take it back, so I turn to Sebastian. "What's tomorrow like for you? We could have lunch." His blank stare sends exasperation zipping through me. "You know, to make up for Friday? I had to finish my English paper?"

I'm in my senior year at Southern Michigan University—Smoo, to us students. This is the last semester before I graduate with my bachelor's degree in history. Not that I know what I'm going to do with it.

Understanding dawns on Sebastian's face, and he pushes his glasses higher up on his nose. "I believe that would work."

"Meet at one? Then I can be done in time for my shift at the library."

Conversation slowly picks up as Silas regains his usual energy. Soon he regales us with tales from his date the night before, and we're all chuckling. My gaze lands on the empty seat at the table, and I wish Meg were here. She's my best friend, our other housemate, and she's as much of a serial dater as Silas.

If anyone could one-up his story, it'd be her, I think as Silas wraps up. I always thought he and Meg might end up together, but that ship has sailed. They hate each other even more than Shawn and I do.

Sebastian's chair screeches as he pushes back from the table, hurrying to take care of his plate before retreating to the living room with his book. I fondly watch him go. I'm in the middle of a steamy romance about a count and his lady that I can't wait to get back to. I can't think of a better way to spend a Sunday night than reading, curled up on the couch next to Sebastian. Especially in snowy February.

One of the many reasons he and I get along so well.

I tune back into the conversation as Steven begins complaining about someone stealing his food at work. Again. The only one of us not still in college, he graduated two years ago with some technical degree, and now works nine to five. I've heard about the food thief every day for the last week. And it's getting old.

"So do something about it," I interrupt. He frowns, and I feel bad about my harsh tone. "I mean...there's got to be some way to catch them."

Shawn leans forward eagerly. "Yeah, make your food like normal then chop up a ghost pepper to put it in."

"That would be awesome!" Silas reaches over to high five Shawn.

A pensive look crosses Steven's face. "That could actually work."

The three of them start plotting, and I push away from the table. I'm sure I'll hear all the details when it goes down. I carefully rinse my plate before I put my sauté pan in the sink. Just because Shawn said he'd do the dishes, doesn't mean I can't do my part.

More than ready for my book, I hurry through the living room where Sebastian is completely engrossed, then I pop into the mini suite I share with Meg. We have our own little sitting room with a cute couch and end tables. My bedroom is on the right and Meg's is on the far left, with a bathroom in between.

This house is perfect for all of us. Bought as an investment by their parents as a hedge against paying for four kids rooming at college, the nearness to campus is an added bonus. The brothers all have rooms upstairs along with another bathroom. The rest of the downstairs we share, and it's nice to have my own space when they get to be too much. Tonight though, I'm ready for some company.

I grab my book, trotting back into the living room where Silas and Steven already have on a basketball game. I don't mind though, knowing I'll be able to tune it out. But I stop in my tracks when I see what book Sebastian is reading now.

The title contains wombats — his latest obsession. He only has so much capacity to learn about plants, then he has to switch to "fluff", as he calls it. His photographic memory imprints all the facts on his brain making him a walking encyclopedia.

A walking, talking encyclopedia.

So far this week I've heard a variety of wonderful facts. Yesterday he asked if I knew that wombat feces are in the shape of a cube. No, nor did I need to know that.

Two days ago, he told me that a group of wombats is called a wisdom, and I still don't know what I'm supposed to do with that information.

I nibble on my lip, not ready for another wombat fact. I decide to grab a bottle of water, if only to prolong the inevitable. But my movement catches Sebastian's attention.

An eager smile lights his face as I bite back my sigh, though I try to keep my expression kind.

"Leah! Did you know that the main defense of a wombat is its rear-end?" He quickly turns the page as he finishes with, "If a predator is around, the wombat will dive into its burrow, using its rear to block the hole. It's mainly made of cartilage and very resilient."

So much weird ass knowledge I don't need. I laugh to myself just thinking about my dumb pun. Aloud, I say, "Neat."

But he only hums, completely engrossed in his book once more. I shake my head, sauntering into the kitchen amidst the clink and thunk of Shawn doing the dishes. He glances my way, but I ignore him, going right to the fridge.

My fingers close around a bottle of water as he exclaims, "Oh, shit," followed by the sound of glass shattering.

"You okay?" I hurry over as he mutters to himself.

"I'm fine," he bites out, reaching into the clear water of the rinsing side of the sink to adjust the plug. The gurgle of water draining fills the air then he yelps, jerking his hand away.

I grab a napkin and hand it to him as I glimpse the blood on his finger. He takes it from me, his lips tight, annoyance all over his face. Without another word, I set my book down then go to the end cupboard where we keep a mini first aid kit for situations like this.

"Everyone all right?" Steven calls from the living room.

I peek my head around the corner and nod. "Shawn broke a glass."

Relief crosses his face before he turns back to his game.

Armed with antibiotic ointment and a Band-Aid, I cross back to Shawn. "Let me see."

"It's just a scratch, Lee. I can put a Band-Aid on myself."

I grab his wrist firmly, saying in my best no nonsense tone, "You might have glass in it. Besides, it's easier with two hands."

He huffs but extends his hand over the sink. I tug away the bloody napkin, turning his wrist one way then the other to be sure the wound is clean.

"All clear." I dry off his finger as best I can then open the Band-Aid and smear ointment on it. It takes no time to wrap it around Shawn's finger, and I make sure the adhesive ends overlap just right. "There you go."

When I look up, Shawn's emerald eyes are so intense, they take my breath away. I back up on instinct, swallowing at my suddenly dry mouth. My gaze lands on the dishes. "Um, I can finish these. So you don't get that wet."

But he blinks, and the hardness returns. "I've got this." Without another word, he faces the sink, dismissing me completely.

I sigh at his stubbornness. "You really shouldn't get a wound wet."

He glares my way, his gaze catching on my book. "Why don't you go bother one of your fictional boyfriends?"

My teeth grind together at the derogatory way he says the words. "What's that supposed to mean?"

"C'mon, Lee," he scoffs, ripping the trash can from beneath the sink before he starts tossing glass into it. "You and Sebastian are the least romantic couple I know. Don't you think you might be compensating for something?"

The accusation pierces me to the core. "Sebastian and I aren't your business, especially our romantic life," I say coldly. I snatch up my book, whirling on my heel, but I pause before I stomp away. "That was crossing a line, Shawn. I thought even you could understand why we're taking it slow."

His head whips up, but his stricken expression does little to mollify me. "Shit, Lee, I didn't mean—"

"I don't want to hear it." I storm toward the door to find Sebastian hovering. The glower on his face tells me he heard at least some of it, and I'm grateful when he glares at Shawn, cutting off any further words from his brother.

Sebastian steps into the living room with me, concern furrowing his forehead. "Are you okay?"

I fight the memories struggling to surface, and my throat is tight as I answer, "I will be." Gratitude surges through me when he pulls me into one of his rare hugs, and I rest in his embrace for several moments. Then I clear my throat and move away. Holding up my book, I say, "I'm gonna hole up for the night."

He nods, and movement behind him catches my attention. Shawn turns away, guilt and remorse all over his face as he returns to the kitchen.

Good. Maybe he'll think about what he says before he opens his mouth.

I wave goodnight to the others before retreating to the safety of my mini suite. I shove the door closed behind me, but it doesn't latch. The finicky doorknob is unreliable at the best of times, and I'm used to babying it. I glare at it for a long moment, wishing I was one of those people who lost their temper. I could rage and scream and slam the door until I beat it into submission.

But that's not me.

Instead, I carefully turn the handle just so, then shut the door gently. The latch clicks into place, the quiet sound taunting my need for self-control. But I ignore it, trudging to my room while trying to tell myself I'm not compensating.

Even if my gut isn't quite convinced.

About the Author

Cass is in love with love, and has been since she peeked at her first romance novel at age fifteen. When an unannounced romance hero walked into her imagination presenting his heroine and pushing her into the spotlight, Cass knew she was destined to become a romance writer. The adventure of a new book and the comfort of an old favorite are two of her most cherished pleasures. When she's not writing or reading, Cass explores the world with her spouse and two kids. She loves chocolate, the Texas Longhorns, and the Oxford comma.

Cass loves to hear from readers. You can find her contact information, website details and author profile page at https://www.totallybound.com

Home of Erotic Romance

Sign up for our newsletter and find out about all our
romance book releases, eBook sales and promotions,
sneak peeks and FREE romance books!

www.ingramcontent.com/pod-product-compliance
Lightning Source LLC
Chambersburg PA
CBHW031109030726
47496CB00002BA/464